FlabberGassed

FlabberGassed

A MISTER PUSS MYSTERY

MICHAEL CRAFT

QUESTOVER PRESS

A weight-loss miracle. A dashing gay architect. A talking cat. What could possibly go wrong?

In the idyllic little town of Dumont, Wisconsin, wealthy widow Mary Questman adopts an exotic stray cat, Mister Puss, who begins to talk to her. At least she thinks so. Mary's young friend, gay architect Brody Norris, soon finds another reason to worry about Mary's judgment when she decides to help finance a bizarre weight-loss enterprise called FlabberGas, the invention of a flamboyant local dermatologist, Dr. Francis Frumpkin.

Brody's skepticism is partially overcome when Dr. Frumpkin commissions him to design the first of a planned chain of FlabberGas clinics. But then, during a public demonstration of Frumpkin's gimmicky new treatment, a volunteer is gassed to death in a hideous mishap that turns out to be no accident. It was murder, all right. Suspects abound. And Brody is drawn into the role of amateur sleuth, assisting Sheriff Thomas Simms.

Funny and tender, thoroughly tangled, with a chilling motive at its core, the mystery comes to a jolting conclusion when Brody pieces together tiny, overlooked details and helps Sheriff Simms name the killer. Along the way, though, Brody himself gets a little help—or so it seems—from the chatty Mister Puss.

"Craft writes in a crisp, lively prose that highlights the quirks of his colorful cast of characters ... The idyllic atmosphere of Dumont—where people don't hold many prejudices even if they can get a bit nosey —is a well-drawn setting, perfect for an exuberant murder mystery ... Craft's talents for characterization and intricate plotting make the novel an entertaining read with delightfully offbeat elements."

— *Kirkus Reviews*

"The new 'Mister Puss' mystery series opens with one of the most intriguing introductions seen in the mystery genre ... *FlabberGassed* is especially strong in its portrait of deadly mischief ... and in its depictions of how a temporary investigator is changed by pursuits far from his comfort zone. Readers used to the usual progression of a murder mystery will find many exceptional twists in this story, from a feline character to a gay architect's involvement in a case demanding skills that he fears he may not possess. *FlabberGassed* is quirky, original, and a delightful read."

— *D. Donovan, Senior Reviewer, Midwest Book Review*

Design and typography: M.C. Johnson
Cover image, parachute: modified from a 1942 photograph
    courtesy of the Library of Congress, LC-USF35-282
Cover image, cat: Adobe Stock
Author's photo: TimCourtneyPhotography.com

Library of Congress Cataloging-in-Publication Data

Craft, Michael, 1950–
FlabberGassed : a Mister Puss mystery / Michael Craft
    ISBN: 978-0-692-13611-9 (hardcover)
    ISBN: 978-0-692-13599-0 (paperback)
    BISAC: FIC011000   Fiction / LGBT / Gay
              FIC022110   Fiction / Mystery & Detective / Cozy / Cats & Dogs
              FIC022100   Fiction / Mystery & Detective / Amateur Sleuth

First hardcover and paperback editions: September 2018
Questover Press
    California • Since 2011

ACKNOWLEDGMENTS

Although writing fiction is largely a solitary pursuit,
I could not have brought *FlabberGassed* to publica-
tion without the help of many friends and associ-
ates, including David Grey, Pamela Johnson, Wayne
Quimby, and Jennifer Thiel, for their guidance with
various plot details; Nancy Cunningham and Larry
Warnock, for their attention to the words on the
page; and Palm Springs photographer Tim Courtney,
for such a flattering author's portrait. As always,
my agent, Mitchell Waters, was generous with his
enthusiasm and wise counsel. And my husband,
Leon Pascucci, has been a steady font of patience,
support, and good cheer. My sincere thanks to all.

— *Michael Craft*

CONTENTS

PART ONE

Doubts and Whispers

On a bright May morning, Mary Questman puttered in her kitchen, fixing breakfast, alone in the grand old house that sat foursquare beneath a canopy of oaks and elms. The trees concealed a world of birds that awoke and sang—fed and preened—then sang some more. Mary had seen some seventy Wisconsin winters melt away, but the vernal swerve of mother Earth's face toward the sun still surprised her with the promise of fresh beginnings.

A breeze riffled the curtains. The back door was open, with only the screen of the storm door separating the kitchen from the leafy universe beyond. Feeling downright girlish, Mary sashayed from the refrigerator to the stove in her cheery yellow housecoat and whistled along with the chorus from the trees.

When suddenly, the birdsong stopped.

Mary paused to listen. Bacon crackled in a skillet, but otherwise, not a sound—as if the birds had been hushed by a cloud of foreboding.

A tentative meow drifted through the screen from the porch.

Mary stepped to the door and peeped out.

The cat hopped up from the stoop and moved toward the door, gazing at Mary with golden eyes. Arriving within an inch of the screen, it sat, looking regal and statuesque, as if pilfered from a pharaoh's tomb. Its ruddy orange fur, short and dense, bore the flecked markings of a wild, much bigger cat, though this visitor was the size of a household tabby.

Meow—its voice was now clear and confident, almost assertive.

Mary chortled. "Someone smells bacon."

The cat meowed again, with a lilt that seemed to ask, Won't you let me in?

Mary cracked the door open. "*Entrez*, Your Highness." Stooping to rub behind the cat's ears, she asked, "And to what do I owe the honor of this visit, Miss Pussytoes?"

The cat stepped over to the stove, sniffing, tail erect.

"Aha," said Mary. "I beg your pardon—*Mister* Puss."

Mary sat at the kitchen table with her coffee, the morning paper, and the plate of bacon. Purring loudly, Mister Puss circled the chair and nuzzled Mary's shins. Mary tried reading the *Dumont Daily Register*, but the novelty of the cat distracted her. Where had he come from? He was so distinctive, she'd have recognized him if he lived nearby. He looked healthy and well cared-for, as well as beautiful—a purebred, she guessed, and valuable—but he wore no collar, no tags.

She broke off some bacon. "Is this what you want?" Mister Puss nipped it politely from her fingers and dropped it to the floor, still purring, which sounded like a growl as he chewed and swallowed.

Mary kept an iPad on the table, using it each morning to check e-mail. Today, though, she Googled a list of cat breeds. And the first to pop up, alphabetically, was the Abyssinian, which originated in Africa, along the Nile, domesticated near modern-day Ethiopia. The photos left no doubt whatever: Mister Puss was a descendent of the cats of ancient Egypt.

"Well, now," said Mary, scooting her chair back and patting her knees, "aren't we special?"

The cat jumped up to Mary's lap and stretched to touch noses.

Mary stroked the cat's neck; the purring intensified. She peered into his almond-shaped eyes and whispered, "How did you get here? Why did you come?"

His warm breath carried the smell of bacon, but deeper from his quivering body rose a potpourri of subtle, more exotic scents. Closing her eyes, Mary inhaled the sandy dryness of a vast desert—plus a trace of something very old and delicate, perhaps papyrus—and a pungent whiff of kyphi, the sacred temple perfume of once-great dynasties.

Mary rubbed cheeks with the cat. She felt his nose climb her face until the fur of his chin touched the opening of her ear. His purr thundered. And soon, from the drone of his purr, other sounds arose. The rustle of reeds in a delta marsh. The ripple of a crocodile plying the great life-giving river. The hiss of an asp. And rising above it all—gibberish—Egyptian gibberish, the babble of an ancient marketplace. Amid the crowd, one voice struggled to be heard.

Hair fire.

Mary blinked, as if snapping free from a trance. She turned and whispered to the cat, "Did you say something?"

Mister Puss found her ear again, and through his purr, the words became clear: *Your hair is on fire.*

"My goodness!" Mary stood, patting her head as the cat landed sure-footed on the floor. Then Mary broke into laughter. "Why, you little so-and-so."

The cat leapt onto the table. Mary lowered her ear to him.

You're so easy.

Mister Puss showed no interest in leaving Mary Questman's lovely home, and Mary had no desire to lose the cat's company. As a girl, she'd had a cat—Boots—but never since, because her late husband, the wealthy Quincy Questman, had been adamant about "no livestock in the house." In the years since his death, however, Mary had begun to rethink things. After four decades of marriage, she rather enjoyed her independence. So if Mister Puss would like to stay, by God, she'd have him.

Berta, longtime housekeeper at the Questman home, did not share Mary's enthusiasm for the cat. While heading out to purchase another list of supplies for the comfort and amusement of Mister Puss, Berta turned in the doorway, asking, "Shouldn't you at least *try* to find the rightful owner?"

Berta was right. "Finders keepers" was childish. Confiscating such a splendid animal was tantamount to theft. So Mary searched the Internet for Abyssinian breeders, locating only two within hundreds of miles. She sent a photo of Mister Puss, asking if they or their clients had lost a cat. Both replied no, and both confirmed that Mister Puss appeared to come from champion stock.

Locally, Mary ran a classified in the lost-and-found column, asking the claimant to phone and describe the missing cat, but no one called.

Now and then, Mary nuzzled up to Mister Puss and whispered, "Don't you want to tell me about your other home?" But he always played dumb. And that settled it.

Within weeks, Mister Puss was no longer the new arrival, but a fixture in the household. A lower cabinet in the butler's pantry was cleared out to accommodate his litter box, and Mary consulted an architect friend, Marson Miles, who designed a circular opening in the cabinet door that would allow Mister Puss ready access for his private needs. Then Mary called in a carpenter, who cut the hole. Then a painter, who refinished the door.

Meanwhile, Mister Puss playfully tormented Berta during her five mornings of chores; later each afternoon, he napped with Mary in her upstairs bedroom, nesting on the pillow, near her ear. Before dozing off, Mary always chatted with him, whispering this and that. Sometimes he responded with only a soothing purr, lulling them both to sleep, but lately, his replies had become more articulate.

One day, Mister Puss mutilated Berta's feather duster. When Mary bedded down with him later, she whispered, "You were a naughty boy today, weren't you?"

His voice spoke through the purring: *Feathers—it's what I do.*

Mary laughed. "I suppose so. But something tells me you don't like Berta."

She's okay. Humorless. Would it kill her to smile?

"She hasn't had an easy life. But she's always been loyal."

Loyal. Dogs are loyal. That's nice.

Several days later, Mary couldn't find her fountain pen, which she used for signing checks. It was kept at the desk in the study, but when she looked for it that afternoon, it wasn't there. She made do with a felt-tip, but the whereabouts of the pen vexed her till nap time, when she lay down with Mister Puss.

She tossed and turned.

What's wrong?

"I can't remember where I put my pen. Any chance you've seen it?"

It's in the kitchen.

She gasped. "Of course. I was making a list for Berta. I left it on the table."

It's on the floor now.

Mary chuckled. While exploring the house, Mister Puss liked to swat at things that would slide on a slick surface. No harm done. She gave him a tender stroke, then left him to snooze as she padded out of the room and down to the kitchen.

After finding the pen on the floor, she sat at the table, wondering. Forgetfulness had troubled her for some years, but she preferred to believe her slips of memory were benign. She wasn't going daft. Not at all. Mental flubs were just a minor, often comical, badge of aging.

With the arrival of the chatty Mister Puss, however, she needed to take stock of her marbles. Was this the beginning of the end? Was this the start of her one-way trek down a blurry road that would lead to diapers and conservatorships and the total loss of her dignity and independence?

Or was she simply—and in actual fact—having conversations with her cat?

A *ping* signaled an arriving e-mail on her iPad. Mary opened the message, from one of the breeders she had queried:

"If you haven't located the cat's owner yet, try taking him to a vet or an animal shelter, where they can scan for a microchip implant. Such a valuable cat, without tags, might have a chip identifying the owner."

Mary slumped in her chair. It had been settled, she'd thought. She and Mister Puss had agreed that he would stay. She couldn't bear the thought of losing him. Even so, if he belonged elsewhere, she needed to know.

James Phelps, DVM, had a quaint, shingled veterinary office on the outskirts of town. Though Mary had never used his services, she had known him forever through the Dumont Country Club, so she booked an appointment and brought in Mister Puss.

The cat stood alert and curious on a stainless steel exam table as Dr. Phelps checked his heart, eyes, teeth. He scoped the cat's ears, took his temperature, and started a chart. "A healthy adult male," proclaimed the vet. "About a year old, I'd say. Seems good-natured and intelligent."

"*Very* intelligent," agreed Mary. "But I have no idea where he came from."

The vet slid a drawer open. "Let's see if he has a chip."

Mary's heart raced. Did they really need to do this?

Dr. Phelps produced a gadget resembling a bulky garage-door controller, switched it on, and dragged the scanner over the cat's coat, trying repeatedly between the shoulder blades. At last, he switched it off. "Nothing. Congratulations, Mary. You've got yourself one crackerjack Abyssinian."

Relieved beyond measure, Mary gave Mister Puss an adoring look.

The vet asked, "Schedule the surgery?"

Mary blanched. "What?"

"About time to get him fixed. Neutered."

Mister Puss turned to Mary.

Mary looked away, averting the cat's gaze. "We'll need to talk about that later."

"We?" The doctor laughed. "You and I—or you and the *cat*?"

"You'll think I'm dotty, Jim, but I do talk to Mister Puss."

"Sure you do. We all talk to our pets."

"But Mister Puss, he"—Mary hesitated—"he talks back to me."

Dr. Phelps weighed his words. "Cats have no physiological apparatus for speech."

"Don't be condescending, Jim. I know that. You see, I speak to him in whispers, and he speaks to me through his purr."

"Ah. Well."

"Mister Puss and I communicate on some special level— perhaps a *transcendent* level." Mary recounted the trancelike circumstances of their first exchange. She explained how they often conversed while slipping into naps.

Tapping his chin, Dr. Phelps asked, "Does the cat ever bring external information to these talks? Or does he just rehash the things you say to him?"

Mary described how Mister Puss had helped her find her missing pen—in the kitchen, not on the table, but on the floor.

The doctor suggested, "But as soon as the cat said it, you remembered where you'd left the pen, correct? And you could've guessed he would knock it off the table."

Mary's head wobbled. "Maybe."

"Consider this. As children, we've all talked with animals, dolls, or imaginary friends—a normal exercise in creativity. Even though such dialogue seems very real, *we* put the words in the *other* party's mouth. Hearing those words come back to us is sort of a mental loop, like déjà vu. I'll bet you've been 'channeling' through the cat to clarify your own thinking. Which is fine. But I'm sure your cat could never tell you something you don't already know." Doctor Phelps turned to put away the scanner, concluding, "For every little mystery, there's always a simple, scientific explanation."

Quack.

"What say?" asked the doctor over his shoulder.

"Quiet, Mister Puss."

Meow.

Going home, Mary stopped to buy some prime beef tenderloin, which would make a nice dinner for Mister Puss. He preferred raw beef over anything else, and now was a time to celebrate— he was staying for good.

That evening, Mary stood in the kitchen, dicing the beef into bloody, bite-size chunks while Mister Puss circled her legs, purring. Mary said, "Dr. Phelps called you a crackerjack Abyssinian. But he doesn't seem to think you have much to say."

The cat jumped to the counter and stretched toward Mary. She leaned to listen.

An exercise in creativity? Channeling through a mental loop? Déjà vu? Please.

Mary shrugged. "It's a frame of mind. He's a man of science."

Science? That was mumbo jumbo.

Testing the doctor's theory, Mary whispered, "Tell me something I *don't* know."

But the cat only purred.

The next morning after breakfast, Mary settled at the kitchen table to review her calendar and plan her day. Good thing she checked. She'd forgotten about the luncheon party at the home of a lady friend, who had asked Mary to bring her filigreed sterling cake server. Better set it out with her handbag—now—in case it slipped her mind again. So she went to find it in the butler's pantry.

When she swung the door open, there was Mister Puss, sprawled on the floor outside his privy with one leg pointed to the ceiling, busily cleaning his bottom. "Oops," Mary mumbled, "excuse me."

She backed out, eased the door closed, returned to the table, and sat. Then her lips sputtered with laughter.

Did I just apologize to a *cat?* she wondered. Granted, Mister Puss projected a distinct air of refinement, but he was indeed a *cat.*

He appeared in the kitchen, having circled around from the dining room, and jumped up to the tabletop, purring. He stretched toward Mary's ear. *Cleanliness is next to godliness, you know.*

"I know. Tell me something I don't know."

Bastet licked herself.

"What? Who?"

She licked herself plenty. Bastet. The cat goddess.

"Oh, come now. That's just a myth."

Do you pray?

"Of course, all the time." Mary paused, reconsidering. "Well, not so much anymore. It's been quite a while."

Your god is a myth, too.

"That's a terrible thing to say."

But you already know it, don't you? Isn't that why you stopped praying?

Mary had no answer. Mister Puss gave her a nose-kiss, hopped off the table, and left the room. Mary listened to the thump of her heart.

Could a cat be guilty of blasphemy? Or had Mary been channeling her own suppressed thoughts through the cat? Perhaps Dr. Phelps was right. Mister Puss was incapable of telling her anything she didn't already know.

Then, through the miasma of her doubts, one trifling detail drifted to the surface. Mary caught her breath. She was certain:

She had never known the name of the cat goddess.

1

Marson Miles glanced at the text message, then looked at me with a wry expression and slipped his phone into an inside pocket of his sport coat. "That was Frumpkin," he said as we got out of the car. "He's running a few minutes late."

I asked my husband, "Any idea what this is about?"

"Not a clue, Brody."

On a Tuesday evening in October, we could have parked within a few spaces of the restaurant's main door, but Marson had chosen a spot near the back of the lot—minimizing the threat of door dings. I had been living with him for nearly two years, so I had given up razzing him about obsessive tendencies that were not only harmless, but also quite charming.

At seven o'clock, the sun had long set, and planets now peeped through the velvety twilight of a crisp autumn night. As we strolled from the car, our shoes crunched loose pebbles on the asphalt. Somewhere in the high branches of a wasting maple, an owl prepared for his hunt, begging the moon to appear. The bird's eerie call, with its note of foreboding, quickened our steps.

I slid my hand to Marson's waist, hooked a finger through one of his belt loops, and exhaled a soft laugh, mixing my warm breath with the cool air.

He turned his head to me. "Hm?"

"Nothing," I said. "Just feeling lucky to have you in my life."

"I'm the lucky one, kiddo."

"Then it's mutual. Lucky us."

"Lucky us," he agreed.

It hadn't always been that way. While I was a boy, growing up in California, my mother and I had visited Wisconsin for a family wedding, and that's when I first met Marson Miles, an architect who was married to my mother's sister, my aunt Prue. Though only fourteen, I underwent two epiphanies during that trip that would set the future course of my life: I knew with sudden certainty that I wanted to become an architect, and I found myself attracted to older, creative men.

More than twenty years passed before I returned to central Wisconsin, to the small town of Dumont, where I would join my uncle's architecture firm. I had established a successful practice in the Los Angeles area with another man—an older, creative man—who was my husband. But his roving eye and irresistible attraction to one of our clients (younger than I was, and wealthy) spelled an end to both our marriage and our firm.

I needed a change of scenery, a new direction.

Meanwhile, Marson's firm in Dumont had hit its stride when he designed Questman Center for the Performing Arts, named after the local widow who had spearheaded the project and written a huge check. The design landed rave reviews and a backlog of new commissions, which meant that Marson needed more help, younger blood.

So the timing was right. A deal was struck.

What I didn't know was that Marson had endured decades of a frustrating and loveless marriage with my aunt. I didn't understand that he, turning sixty, was also in need of a new direction. At a conscious level, neither did he.

But that all changed on New Year's Eve, not yet two years ago, when we met at a restaurant to celebrate my arrival. With five of us crowded around the small table of a corner booth, I was seated next to Marson, and beneath the draped white linen of the tablecloth, our knees eventually—inadvertently—touched. In the dry, wintry air, a spark of static electricity leapt between the fibers of our woolen slacks with an audible crack. And that spark brought with it an understanding that profound changes lay ahead for both of us.

We now walked through the parking lot of that same restaurant, where we were scheduled to meet Dr. Francis Frumpkin, a dermatologist and cosmetic surgeon of some renown whose main practice was located in Milwaukee, with a satellite office in Dumont. Our dinner meeting had been set up by Frumpkin's adult daughter, Sarah Frumpkin Ward. I had never met either of them, and Marson knew them only as passing acquaintances, so our get-together had neither a precedent nor an apparent purpose. When Sarah had phoned our office, she'd simply explained, "Dad and I would *love* to talk to you."

As Marson held the door open for me to enter the restaurant, Ginger, the hostess, stepped out from behind her podium to greet us both with a hug. "You *two*," she said. "You're just perfect together. Hang on to each other."

I assured her, "We plan to."

Marson said, "We're meeting Dr. Frumpkin and his daughter, but they're running late."

Ginger nodded. "They called. Let's get you settled." She gathered a few menus, as well as a large manila envelope, from a shelf below the podium, then led us into the dining room, past the bar, and straight to the same corner booth where a slip of the knee had changed my life. Ginger said, "They requested a quiet table where you could talk."

"This looks just fine," said Marson as he and I slid into the booth, squeaking on the burgundy-colored leatherette.

Ginger arranged the four menus, then handed the envelope

to Marson, explaining, "Someone from Dr. Frumpkin's office dropped this off and asked me to give it to you."

Marson thanked her with a nod. "Mission accomplished."

As Ginger returned to the lobby, Marson turned the envelope in his hands. The back flap was secured with a brass fastener. On the front was a typewritten label: MILES & NORRIS, ARCHITECTS. Marson set aside the envelope and looked about for a waiter—it was cocktail time.

I nudged the envelope toward him. "Gonna open it?"

With a shrug, he picked up the envelope, opened the clasp, and slid out what appeared to be an eight-by-ten photograph, which he drew close to his face. I watched from the backside of the photo as he examined it. Over its top edge, his brow furrowed.

"What?" I asked.

He flipped the photo in his fingers and handed it to me. It looked like a newer copy of an old Kodachrome print—soft focus, soft palette, tinged yellow by age. Through a quizzical squint, I gazed into the picture:

On a windswept expanse of lonely terrain, a group of men in white jumpsuits struggled to prevent a billowing parachute from dragging them to their knees in the dirt. It looked like a game, a spirited tug-of-war against the powerful but benign forces of nature. The strange attire, coupled with the barren setting, lent the image a surreal quality that looked more like a painting than a photograph. Everyone in it was intent on the task at hand, except—conspicuous among the others—a man in a gray business suit.

He looked directly out to the camera.

A waiter approached the table with a bottle of champagne in an ice bucket, which we had not ordered, just as Ginger emerged from the lobby, escorting in our direction a man and a woman who I assumed were Dr. Frumpkin and his daughter.

I knew from a prior conversation with Marson that he and Frumpkin were about the same age, which left me surprised by Frumpkin's appearance as he neared the table. He looked impossibly young for his sixties, vigorous and tanned, with a huge head of processed hair, streaked various shades of gold and silver. In the dim light of the dining room, his ear-to-ear smile glowed with stunning white porcelain. Marson leaned close to whisper, "He's had a lot of work done." Completing the picture, Frumpkin wore a nubby-silk blazer of shocking crimson. Joking with Ginger, he let out a hoot of laughter that turned every head in the room.

By stark comparison, his daughter was unremarkable. Not plain, not blah—just normal. Mid-thirties, I guessed, about my age. Of svelte build, she was well turned-out and seemed comfortable in her own skin, but both her prim hairdo and her twill suit projected an air of no-nonsense. I wondered if she had recognized the manifest futility of any attempt to out-peacock her father. Or had something in her nature pushed her to the background, where she found refuge from her father's limelight?

Ginger brought them forward, announcing, "Look who's here. Enjoy the champagne." She disappeared as the waiter popped the cork.

Marson and I began sliding out from the back of the booth to greet our dinner companions.

"Please," said Frumpkin with a lavish wave of both arms, "don't get up, gentlemen. No need for formality, not tonight." He slipped into the booth next to me, touching knees. His daughter sat opposite him, next to Marson, as the waiter poured a first round of Cristal—pricey stuff, I didn't even know they carried it. Frumpkin explained, "I took the liberty of ordering earlier. Hope you don't mind. But tonight should be cause for celebration."

Marson and I exchanged a puzzled glance.

Frumpkin raised his glass and clinked mine. "Pleased to meet you. *Very* pleased. I'm Francis Frumpkin."

"My pleasure, Doctor. I'm Brody Norris." I offered my hand.

He shook it. "Now, now—I insist—it's *Francis*."

Marson took over. "Sarah, I don't believe you've met my husband, Brody Norris. And Brody, this is the doctor's daughter, Sarah Frumpkin Ward."

I reached across the table to shake Sarah's hand. We lobbed a few pleasantries. If I'd expected her to be timid or retiring, I was wrong. She said, "Sorry if things seem a tad mysterious tonight. Dad's always suffered from an acute sense of theater." I liked her.

Marson laughed. Lifting the photo from the table, he said, "*This* is certainly mysterious."

"Aha," said Frumpkin, flashing that big, manufactured smile. "I admit, it was meant to be a bit of a tease, so I'm delighted it's piqued your curiosity. Now, take a closer look at it."

Marson set the photo in front of me, where we could both study it.

I said, "It looks like a class of some kind—student pilots, a flight school."

"Civilian," said Marson, tapping one of the white jumpsuits. "It's obviously old, I'm guessing before World War II—otherwise they'd all be in uniform."

"Very good." Dr. Francis Frumpkin traced a finger around the rim of his champagne flute, then leaned nearer, huddling over the photo with us. "In the summer of 1941, they could enjoy that day's lesson while joking about the imagined thrills and glamour of their calling to the wild blue. Not one of these half-dozen trainees, so lean and youthful, had even *heard* of Pearl Harbor.

Within a year, though, they'd be wearing different uniforms—all of them. And within four years, only half would remain to know the dark victory of Hiroshima." Frumpkin paused. "And what about the man in the middle, the man in gray?"

Marson and I peered closer but said nothing.

"He was an aeronautical engineer, some say a genius—Dr. Archibald Frumpkin. He grew up flying planes over long, desolate stretches of the family ranch. Then, leaving home for school, he traded his Stetson for a leather aviator's helmet. His later writings included some provocative theories, never proven, regarding the effects of altitude and oxygen on human metabolism. Archibald was my grandfather. His son—my father—snapped this picture when he was a boy. Back in Texas."

Our waiter returned to top up our glasses and recite a few specials. Though we had not yet looked at the menus, Frumpkin commanded, "Get them the best steak in the house. In fact, make it three—a chilly night always makes me hungry for meat." We offered no protests.

"And the lady?" asked the waiter. "The porterhouse as well?"

"I think not," said Sarah with a tidy shake of her head. She opted instead to start with a cup of asparagus soup, but only after being assured by the waiter that it contained no cream. For her main course, she requested a plate of fresh greens—arugula, escarole, kale, mâche—with a few lemon wedges instead of dressing.

"Sounds tasty," I said as the waiter left.

Sarah smirked. "Trust me—I splurge now and then."

Her father said, "And you *deserve* it. Sarah, honey? Perhaps you could stand up and give us all a good look."

With a wave of apprehension, I wondered, What the hell?

Sarah stood, straightened her skirt, opened her jacket. Then she took a step away from the table, twirled, and returned, striking a pose.

"Bravo," said Frumpkin, miming silent applause. He turned to Marson and me with raised brows. "Not bad, right? Perfectly trim. Well proportioned. A figure anyone would envy."

With a dumb, numb nod, I agreed, "Very nice."

Sarah ran the fingers of both hands along the sides of her torso. "It was all Dad's doing."

Marson struggled to ask, "Liposuction?"

She shook her head. "Nope. FlabberGas."

My jaw sagged. "What?"

She enunciated: "Flab-ber-Gas." Flinging her hands to the ceiling, she announced, "I've been FlabberGassed!"

Squinting, I repeated, *"What?"*

Sarah plopped back into the booth, telling us, "It's the most marvelous new *gas* treatment that accelerates weight loss. So Dad has branded it FlabberGas. We're planning to build a stunning new clinic to promote it."

Frumpkin got to the point: "And we need a top-notch architect."

"For a fat clinic?" asked Marson, sounding dismissive. "Maybe you could try Frank Gehry."

With a quiet laugh, Sarah explained, "I know, at first blush, it all sounds preposterous. But trust me—we have ambitious plans. The new clinic will serve as a prototype for FlabberGas franchises in every resort destination in the world. This is *big*, Mr. Miles."

"Ahhh," said Marson. "In the immortal words of Daniel Burnham, 'Make no little plans; they have no magic to stir men's blood.'"

"Right *on*," said Sarah, oblivious to Marson's sarcasm.

Frumpkin added, "So you see, gentlemen, we're looking for

a singular talent who can handle the challenge of unrestricted design freedom to create a structure *worthy* of being replicated all over the world. And not to sound crass, but as the franchise network spreads, your commissions would multiply."

Marson caught my eye—the money sounded good.

Sarah said, "So we *have* to get this right the first time. Dad is planning a move to Palm Springs, and that seems like the right location for the prototype clinic."

I chimed in: "Makes sense. The population skews a little older there—and gay, of course. Shall we say, cosmetically aware?"

Frumpkin howled with laughter. Heads turned again.

Sarah jabbed at the tabletop with her index finger. "We need vision. We need style. We need adventurous thinking in the great tradition of California modernism. In short, we need balls-to-the-wall pizazz."

Marson blew a long, low whistle. It was the sort of project that would tempt any architect—the opportunity to create something magical and truly original, like Frank Lloyd Wright's Fallingwater or Gustave Eiffel's tower or Frank Gehry's museum at Bilbao. I could tell that Marson's resistance was wearing thin. He hesitated, clenching his lower lip with his teeth. Then he said, "I'm sorry. Things are really busy right now—I've got a ton of new work in the hopper. But more to the point, I'm not well versed in the design idiom you have in mind."

Under the table, Frumpkin rested his hand on my knee. "But *you* are, aren't you, Brody? You're from Southern California. You live and breathe modernism."

"Of *course*," said Marson, "stupid me." Breaking into a broad smile, he rested his hand on my other knee. "Brody, the project sounds perfect for you."

It did indeed. Within a few moments, I was busy with a borrowed pen, sketching an idea on the back of the big envelope while Frumpkin prattled on about his plans.

"As you may have guessed," he said, "I'm gay."

No kiddin'.

"It was a later-life awakening. My wife passed away long ago, but I didn't dare act on my feelings till Sarah left the nest and started a family of her own. Looking back, it seems odd that I felt the need to 'protect' her—or anyone—from the truth. Amazing, isn't it, how we can delude ourselves with mental games and kick our happiness down the road? But: better late than never."

"I'll drink to that," said Marson, raising his glass to the doctor. "My journey was similar. But it's the ending that matters." He winked at me.

Sarah said, "Forgive the cliché, but Dad seems to have a new lease on life. He's never been more energized."

With a low chortle, Frumpkin stretched his pinkie under the table to trace little circles on the side of my knee.

I clenched my legs and focused on my sketch.

Frumpkin told us, "Not many of us are given a second chance to start over, and that's how I see my situation. My practice here is in good hands—Sarah has managed the Dumont office for the past ten years, and her husband, Jason, is a top-notch physician. I've been grooming him to take over from the start. Plus, there's Dahr."

"Who?" asked Marson.

Sarah explained, "Dahr Ahmadi is our certified nurse practitioner. He's Iranian. Name's Dariush, but he goes by Dahr."

Frumpkin sighed. "A lovely young man."

"He's *my* age," said Sarah.

He's *my* age, I thought.

"In fact," said Frumpkin, "he's *almost* as gorgeous as Brody here. We've been 'talking' lately. So the time is right. I'm ready to make a move to Palm Springs, become a happy Californian—hopefully with Dahr—and begin promoting FlabberGas to the world."

"I hesitate to ask," said Marson, "but what exactly *is* Flabber-Gas?"

Frumpkin swirled the champagne in his glass. "It's the most important discovery to hit the weight-loss industry in decades."

Sarah cleared her throat, drawing our attention. "It's a weight-loss *miracle*." With a grin, she added, "It's oxygen."

"An oxygen *treatment*," her father stressed. "When combined with a medically supervised diet-and-exercise program, Flabber-Gas is approved as safe and effective for loss of weight."

While doodling a few palm trees in the background of my sketch, I said, "Diet and exercise make sense. What does the oxygen do?"

Frumpkin's tone turned coy. "It contributes a glorious aura of well-being. Some of my patients describe it as bliss. The oxygen is administered in a hyperbaric chamber, which enhances the perceived efficacy of the weekly treatments."

Sarah said, "As noted earlier, my father has an acute sense of theater."

"Guilty," he said with a laugh. "Medicine is largely science, but it's also an art."

I looked up from my drawing. "The same might be said of architecture."

"Yes," agreed Frumpkin, "but perhaps the proportions are in-verted—the science takes a backseat to your art."

I handed him my sketch. "*Very* preliminary. Just brainstorm-ing a concept. Is this at all what you had in mind?"

He gasped. "Genius. Pure genius." Passing the envelope to his daughter, he told me, "It's whimsical, it's space-age, it's orig-inal—you've nailed it."

In truth, it wasn't all *that* original. I'd combined one classic idiom of midcentury-modern design (the inverted butterfly roof) with another (slanted exterior walls), creating the appearance of a building with a cinched waist. A huge neon FLABBER-GAS sign rose from the roof, with its letters angled upward to accentuate the tightening below. The overall effect was something of a cross between a Jetsons drive-in and a swank supper club. It would look right at home along the main drag in Palm Springs, where the weight-conscious gentry could stroll in for a gas treatment after brunch or before cocktails.

With a hearty laugh, Marson passed the drawing from Sarah back to Frumpkin. "It looks like the building's on a *diet*."

Nodding, Frumpkin repeated, "Pure genius."

Dead serious, Marson said, "I agree. Brody is a man of many talents. Top of the list, he's a first-class problem-solver. And that's what design boils down to: problem-solving."

"Same with medicine," said Frumpkin. "Same with all of life's many mysteries: problem-solving."

During dinner, Sarah mentioned, "Our business plan is sound. The numbers, promising. Eventually, we'll sell actual franchises; they'll provide the main income stream. But first, we need to develop the prototype clinic and get it built. Dad plans to fund the bulk of that himself."

"To do it *right*," said Frumpkin, "I'll take on a few early investors as stakeholders in the entire enterprise. Mary Questman is interested."

Marson set down his fork. *"Mary?"* he said, sounding astonished. "Mary wants to put money in FlabberGas?"

"She's been a patient for years—regular skin checks, nothing major."

Mary Questman was the wealthy widow who had given Marson the greatest design opportunity of his career. She was not only our most important client, but one of the sweetest women I'd ever known.

Frumpkin continued, "She came to me for a diet plan, so I asked her to try my new oxygen treatment. She was thrilled with it. So much so, she's offered to host a reception at her home, where I can pitch FlabberGas to prospective backers." Frumpkin turned to me. "The presentation is Friday. Any chance you could work up something by then?"

"A conceptual presentation, maybe. Working drawings will take far longer."

"Yes, of course."

Marson seemed unable to compute what he'd heard. "Mary's been *FlabberGassed*?"

"Several times," Frumpkin assured him.

Sarah said, "She was so grateful for the results, she invited us to dinner at her home. One thing led to another, and by the end of the meal, she was asking about investment opportunities."

"Really?" said Marson.

With an exaggerated wink, Frumpkin told us, "Her cat had no objections."

2

Chicken casserole may not be the height of culinary sophistication, but as comfort food, it has a retro, homey appeal second to none (well, maybe pot pie). And it would be the perfect antidote to the prior evening's porterhouse overload with Dr. Frumpkin. So Marson and I made a last-minute decision to spend Wednesday night at home.

Although he had praised me as a first-class problem-solver a mere twenty-four hours earlier, the task of concocting a casserole from scratch now fell to him. A man of discipline and precision, he normally approached cooking with the exactitude of a chemist, but our sudden hankering to "eat in" that night not only allowed, but required, some improvising. For guidance, he turned not to Julia Child or Ruth Reichl, but to a tattered old Betty Crocker. He rummaged in the cupboards and the fridge. He opened a can-of-this and a jar-of-that.

I, meanwhile, moiled at my computer. My problem-solving skills had been focused all day at the office—and now at home—on developing a pair of perspective drawings of the prototype FlabberGas clinic, needed for Friday's pitch session. The ease and the whimsy of sketching my initial concept on the back of a manila envelope were now replaced with the nuts and bolts of engineering the shell of a space that would not only accommodate the various needs of the clinic, but also hold up the roof—and still look fabulous.

"How's it going, kiddo?" asked Marson from the open kitchen of our loft.

"Getting there." In fact, I was thrilled with how the renderings had shaped up, but I didn't want to jinx my progress with any semblance bragging. I asked, "And the casserole?"

"Hope you like peas."

"If they're buried in cheesy goo." With a swipe of the mouse, I dragged and dropped another palm tree into the mountainous background of the clinic.

"Okay. More goo." He clattered around the kitchen.

Sitting back, I watched Marson at work in the sleek, spare surroundings of our temporary home.

By Dumont standards, our First Avenue loft, which we converted from an old haberdashery, was cutting-edge—exactly the sort of space in which two architects might be expected to devise their living quarters. The ground floor of the loft included the kitchen along the rear wall, which opened to a dining area, separated by a couple of steps from the main living space in front, with its two-story wall of windows. The shop's former mezzanine, over the kitchen, was now our sleeping area, accessible by a spiral metal staircase. The decorating scheme was largely black and white; the materials leaned toward leather, glass, and stone. In a word, the look was industrial.

We weren't trying to be hip. To us, these choices had been more a default than a preference. Not quite two years ago, when our unexpected attraction led quickly to love and then commitment, when Marson's life and his marriage of thirty-odd years were upended, we needed housing—our first home together—on short notice. And the downtown loft checked all the boxes. It was near our office. It was clean and comfortable, with neutral styling that would allow us to discover, over time, a shared sense of aesthetics. It was *ours*.

Now we were married—since June, only a few months ago. But all along, it had seemed inevitable that, once we were feeling more settled, we would again contemplate new surroundings, a home reflecting a more defined expression of our evolved tastes as a couple. We referred to that next project not merely as our dream house, but with brazen immodesty as "the perfect house," one we would build from the ground up. And in fact, construction had just begun.

"Taste," said Marson. He had ambled over to my computer with two glasses of wine, extending one.

I sipped, swallowed, smiled. "Nice."

"I thought a dry rosé might work with the chicken—a little more substance than a white—just *too* predictable."

I got up from my chair and pulled him close for a kiss. "You chose well."

He touched his glass to mine. The chime of crystal drifted through the cavernous space of the loft—and vanished.

"Take a look," I said, offering the chair at my computer.

He sat, peered at the screen, and grinned. Setting down his wine, he tapped the mouse to zoom the view. "Marvelous, Brody. I could *never* have come up with this. So fresh, so spirited. Frumpkin will love it—you had him sold with that first sketch."

I had already told Marson about Frumpkin's fancy fingerwork beneath the tablecloth. Now I noted, "I think he was sold *before* the sketch."

Marson leaned back, looking up to study me. "You're an attractive man—desired by many. The night we met, the memory of that, it still leaves me breathless."

The memory he invoked left *me* not only breathless, but suddenly needy. Our two years together had been a steady journey in building our shared trust, companionship, and dreams. But that adventure had begun with a spark of lust, pure and simple—an impulse driven by physical, mutual attraction, a craving that, to this day, has not withered in the least. I fixed him in my stare. "How much longer for that casserole?"

His eyes widened. His voice turned dry and throaty: "Twenty minutes. Thirty?"

"Plenty of time."

The casserole turned out crustier than planned, a tad crunchy around the edges, but the delightful rosé made the food's shortcomings easy to dismiss. Marson had also made a simple salad and whisked a masterful vinaigrette that, combined with the rest, made a modest but elegant meal for a chilly autumn night at home.

We hadn't bothered getting dressed again, wearing cozy bathrobes at our dinner for two as we perched on stools at the kitchen island. Huddled with a few candles, we tippled as we ate and gabbed.

"On the one hand," said Marson, "he's a showboat. On the other hand, he's a successful, ambitious businessman thinking outside the box."

"He's a doctor," I said. We were speaking of Francis Frumpkin. "Somehow, I've never associated medicine with business savvy—or thinking outside the box. Doctors follow established protocols."

"X-rays, penicillin, DNA—those discoveries came from thinking outside the box."

"True." I gave my wine a swirl, sliding the base of the glass in lazy circles on the granite countertop. "But Frumpkin's not a researcher. He's a practicing dermatologist and cosmetic surgeon."

Marson reminded me, "He's on the verge of retirement. He wants to move to Palm Springs. He intends to try something different for his chapter two."

"I'll say. He wants to start over with his nurse—what was his name?"

"Dahr. I assume we'll meet him at the doings on Friday. And if things work out for Frumpkin—with FlabberGas *and* with Dahr—he'll be able to walk away from the daily grind of the practice, turning things over to Sarah and her husband. In short, Frumpkin has a plan."

I found Marson's logic reassuring. At some level, I was tempted to dismiss Frumpkin as a flake, which gave me qualms about designing his FlabberGas clinic—did I really want my name tied to a project that sounded like a joke? But Marson was right. Frumpkin exuded an astute sense of marketing, so perhaps his silly branding concept would be just the ticket to drive throngs of the flabby to his door. And along the way, I'd landed a commission that was potentially lucrative and uncommonly fun.

Marson concluded, "Enjoy the ride with Frumpkin. What could possibly go wrong?"

Lacking foresight of the magnitude of what would indeed go wrong, I ignored his question and responded with another: "How's the museum coming along?"

Marson brightened. He set down his fork. "I wish you could have gone to the site with me today."

"Sorry." Lamely, I added, "FlabberGassed."

"Understood, kiddo." He patted my hand. "Anyway, they'll have the museum closed-in before winter. All the visual massing is in place now. And the juxtaposition with Questman Center is stunning—as planned."

A few years earlier, when Mary Questman had chosen Marson to design the performing-arts center, many were skeptical of her decision to award such a significant job to small-town talent. But when the design was unveiled, critics were won over by Marson's flawless integration of the theater complex into the rocky ravines of an old city park, donated by the county as the building site. Later, when Questman Center opened, it was acclaimed an instant landmark—not only in sleepy little Dumont, but among the larger world of the architectural cognoscenti.

Then, last year, when the board of the Dumont County Museum decided to phase out their cramped old building and construct a larger, more modern facility, the county donated additional land near Questman Center, which would now serve as anchor to an expanding cultural campus that would eventually include a new main library as well. The theater complex had been such a hit, there was no question that Marson would be tapped to design the new museum, now under construction. That was shortly after I had entered Marson's life—living with him as well as working with him. And one night, as I was lying in Marson's arms, he turned to tell me, "When they get around to the library, that one's yours, Brody. That will be *your* masterpiece."

Awesome. But first things first. I had a FlabberGas clinic in the works.

There in the kitchen, Marson poured more wine for me, then sloshed the remaining inch or two into his own glass. "Any news about the house?"

Aha. The perfect house. I answered, "Yes, in fact. After you went out to the museum, Carter called the office." Clem Carter was the owner of Carter Construction, our general contractor. "They finished the grading today. He asked me to take a look."

"Great," said Marson. "The first hard freeze can't be far off."

"I'll check it out tomorrow."

"Have enough time?" He reminded me, "FlabberGas."

"I'm in good shape. Today was productive. No problem getting everything to Frumpkin on Friday."

"You are one *driven* young man. I'm impressed." Marson got

up, kissed the top of my head, and carried a few dishes to the sink.

I followed him with the flatware and empty glasses. "Actually, I was already planning to drive out there tomorrow. I'm taking Glee. She's dying to get a look."

"Not much to see. Nothing's built yet."

"That's the point. She wants some 'before' shots."

"I'll just bet she does." Marson started rinsing things. It creeped him out to put dirty dishes in the dishwasher.

We were talking about Glee Savage, a good friend who worked for the *Dumont Daily Register*. A year earlier, she'd run a story about our "repurposing" of the loft (a first in Dumont), and now she was intent on documenting the building of our house, which she deemed all the more newsworthy.

"But a word of warning," said Marson. "Watch out for Glee."

"Why?"

His tone was facetious: "She's a killer."

Glee Savage was not a killer. Or at least, no one had proved it. There'd been talk, many years before my arrival in Dumont, that she was responsible for the untimely death of an old foe, Gillian Reece. A shrew of a businesswoman, Reece had no shortage of enemies—any one of whom might have been motivated to shove her over a balcony in her magnificent new home and send her plummeting to the limestone floor two stories below. The fall proved fatal, denying Reece the payback of naming her assailant, so the mystery death was never solved. But Marson had maintained all along that it was preposterous even to consider Glee Savage a killer. And that was good enough for me.

Glee Savage did, however, have a killer sense of style. Well into her sixties now, closer to seventy, never married, she had worked at the local paper for more than forty years, weathering the digital tsunami that still redefined the delivery of news. Whether by shrewd planning or by lucky happenstance, Glee had managed to carve out a niche.

With her big hats and big purses, with her ruby-red lips and high-heeled strut, with her bounce, her panache—Glee was the long-established voice of culture sounding in these timbered hinterlands. She had played many roles at the *Register,* which must have been the key to her longevity. By serving as everything from beat reporter to gal Friday to women's editor to arts reviewer, she had now been elevated to the ranking position of features editor, one of the few bones left on the newspaper's skeleton staff.

Thursday morning, Glee phoned me at my office, confirming our plans to tour the building site. She asked, "Shall I meet you there?"

Everyone in town knew her car, a honey of an ancient Gremlin hatchback with a fuchsia paint job, pristine whitewalls, and baby moon hubcaps. I struggled to envision it negotiating the ruts and mud of the undeveloped land I would eventually call home, so I suggested, "Let me pick you up. I'll borrow Marson's Range Rover."

"Sounds wonderful, love. I'm working from home today— seems to be the trend."

"I'll swing by at eleven. And be sure to wear flats."

Which gave me another hour to tinker with the pair of computerized drawings I was finishing for Dr. Frumpkin. One of them was rendered as a basic two-point perspective, detailing the building itself. The other was a more elaborate three-point perspective, looking up from ground level to accentuate the clinic's zany angles, set against a fanciful backdrop of palms and mountains and sapphire sky.

Last night after dinner, I had worked late on them at the loft, so there was little left now but tweaks. Before long, I added our logotype, MILES & NORRIS, ARCHITECTS, LLC, to a lower corner of each image. Then I sent the electronic files to be print-ed, laminated, and mounted. Because Frumpkin wanted impact, I ordered them four feet wide.

There's something about an October sky—the angle of the sun, maybe. With summer's haze long gone, the intense late-morn-ing blue verged on indigo, rivaling even the storybook sky I'd dropped into the drawing of the FlabberGas clinic. And this wasn't la-di-da Palm Springs, but central Wisconsin.

At the wheel of Marson's whopping hunter-green Range Rover, I drove the few blocks from downtown Dumont to the quiet side street where Glee Savage lived alone in a tidy Crafts-man-style bungalow, which she had perked up with fuchsia trim. Potted pink geraniums lent pops of color to the front porch. Flanking the gate at the sidewalk, huge bushy stalks, at least ten feet tall, sprouted spectacular palmate leaves, an exotic look for this small Midwestern town; these were some of Glee's prized castor plants. She made a hobby of harvesting their beautiful beans—the source of deadly ricin—and stringing them into necklaces and bracelets that provided primitive accents to her ever-changing wardrobe, which was both fearless and chic.

That Thursday was no exception. She was waiting for me in-side her gate when I pulled up at eleven and got out of the SUV to greet her. As she stepped outside the gate, I noticed that she'd heeded my advice to wear flat shoes, and I couldn't recall if I'd ever seen her *not* wearing spike heels. Today she wore strappy low-heeled boots that rose almost to her knees; shocking Mer-curochrome-colored slacks that otherwise resembled jodhpurs; a glittery, feathered hat (always a hat) that might once have been a pith helmet; and something like a flak jacket, gussied up with a sizable broach of rose quartz and a double string of castor beans. With the Range Rover idling at the curb, she looked ready for a swingin' safari.

"*Brody* sweets," she gushed, delivering a kiss, "you look amazing, as always."

I was wearing what I normally wore to the office—sport coat and tie—nice enough but nothing special. And I'd ditched the Italian loafers for a pair of clunky Wolverine work shoes I kept under my desk for visits to building sites. With a laugh, I told Glee, "I can't compete with you, doll."

Her simper seemed to tell me, Get real. She said, "Gorgeous green eyes, thick sandy hair, body to die for—you'd look great in *anything*."

I rolled my eyes. Then I helped her up into the vehicle.

As we pulled away from the curb, I asked, "Did you bring a camera?" She always carried a huge, flashy purse; she seemed to have hundreds. As for today's, she could've stashed a tripod and super-telephoto lens inside it.

"No need for a camera. They have us taking pictures with our *phones* now, if you can believe it. There's only one real photographer left on staff, and he's pretty much limited to studio work."

"And yet," I said, "the *Register* is a fine little paper. Not many small towns even *have* a local daily anymore. You should be proud."

Glee reached across the console to squeeze my elbow, a silent thank-you that spoke volumes. She might have been wondering which would expire first—her lengthy career at the *Register*, or the paper itself.

Our drive lasted barely ten minutes, but it took us out beyond the edge of town to a parcel of land that few people even knew existed. It had been part of the expansive holdings of the Questman family, whose name was still synonymous with the timber and paper empire that had been Dumont's original raison d'être. Mary Questman had first shown it to Marson a few years earlier, when he was designing the performing-arts center. Later, after I entered his life, he bought the land from Mary, surprised me with the deed and a topographical survey, then challenged me: "Design the perfect house."

Glee had seen the house plans, but not the land. "Good heavens," she said as we got out of the SUV, "it's breathtaking."

The site was lightly wooded with birches where it opened to a prairie, which was held in trust by a conservancy. A stream ran through a craggy ravine, forming a playful waterfall of perhaps twenty feet where some Ice Age mischief had cleaved upper and lower plateaus. When Marson had first taken me there, my heart skipped a beat, and I knew how Frank Lloyd Wright must have felt on his first visit to Bear Run in Pennsylvania. The similarity of this setting was arresting, and I quickly formed a mental image of the vista that would be enjoyed from a house perched on the upper plateau—a prairie view that would never change, never be developed, preserved for posterity.

In a hushed tone, Glee asked me, "Know what this reminds me of?"

I put an arm around her shoulders as we looked up at the stream's gently falling water. "Of course," I said. "You've seen my drawings of the house; the inspiration was pretty obvious."

"But you took a more minimal approach. Wright's concept was to make the house seem like an outgrowth of nature. Yours is more … polished."

I recalled, "Marson called my design 'a faceted jewel in the woods.'"

"Yes!" said Glee, flinging her arms wide. "Brody, you've just given me the headline for my story." And with that, she whipped the phone out of her purse and went to work snapping pictures.

Meanwhile, I inspected the grading that had been completed on Wednesday—the main footprint of the house on the upper plateau, as well as the sloped access that would eventually become the driveway. Orange stakes protruded from the ground, delineating the outer walls of the house and the anchor-points of the cantilever that would extend over the water. I stepped into our "living room" and surveyed the view.

"How's it look?" asked Glee, approaching me from behind.

I turned to her and grinned. "Perfect."

Back in the Range Rover, I managed to turn us around and began a slow exit of the property, following the tracks left by construction equipment the day before. Glee was dashing off something in shorthand on her spiral-bound steno pad. The chain attached to her reading glasses swung at the sides of her neck as the vehicle found its footing. She asked, "How did Marson convince Mary to sell the land? It's a little slice of paradise out here."

"Off the record?"

She closed her notebook.

I explained, "When Mary first showed him the land, she told him she'd been tendered many offers for it over the years, but she'd never felt right about parting with it. Then, after I entered the picture, Marson approached her with an idea—our perfect house—and she was all in. She sold him the land for a song. They sealed the deal then and there. As a deposit, Mary took whatever cash Marson had in his pocket."

Glee let out a loud laugh. "That is *so* Mary."

"I guess she likes us."

Glee paused. When she spoke, her voice carried a note of concern. "So you and Marson, you genuinely *care* about Mary, right?"

"Absolutely."

Glee explained, "I've known her forever. Not that we run in

the same circles, but we're at all the same charity events—I write the stories, she writes the checks. And over the years, we've grown to be close friends. Two tough old birds. Bosom buddies. So I can't help feeling a bit worried."

"Why?" I eased off the gas and turned my eyes from the road to look at Glee. "Is something wrong?"

"Well, I hope not." With a little snort of laughter, she added, "It's just—that *cat*."

I shared the laugh and returned my attention to the road. "Mister Puss? He's a cutie pie. What's the matter—allergic to him?"

"Brodie." Her castor beans rattled as she pivoted in her seat to face me. "You know very well that's not the issue. She *talks* to him. More to the point, *he* talks back. At least she thinks he does."

"Maybe he does."

"Brody. I'm serious—don't you find this at all disturbing?"

I hemmed. "These last few months, Mary's had a new spring in her step. The cat brings her pleasure. If she has conversations with Mister Puss, that's harmless enough."

"I suppose," said Glee. "Although sometimes, you have to wonder."

With a chuckle, I asked, "Did Mary tell you? Mister Puss gave her the thumbs-up to invest in FlabberGas."

Glee froze for a moment, suddenly on full alert. She removed her glasses. "What?"

Oops. I said nothing.

"Brody? Sweetie?" The inflection of her kindly words carried an undisguised lilt of menace.

So I told her all about it.

She had her glasses back on—she was taking notes again—when she asked with delicious anticipation, "And the presentation at Mary's place is *when*?"

"Tomorrow afternoon, four o'clock."

She clicked her ballpoint. "I'll call her. Maybe I can finagle an invitation."

"From your bosom buddy? I should think so." I slowed the SUV as we approached downtown Dumont on First Avenue.

Glee glanced at her watch. "Hungry? I owe you lunch."

"You got *that* right."

Friday afternoon, Marson and I arrived at Mary Questman's house on Prairie Street around three o'clock, an hour before the scheduled start of Dr. Francis Frumpkin's presentation, pitching his chain of FlabberGas clinics to potential investors. Mary greeted us at the door with a kiss and a cheery "Welcome, boys—do come in." As we stood in the open doorway, Mister Puss circled Mary's ankles, purring.

Marson asked, "Aren't you afraid he'll take off?"

"Oh, *no*. Mister Puss would never pull a stunt like that—he promised."

Marson laughed with Mary and turned to give me a wink.

As Mary closed the door, the cat left her ankles to investigate mine. His purring grew louder as he peered up at me.

I crouched to give him a rub behind the ears. "How's every little thing in *your* world, Mister Puss?" He reached a front paw to my knee and stretched his head to my face, touching his nose to my chin. His purr grew so intense, it gurgled.

Mary twittered, "Someone has a new friend."

"Me?" I asked. "Or Mister Puss?"

"*Both* of you."

He seemed to want me to pick him up—odd for a cat, I thought—so I did, lifting him with one arm as I stood again.

We weren't the first to arrive. Mary said, "Francis is in the living room. Can you show yourself in? I need to check with

Berta in the kitchen."

"Of course," Marson told her. "We'll be fine."

Mary retreated to the back of the hall and through a swinging door as we made a turn and stepped through the double doors to the living room.

A grand and gracious space, it bespoke old money, with softly patterned wallpaper, white enameled doors and trim, and tall windows draped in bone-colored silk. A nine-foot Steinway anchored one end of the room, with a stately marble-faced fireplace dominating the opposite wall. Three matching chandeliers hung overhead; thick wool carpeting stretched underfoot. In the middle of the room, a large grouping of upholstered furniture had been spread apart to form a clearing for the two easels that held my drawings, delivered earlier that day.

As we entered, Frumpkin turned from the easels, where he stood with another man, and beamed that perfect, manufactured smile. In his cashmere jacket—peacock blue, with a poofed-up yellow pocket silk that looked like a canary perched near his shoulder—he bounded across the room to greet us. *"Brody,"* he bellowed, "I couldn't be more *thrilled* with your work!"

As he neared us, Mister Puss squirmed from my arms, dropped to the floor, and retreated to the foot of an overstuffed armchair, where he sat and watched.

Frumpkin pumped my hand, holding on too long while turning to tell Marson, from the side of his mouth, "What a *talented* young man you've got."

Marson responded dryly, "Thank you, Francis."

I said to Frumpkin, "Glad you're pleased."

Leading us over to the easels, he said, "You need to meet Jason, my son-in-law."

Dr. Jason Ward, husband of Frumpkin's daughter, Sarah, was about my age or so, maybe forty. Reasonably good-looking, lean, and very clean-cut, he fit the visual stereotype I've often associated with doctors. As we conversed, I found him well-spoken but not animated, certainly not in comparison to Frumpkin, whose presence seemed to command all of the energy in any setting. In that sense, Jason was a good match for Sarah, both of them living in the shadow of—and working for—the flamboyant Dr. Frumpkin.

Jason pondered the drawings for a moment. "Hard to believe this is about to get off the ground. To be honest, the idea struck me as far-fetched at first. But now? The sky's the limit."

"If"—Frumpkin, raised a cautionary finger—"if, and only if, we can convince a few members of the investing class that the potential rewards are worth the risk."

I reminded him, "Mary seems sold."

"Bless her heart," said Frumpkin with a grin that made me uneasy.

The doorbell rang, and I heard some to-and-fro in the hall as Frumpkin questioned Marson about construction lead times.

"Start to finish, a year ought to do it."

Berta, Mary's housekeeper, led Sarah Frumpkin Ward into the room, along with a little girl and an attractive (*very* attractive) middle-aged man. Berta watched as Mister Puss skittered behind a sofa, then she flashed him a scrunched, ugly face before leaving for the kitchen.

Sarah told the girl, who hung behind her, "Say hi to Grampa."

Frumpkin crouched and waved the girl forward, "Come on, Olivia. Grampa wants a kiss."

She skipped over to him, delivered the requested peck, and pulled back again.

Jason crouched. "Hey, princess, what about Daddy?"

But Olivia wasn't interested. She'd spotted Mister Puss and was stalking him from the far side of the couch.

Introductions were made. I learned that Olivia was seven years old, in second grade, and "a bit of a problem these days," according to her mother. The attractive man, as I had guessed, was Dahr Ahmadi, Frumpkin's certified nurse practitioner. Because both Frumpkin and his son-in-law had earlier driven their cars to Mary's house, Dahr had driven Sarah to pick up Olivia after school.

It was easy to see why Frumpkin was so taken by Dahr, with his natural body tan and a hint of the exotic in his Persian features. I didn't know much about his culture, but I knew it wasn't gay-friendly, so I had to wonder if Frumpkin was barking up the wrong tree. Nonetheless, my trusty gaydar was sending signals that Frumpkin was on the right track. Marson sensed it, too— he couldn't take his eyes off the guy.

Dahr shook our hands. "You're the architects? Really great to meet you." Tuesday evening, Sarah had mentioned that Dahr was Iranian, but he spoke with no accent at all, so I gathered he had moved here long ago.

Marson replied, "It's our firm, yes. But Brody designed *this* project."

Dahr looked at the drawings. "Amazing, Brody! Francis has talked of nothing else since your dinner meeting. He says you're a genius. I agree."

I liked him. I'm easy.

Next to arrive was Thomas Simms, our county sheriff. A tall black man with a graceful bearing and a refined workday wardrobe of natty business suits and eye-popping rep neckties, Simms defied every stereotype of the small-town cop. He had also defied all the odds of rising from the rank of detective and being elected top lawman in Dumont County, where the white-bread demographics were as rooted as the region's timbered past. With his modest nature and a caring spirit, Simms had coasted to that first election while still in his thirties. Now in his early forties, he was up for reelection within a few weeks, in November.

Not long after my arrival in Dumont, when I first met the sheriff at a chamber luncheon, I had asked Marson if Simms was gay. "No," said Marson, "not unless his wife, Gloria, and their little Tommy are parties to an elaborate sham."

Gloria and Tommy were with the sheriff today as Mary escorted them into the living room. Gloria, like her husband, had a sharp sense of style, never looking less than sensational; she managed to make most other women in Dumont look frumpy. Their well-mannered young son was adorable in a tiny blazer and dressy wool slacks.

Mary asked, "Do you know everyone, Thomas?"

"Yes, Miss Mary, I think so, except Dr. Frumpkin. Don't believe I've had the pleasure." He and Frumpkin shook hands and exchanged pleasantries. The sheriff wished the doctor good luck with his new business venture; the doctor wished the sheriff good luck with his reelection.

Although Simms had not previously met Frumpkin, he and Gloria were already on a first-name basis with Frumpkin's daughter, Sarah, and her husband, Jason. This struck me as curious, till I realized that little Olivia and little Tommy were both in second grade at the same school. And it seemed they all attended the same church, St. Alban's—a reminder that Dumont was indeed a small town.

Berta appeared with a tray of filled, chilled champagne flutes, and we all gratefully partook (not the kids, of course, who got ginger ale). I stepped over to Frumpkin, clinked his glass, and said, "Nice touch, the champagne."

With a knowing nod, he replied, "No harm in a bit of lubrication prior to the pitch."

Marson and Mary huddled nearby with the sheriff, who was telling them, "Don't want to sound overconfident, but I'm starting to think the election's a done deal. I met with the *Register's* editorial board this week, and from the tone of it, they seem to think so, too."

I stepped into the conversation, telling the sheriff, "I don't know much about your opponent. Alex Kastle—he's in your department?"

Simms exhaled a weary sigh. "Yeah, he's a deputy. A deputy with ambitions." He said no more.

"Well," said Mary with a touch of indignation, "if his ambition is to replace *you*, Thomas, he'll be mighty disappointed. If your funds run short, just let me know."

"Thank you, Miss Mary. You've been way too generous already."

Marson said, "The election's still a month away. You can coast for a while and see if Kastle gets any traction—which he won't."

Simms reminded him, "The election may be a month away, but early voting starts two weeks from Monday."

The doorbell rang, and Berta went to answer it. While leaving the room, she paused just long enough to stamp a foot near the back of the sofa where Mister Puss had retreated from Olivia's pursuit.

Marson asked Simms, "So, Thomas—are you thinking of investing in FlabberGas? Or are you just here for the show?"

Mary answered for him. "Thomas is here because I invited him. He's always welcome in my home. And if he happens to sniff an opportunity that's of interest, all the better."

At that moment, Mister Puss let out a yowl and raced to the middle of the room. Olivia followed, yelling, "I. Said. *Here, Kitty!*" With her little-princess dress, reddened face, and bared teeth, she looked possessed.

Sarah marched forward and grabbed her daughter by the arm. "You behave right *now*, young lady. Are you ready for a time-out?" The child seethed at her.

Tommy Simms, standing next to his mother, froze ramrod stiff, watching with unbelieving eyes.

Mister Puss, looking proud to have vanquished his tormentress, sauntered over to Tommy and nuzzled his shins. The boy stooped to pet the cat, whose purr rumbled in the silenced room.

Dahr stepped over to Sarah. "Why don't I take her outside?" Sarah nodded. Dahr offered his hand, which Olivia took, and they left quietly together.

When the chatter resumed, Jason brought Sarah a fresh glass of champagne, telling his wife, "Doctor's orders." She mustered a weak laugh, thanked Jason, and drank.

I followed Mary as she joined them. She said, "I do hope your daughter finds herself in better spirits soon. It can have its rough spots—childhood."

Jason said, "I'm sorry she was so disruptive, Mrs. Questman."

"Nonsense, dear. She's precious."

Precious? I thought Tommy Simms was precious, the embodiment of a model child. But Olivia was an absolute hellion.

Sarah said, "She's gotten into this phase of 'acting out.' The only *good* thing about phases—they pass. At least that's what they say. Any time now, I'm ready."

Jason asked, "Any word from Dr. Hammond?"

Sarah brightened. "Yes, in fact. His office called while I was in the car." She turned to explain to us, "Since all of this started, about six months ago, Jason and I have been taking Olivia to a number of child psychologists, as far away as Milwaukee, but as you've just seen, not much progress. So we've been *trying* to get in with Dr. Hammond in Green Bay, one of the best anywhere.

He's busy, naturally, and with schedules and school, we haven't been able to land an appointment. But *now*"—she pivoted to her husband—"they just had a cancellation, so there's an opening tomorrow at one."

"Honey, I'm *slammed* tomorrow. We can't rebook that many patients *now*, on Friday afternoon."

"I'll take her."

"We're a *family*. We're in this together. I want to be there for both of you."

"I know, sweets," said Sarah, "and I appreciate your commitment. But God only knows when there'll be another opening on a Saturday. So I'm taking her."

Jason shrugged, but he didn't look happy to be left out.

Over the next quarter hour, guests continued to arrive, some of them known to me—a banker, a lawyer or two, and Clem Carter, who was building our house—but there were several others I didn't recognize at all, conspicuously older, who must have been denizens of the moneyed elite invited by Mary from surrounding towns. The presentation was not set to begin for another ten minutes, so everyone mingled and gabbed, gravitating near the drawings on the easels, which drew both high praise and muffled snickers. In any other circumstances, I would have taken umbrage at having my work laughed at, but given the whimsical nature of the FlabberGas project, I took it as a compliment.

Berta continued to circulate with a silver tray bearing finger food—shrimp, tiny crab cakes, and inch-sized cubes of rare beef tenderloin on toast points. Mister Puss followed at her heels; she looked down now and then to hiss at the cat or tell him to scat. When Berta approached me with the tray, I said, "Looks like someone must enjoy your cooking. Or is it just the fish?"

Deadpan, Berta informed me, "His Majesty prefers beef."

"Then I'll have to try it." Which I did, finding it sublime. The cat moved from Berta's ankles to mine.

Berta leaned near as I chewed and swallowed, telling me, "And not just *any* beef, mind you, not for His Majesty. Mary added ground sirloin to my shopping list, with a note that said, 'Mister Puss might enjoy it, but make sure it's good and lean.' So I brought back a pound. Next day, another note: 'He didn't care for it. Better pick up a nice tenderloin. Help yourself to the ground sirloin for lunch.' So I ended up eating His Majesty's leftovers."

I tried not to laugh. Marson had always described Berta as "impertinent," but I thought a better adjective might be "woebegone." I said to her, "Mister Puss has highly refined tastes. It's excellent, Berta." And I took another.

Berta flashed me a wry smile, then turned to other guests.

As she moved away, I ate the toast and gave the meat to the cat. He ate it with such rapture, he quivered. When he finished, he reached a paw to my knee, so I picked him up, holding him with one arm. As I carried him about the room, he seemed to appreciate the elevated perspective of the proceedings, purring in response to the tweaks and twiddles that others offered while we moved through the crowd.

"A fine animal, isn't he?" The man who made the comment had a deeply lined but kind, smiling face and wore a corduroy sport coat with knotted-leather buttons. He looked about sixty or so and seemed, for lack of a better word, somewhat countrified, slightly out of place but totally at ease in Mary's elegant living room.

I introduced myself.

He said, "Jim Phelps. I'm Mary's vet. I mean, I'm the *cat's* vet." He laughed.

Mister Puss got squirmy, so I reached down and dropped him

the last foot to the floor. He stretched, found his land legs, and wandered into the crowd.

I shook the doctor's hand. "She really dotes on Mister Puss. And why not? He's a great little guy."

"A fine animal," the vet repeated. Leaning close, he added, "And *highly* intelligent."

I thought, Did he just wink at me? He did. He knows. He knows that Mary thinks the cat talks to her.

Without explanation or context, I asked him quietly, "Should I be concerned about Mary?"

With the slightest shake of his head, he said, "Nah. On balance, the cat's good for her."

"My thoughts exactly."

"On the other hand," said Phelps, "I *am* concerned about Mary buying into this FlabberGas nonsense."

"You think it's nonsense?" I wasn't being defensive; I wanted to know.

"Well, *yeah*. Granted, I'm here to learn, and I'll keep an open mind. But on the surface? It sounds *nuts*."

His down-to-earth logic shook me. Had I gotten myself involved with a project I should have turned down at the outset? I shook his hand again. "Glad to meet you, Jim." And I stepped away, plucking from my sleeve a few stray hairs from Mister Puss—without ever having mentioned that I was Frumpkin's architect.

Dahr Ahmadi returned to the living room with Olivia in tow. The girl looked calm now, but there was something about that princess dress that stressed me. Why, I wondered, were parents now letting little kids wear "costumes" as normal attire? Halloween was just around the corner—couldn't it wait? And the *worse* infraction, at least to my mind, was that the dress looked ratty. If you're doing the princess-thing, glam it up. But Olivia's Cinderella appeared to have stepped from the scullery, not the ball. Were her parents blind to this, or was Olivia simply incapable of getting through the day without making a mess of herself? Honestly, she'd have looked better, *prettier*, in jeans and a sweater.

I watched as Dahr delivered Olivia to Sarah, who sat down with her daughter on the piano bench and tried to fix her hair, spruce her clothes.

Then Dahr moved over to Jason Ward and huddled with him in conversation. But Jason quickly backed off and raised his voice. Dr. Frumpkin must have sensed trouble, so he stepped in, as did I. Jason was saying, "When I want advice, Dahr, I'll ask for it."

Frumpkin, sounding testy, reminded them, "This isn't the time or the place."

Dahr said, "My apologies, Francis. Just trying to help."

"Help?" said Jason. "You're incompetent."

Frumpkin told Jason, "You *know* that's not true." He checked his watch. "We need to get this rolling soon. Let's shape up and look smart."

Dahr went over to the piano bench and helped with Olivia's hair.

Frumpkin stepped aside with me, confiding, "My son-in-law has become jealous of my nurse practitioner."

I wasn't sure I'd heard him correctly. "Why would Jason be jealous of Dahr?"

"Simple," said Frumpkin. "I've made no secret of my efforts to woo Dahr, and although I've had little success—so far—Jason seems to fear that my relationship with Dahr will bring him into the family and into the business. I'd like that. Jason wouldn't."

As Frumpkin moved over to the piano to review his notes

with Sarah, I noticed that the room had grown dusky. At four o'clock in October, it was still a couple of hours till sunset, but the day had been gray, and a full canopy of trees surrounding the grand old home was an effective barrier to the remaining sunlight.

Mary entered the room from the hall and, noticing the dim surroundings, switched on the chandeliers, which drew a gasp of surprise from the guests, perhaps twenty of us. "That's better," she said, although to my eye, the room now seemed too bright.

At her side was Walter Zakarian, a portly but elegant man who had recently returned from a hush-hush birthday trip to Puerto Vallarta, celebrating his fiftieth.

Some said he had a shady past—there were rumors that his long-ago ancestors had dabbled in the slave trade with Persians and Turks. His version of the story was different—his forebears had built their wealth as honorable traders of spices, then silk, and finally rugs. To this day, he carried on that tradition in Dumont, where he owned the region's largest flooring and carpeting business. In his cable commercials, he called himself the Karastan King.

A clotheshorse with a taste for custom tailoring, he often donned a tux and served as escort to several of the town's wealthier widows, including Mary, but the lifelong bachelor fooled no one. Deeply closeted, he maintained his charade in Dumont, fearful that doing otherwise would be bad for business. Marson and I found this attitude ridiculous. "Who cares," Marson once asked me, "if the guy selling you a rug is gay?"

But Zakarian cared, so he bottled up his desires and packed his bags for occasional quick getaways to a condo he owned—south of the border. A year ago, one of these escapades had gone seriously awry, and the trouble followed him back home. As a result, he still limped. Which gave him an excuse to augment his vast wardrobe with a collection of antique walking sticks. Today's was made of rosewood, capped with the head of a toucan, carved from jade. He squeezed its beak as he hobbled in my direction.

From a few feet off, Sheriff Simms watched with a grin as Zakarian closed in on me.

"Wonderful so see you, Brody." Zakarian shook my hand. "It's been too long."

"Just back from Mexico, Walter? You're looking tanned and rested."

"Yes, yes, it was lovely, thanks. The birthday was a gruesome milestone, but it beats the alternative. I tried to make the best of it." He shifted his weight as he spoke. The tip of his cane poked dimples in the deep wool pile of the Karastan he'd sold Mary.

I asked, "Are you here to learn about FlabberGas? Or just keeping Mary company?"

"Both, I guess. She says it might be a good investment opportunity, so who knows? Never hurts to get in on the ground floor." He paused, scowled. "Except ..."

I noticed that Dr. Frumpkin was watching our conversation. I asked Zakarian, "Except what?"

The direction of his glance told me that he, too, had noticed Frumpkin watching us. "I just don't like him—Francis Frumpkin. We've had issues."

"Oh, really?" I was tempted to add, What sort of issues? But I refrained.

"Yes, really. So be careful with him. I know you're working for him."

Zakarian's choice of words—that I was "working for" Frumpkin—gave me pause. Was that how people saw it? To my mind, I had merely taken on a design commission.

"Speaking of which," said Zakarian, "I'm dying to see what

you've cooked up for Francis. Excuse me while I go take a look at your drawings." And he shuffled off toward the easels, where people were starting to gather for the presentation.

Sheriff Simms stepped over to me and asked, "How's our friend doing?"

"With Walter," I said, "how can you tell? I've never known anyone more guarded, more circumspect. Beyond all the beautiful clothes and well-chosen words—deeper than that, there seems to be *nothing*. At least, nothing he's willing to reveal."

"And that was the problem, wasn't it?" said Simms.

He was referring to the incident a year ago, when Walter had been the target of mischief that could have proved deadly. Though he survived, he had offered no cooperation in helping the investigation get to the bottom of what had happened. Because aspects of the case had pointed to Walter's closeted "other life," Simms had come to rely on Marson and me for insights and advice.

Watching Walter, who was now huddled with Sarah Frumpkin Ward, I said to Simms, "That was the problem, all right. How do you save a man who refuses to be helped?"

Simms patted my arm. "But you solved it, Brody. Still don't know how you figured it out, but you helped close the case."

With a soft laugh, I recalled, "Just the other night, Marson was bragging on me. He told Dr. Frumpkin that I'm 'a first-class problem-solver.' And now? I'm designing—of *all* things—a FlabberGas clinic."

"Works for me," said Simms. His radiant smile rivaled Dr. Frumpkin's—without the cosmetic upgrades. Then he stepped away to join his wife and their young son.

I checked my watch and saw that it was a few minutes past four. Spotting Marson near the edge of the group in the middle of the room, I moved to join him, asking, "Are the natives getting restless?"

"Hardly. The champagne is still flowing. They're fine."

"Where have you been?"

"Circulating. Singing your praises."

"Too kind." I paused. "Is there actually any interest in Flab-berGas?"

He chuckled. "We'll soon find out, won't we?"

And then, Glee Savage arrived.

Mary spotted her from the far end of the room, where she stood with a banker friend, holding Mister Puss. With a yoo-hoo, she called, "Welcome, love! I was afraid you might not make it." All heads turned.

Standing in the doorway to the hall, Glee removed a little fur shrug, handed it to Berta in exchange for a glass of champagne, and strutted into the living room on five-inch heels. "Hellish day at the office," she said. "Did I miss anything?"

"Just the appetizers," said Mary, meeting her halfway, kissing cheeks. "But the show's about to begin."

"Fabulous." Glee leaned in to touch noses with Mister Puss. "I'd like to nab Dr. Frumpkin for a few quick questions first, or should I wait?"

"Suppose we go ask him," suggested Mary.

But Frumpkin was already barreling toward them. Stepping between the ladies, he asked Glee, too loudly, "What are *you* doing here?"

"It so *happens* I was invited." She flashed him a stiff smile, then sipped her champagne.

Mary set down Mister Puss, telling Frumpkin with measured patience, "This is my home, Francis. Glee is my guest."

I was standing nearby with Marson. The cat came over and sat at my feet, watching the confrontation—along with every-one else in the room.

Frumpkin looked steamed, but restrained himself. He explained, "Forgive me, dear Mary, but it makes me a bit uneasy to include a member of the working press."

With innocent curiosity, Mary asked, "Why? I thought the whole purpose today was to *promote* your project."

"Certainly ... yes," said Frumpkin, careful with his words, "but the message we want to send to the public is one thing. It's different from our messaging to potential investors. Today we'll discuss strategies, numbers—nuts and bolts intended *only* for those of us here in this room."

"Well," said Glee, stating the obvious, "I'm *here*. Here in this room."

Frumpkin gave Mary a pleading look.

She repeated, firmly, "Glee is my guest, Francis."

Frumpkin turned to the reporter. His tone was menacing: "There's a lot at stake here. I do *not* want you writing *anything* about this—not yet. Do you understand?"

The crowd was hushed. The room bristled with an electric sense of anticipation. Even Olivia, the little princess from hell, seemed to smell blood, watching with a hungry stare and bared teeth.

Frumpkin again asked Glee, "Do you understand?" His question sounded more like a command.

She waited a tantalizing moment and glanced at me with a crooked smile before telling Frumpkin, "I understand your wishes."

"Good," he said with a brusque nod. Affecting a breezier tone, he suggested, "Then let's get started, shall we, everyone?" He stepped to the center of the room, joining his daughter in front of the easels. There were now three easels instead of two, one of them draped.

The eyes of the crowd followed his movement as he took position for his opening remarks. Mister Puss wandered off, perhaps for a better view.

Back on the sidelines, Glee stepped over to Marson and me.

Speaking low, she told us, "I may *understand* Frumpkin's wishes, but in the immortal words of Mick Jagger: you can't always get what you want."

Marson suggested, "Maybe just sit on it awhile?"

Glee shook her head. "Can't. I've already drafted the story, and my editor loves it. Couldn't stop it if I wanted to—which I don't. I'd hoped to interview Frumpkin and get some missing details. Instead, I'll just use a few quotes from his spiel."

And the spiel had begun.

I found Frumpkin's presentation predictable—I'd heard most of it at the restaurant on Tuesday night. No question, the man had an innate knack for showmanship. He knew how to tell a good story, and today, he had my drawings to back up his pitch, which made the FlabberGas concept seem less bizarre and more tangible.

At Tuesday's dinner, Sarah had told me, "Dad's always suffered from an acute sense of theater." And today, those instincts were on full display as he whipped the draping from the third easel and revealed a huge blowup of the photo depicting his grandfather, Archibald Frumpkin, with the student pilots and the parachute. I had no way of knowing if the man in the photo was truly his grandfather. I had no way of knowing if his grandfather had actually floated provocative theories regarding the effects of altitude and oxygen on human metabolism. Whether fact or hokum, though, these particulars lent a folksy charm to the backstory of Frumpkin's inspiration. He told the crowd that his grandfather was a genius. He then called *me* a genius, pointing me out as the architect of the proposed clinic. Applause filled the room.

While acknowledging the tribute with a wave, I noticed Jim Phelps, the veterinarian, looking at me, puzzled, perhaps dismayed. I gave him a sheepish shrug—and regretted not informing him earlier, when we'd met, that I was designing Frumpkin's project, which Phelps had called "nuts." As Phelps returned his focus to the presentation, Mister Puss moved out of the crowd and settled near the vet's feet.

Then Sarah took over, offering to answer questions from the group. At once, hands shot up, waving eagerly. I thought, My God, they're *buying* this.

Sarah called on one of Mary's friends, a decked-out matron who asked, "I find all of this so *fascinating*. If FlabberGas does what you say it does, this could be bigger than Weight Watchers! But I don't quite understand how the gas treatments work. Can you tell us more?"

Sarah said, "That's a natural question at this point, since FlabberGas is such a revolutionary development. As to how it *works,* that's a little beyond my paygrade." Everyone laughed. Sarah continued, "Dad? Can you review this for us?"

"With pleasure." Frumpkin indulged in a dramatic pause, waiting till all eyes were trained on him. "FlabberGas," he began, "is the registered trade name for an overall treatment process that combines diet, exercise, and the administration of oxygen. The program is approved as safe and effective for loss of weight. What does the oxygen do? It contributes a glorious aura of well-being. And the hyperbaric chamber enhances the perceived efficacy of the weekly treatments."

Quack.

Dr. Frumpkin flinched. A nervous titter rippled through the room. Heads turned in the direction of Jim Phelps.

He stood only a few feet from me, at the back of the crowd. The rude comment did seem to have come from him, as if uttered under his breath. He bobbed his head around, making an unconvincing display of wondering who had spoken. Even Mister Puss looked up at him with an accusing stare.

"Uh, Jim," Frumpkin asked the vet, "did you say something?"

"Nope." He chuckled. "Not me."

"Anyway," Frumpkin told everyone, "I realize the FlabberGas concept can be confusing, or even sound a bit crazy. *But:* seeing is believing. So I want to invite all of you to a demonstration of the technique later this weekend." His words were received with excited chitchat and scattered applause.

The vet strolled over to Marson and me.

I said, "It seems Frumpkin didn't win you over. To be honest, I'm not so sure myself."

He rested his hand on my shoulder and looked me in the eye. "Brody, he's a huckster. It's a fraud." Removing his hand, he added, "Frankly, it should be stopped." Then he nodded good-bye, stepped away, and left the room.

Marson leaned near to ask, "Are you really having second thoughts about this?"

"I just don't know."

Frumpkin explained that the demonstration would be held at noon that Sunday at a small surgical clinic that he owned on the outskirts of town. He and several other doctors used it to perform various outpatient procedures, and it had a single hyperbaric chamber, which Frumpkin had been using for the testing and development of FlabberGas. On Sunday, of course, our little crowd would have the facility to ourselves.

"Now, here's the exciting part," said Frumpkin. "Maybe I should hold a raffle or an auction for this, but I need a volunteer to be the 'subject' of our demonstration."

Someone joked, "You mean 'victim,' don't you?"

Everyone laughed, including Frumpkin, who said, "No, not at all. 'Guinea pig?' Maybe."

Mimicking a carnival barker, Sarah told the crowd, "All right, ladies and gentlemen, you heard the man. We need ourselves one—count'em, *one*—one brave guinea pig who won't mind losing a little weight."

The laughter waned. No one volunteered.

So Mary Questman herself came to the rescue. Stepping to the front of the crowd, she said, "I'll be your guinea pig, Francis. But I'm not sure if I qualify—I've *done* this before."

"Indeed you have." Frumpkin beamed. "And of *course* you qualify. We'll be honored to have you serve as our guinea pig on Sunday."

Everyone applauded. Mary flopped a hand to her bosom, telling them, "Well, it's not as if I can't afford to shed another *pound* or two." They laughed.

Marson and I exchanged a wary glance. I found it difficult to imagine our dear friend, Dumont's doyenne philanthropist, laid out in public view with her open-toe Ferragamos peeping up through the plastic lid of a hyperbaric chamber. What was she *thinking?*

Mister Puss had made his way through the crowd and approached Mary, who lifted him from the floor and held him in her arms. As she prattled with her guests, the cat's rumbling purr seemed to fill the room. He wriggled up her chest and stretched his snout to her cheek. Then he stuck his nose in her ear.

The next day, late Saturday afternoon, I was home at the loft with Marson, having returned together from the office after a few hours of catching up on various projects—the county museum, our perfect house, a proposal for a new university building in Appleton, and another for a civic center in faraway Oregon. Demand for the Miles & Norris design brand was definitely in expansion mode. Lucky us.

But I'd been troubled all day by the FlabberGas project—not only my involvement with it, but also Mary's. At home now with Marson, I continued to pester him with my misgivings as we attempted to enjoy an early cocktail before heading out to dinner with friends. "Would it be unethical," I asked my husband, "to withdraw from the project? I could refuse payment, take back the design, and be done with it."

Marson swirled his drink. "No, I wouldn't call it 'unethical.' But it might be stupid."

I raised an inquisitive brow.

"Frumpkin would feel betrayed. This is a small town. Why create rifts? Plus, realistically, what are the chances he'll ever get this built? If the project has no merit, investors won't sign on. But if it *does* have merit, then all's well. Meanwhile, collect your payment and take pride in your design—you deserve both."

I had to admit, "I like your logic." Then I frowned. "But what about Mary?"

Again the voice of reason: "She was involved with this before you were. She's entitled to make her own decisions. She often confides in me, and if she were feeling bilked, I'd know about it."

Right on cue, Marson's cell phone rang. Glancing at the screen he said, "Speak of the devil." Taking the call, he said, "Hello there, Mary! We were just talking about you. *Yes*, of course, all of it good. What can I do for you?"

Listening to his side of the conversation, I couldn't get the gist of it, as she seemed to be doing most of the talking. Finally, he said, "Okay, Mary, we'll try to take care of it. Don't give it another thought. Bye, love."

"Well?" I said as he took another sip of his drink. "Is she feeling bilked?"

"Not at all." He was toying with me.

I gave him a look that said, Would you *please* get to the point?

He said, "Mary's having second thoughts about being the guinea pig."

"Thank God." Relieved beyond measure, I added, "Glad it

finally dawned on her—the indignity of putting herself on display like that."

"No, that's not the reason." He rattled the ice that remained in his glass. "You see, Mister Puss told her not to go through with it. He's been bugging her about it since last night."

Mary had phoned Marson because she had already called Dr. Frumpkin several times and couldn't reach him. She wondered if we could get in touch with Frumpkin's daughter and let her know that Mary was backing out. I told Marson, "I can handle that—*I'm* the one getting paid."

So I phoned Sarah Frumpkin Ward at home. She answered on the first ring, and I gave her the news.

"Ugh," she said, "it's always something, right? But hold on a sec."

Her husband was there with her, and I heard her apprise him of the situation.

"No problem," said Jason. "I'll just do it myself."

"Thanks, sweetie, that makes it easy." Then she asked me, "You heard?"

"Yeah, great—didn't want to leave you in the lurch."

"All set, then. But why did Mary change her mind? Isn't she feeling well?"

I hesitated. "Nothing like that. She's fine. I'm guessing she felt the demonstration might come across as unladylike—she's sorta old-school."

"Such a sweet old soul," said Sarah.

I couldn't bring myself to tell her that the plans had been nixed by Mary's cat.

4

Glee Savage had told us, on Friday afternoon, that her editor at the *Dumont Daily Register* "loved" the draft of her FlabberGas story. She hadn't exaggerated—her editor's enthusiasm for the finished story proved sufficient to bump the lighthearted feature to page one of the Sunday edition.

While Marson and I woke up that morning with our coffee, we passed the paper back and forth for another read, and our initial appreciation of the story's levity gave way to the sinking feeling that Dr. Frumpkin's displeasure with its timing would surely be compounded by the story's flippant tone, which verged on ridicule.

FlabberGas, anyone?

Local doctor to launch chain of gas clinics,
claiming new technique sheds flab

By Glee Savage

·

OCT. 10, DUMONT, WI—Dr. Francis Frumpkin, a noted dermatologist and cosmetic surgeon with offices in Dumont and Milwaukee, has a big idea for a smaller you. It involves a gas treatment administered in a hyperbaric chamber, inspired by the writings of the doctor's grandfather, Dr. Archibald Frumpkin.

The elder Frumpkin's field of practice was neither medicine nor weight loss, but aeronautical engineering. Though the connection may seem tenuous, Dr. Francis Frumpkin explains that his newly developed method "contributes a glorious aura of well-being" to the otherwise unpleasant rigors of dieting and exercise.

Too good to be true? Speaking to a group of potential investors on Friday, Dr. Frumpkin acknowledged, "I realize the FlabberGas concept can be confusing, or even sound a bit crazy."

To counter some overtly crude skepticism expressed by one of the attendees, the doctor has arranged a demonstration of an actual gas treatment. Investors can then judge for themselves if there's more than hot air to FlabberGas …

The column continued in this vein, tongue-in-cheek, to the bottom of the page. Marson blew a low whistle. "At least Glee didn't give the time or location of today's demo."

I nodded. "And even though she hinted, she didn't spill the beans that the mystery gas is nothing but plain old oxygen."

"Now, *that*," said Marson, "that would be grounds for murder."

We both laughed.

Shortly before noon, Marson drove us out to the edge of town, where Associated Surgery Center was located along a woodsy stretch of county road. The building was hidden as we approached, but a sign at the roadside marked the entrance. It listed some eight or ten doctors who made use of the clinic for their outpatient procedures, including a gynecologist, an oral surgeon, and an ophthalmologist. But the biggest name, at the top, was Dr. Francis Frumpkin, who owned and had built the facility.

As we pulled into the parking lot, the first thing I noticed was the squad car.

It caught Marson's eye as well. "Sheriff's department. I wonder what's up—Simms never drives one of those."

A dozen or more other cars had already arrived, some of them known to us: Mary Questman's spiffed but unpretentious Buick, Walter Zakarian's massive Lincoln Navigator, Dr. Frumpkin's sporty Mercedes, and a tan, anonymous-looking Chrysler that looked like the sedan normally driven by Sheriff Simms. With a measure of relief, I did *not* spot the distinctive fuchsia hatchback owned by Glee Savage. Marson parked his Range Rover between the tricked-out police cruiser and a silver Lexus that I didn't recognize.

As we entered the lobby, we were "greeted" by a sheriff's deputy with a clipboard who told us to identify ourselves. When we gave him our names, he scratched at the list and admitted us with a jerk of his head, sporting one of those Nazi haircuts with buzzed sides, so fashionable now among the alt-right and other white supremacists. Younger than I am, maybe thirty, he wore full trooper's regalia, carried one too many guns, had spent obsessive hours at the gym, and took himself very seriously.

Once inside, out of earshot, Marson said, "Did you notice the name tag?"

"Indeed I did." It was Alex Kastle, the election opponent of our friend Sheriff Simms.

Marson looked appalled. "How could Thomas ever hire such a creature?"

"I doubt that he did. Kastle must've already been on the force when Thomas took over." I paused before adding, with a little growl, "Kinda hot, though."

Marson rolled his eyes.

I was kidding, of course. While it was easy enough to imagine the deputy in some gay-porn scenario, I got the definite impression he just wasn't into that. Maybe it was the dirty look that had washed across his features when I identified myself as Marson's husband.

"Welcome, guys," said Sarah Frumpkin Ward as she approached with a smile. She gave us each a little hug. "So glad you're here. Big day, huh?"

Marson couldn't wait to ask, "What's with the storm trooper at the door?"

"Dad's idea. He wanted a little extra security today—did I mention his flair for the dramatic? The deputy's off duty. Moonlighting, I guess."

I said, "You'd never know it—talk about dressed to kill."

Sarah glanced at Kastle, who was giving the next guests a going-over. With a grin, she said, "Dad may have gotten more than he bargained for." Then she moved on to greet the new arrivals.

I had meant to ask her if her father had seen that morning's paper, but I knew there was slim chance he had missed it. Everyone in town seemed to subscribe, and the paper had hit the streets some six hours earlier.

Marson and I worked our way through the waiting room, which was getting crowded, having never been intended for such a gathering. In Mary's gracious living room, these same twenty-some people had mingled with ease, but here in the clinic's reception area, it was tight quarters.

Mary Questman was holding court in the far corner, gabbing with a clutch of country-clubbers. Spotting us, she trundled over for smooches, which we happily delivered. She bubbled, "Such lovely weather, isn't it? It *must* be a good omen for Dr. Frumpkin's big plans."

She'd left Mister Puss at home, of course, but not Berta, who stood nearby with her perpetual scowl. Marson said hello to her. The housekeeper responded, "I can think of better ways to spend a Sunday afternoon, but I thought I'd better drive."

With a touch of concern, I asked, "Why's that?"

She leaned near. "Haven't you noticed? Mary's not as … *grounded* as she used to be." Berta gave us a knowing nod. "If you have any doubts, just ask His Majesty."

We drifted away. Marson's patrician hackles were up. He said, "That woman has *always* irked me. Can't imagine why Mary keeps her around—such impertinence."

I noted, "They've been together forever. The status quo can be comfortable—better the devil known."

Dr. Francis Frumpkin himself emerged from the crowd to greet us. "Brody! My genius young architect!" He clapped an arm over my shoulder and left it there, telling my husband, "Don't let go of *this* one, Marson."

"Wouldn't think of it."

Easing out of Frumpkin's clasp, I reminded him that he had other fish to fry: "We enjoyed meeting Dahr yesterday—seems like a great guy." Dahr was moving in and out of the reception area, checking on things, carrying an iPad. On Friday, I had judged him a handsome man, but now he looked especially dashing in black dress slacks, a tailored white lab jacket that was cut like a blazer, and the obligatory stethoscope draped from behind his neck.

Frumpkin gave him a wistful look.

Marson asked, "He does have 'feelings' for you, correct?"

"Oh, *yes*," said Frumpkin. "But I can't seem to convince him there's a future for us—a life together. And it's not what you think. It's not the age difference, at least not per se. You see, Dahr wants a family. But me? I've done that. I'm content to enjoy being a grandfather."

As far as I knew, he had but one grandchild, and I found it difficult to imagine her as a source of either joy or contentment. Thank goodness, the dreadful Olivia didn't seem to be around that day.

"Speaking of grandfathers," said Frumpkin, pointing behind us, "did you notice?"

We turned. Hanging on the opposite wall of the lobby was the enlarged photo of Archibald Frumpkin with the parachute, framed and spotlighted.

Our host explained, "The first of many, let's hope. We'll display that tribute in the lobby of your fabulous building, Brody—and in every FlabberGas clinic built from that day forward." He glowed.

Stepping over to an open doorway, he pointed down a hallway to a sign affixed to a door, reading "FlabberGas Station #1." He told us, "The sign, that's just a mockup for today, but we will in fact call the treatment rooms 'FlabberGas Stations.' The prototype clinic will have three, but once we get rolling, the franchises could have as many as six."

Somehow, this aspect of his marketing plan struck me as ... off. Suppressing a laugh, I told Marson, "Good thing Glee didn't get ahold of *that* detail."

Marson laughed.

But Frumpkin didn't. "That hack. That *bitch*. I have half a mind to sue the *Register* for slandering my practice." Calming himself, he said, "Excuse me, gentlemen," and retreated down the hall.

A mellow, familiar baritone voice asked, "What was *that* all about?"

Turning back to the waiting room, we found Sheriff Thomas Simms looking past us, watching as Frumpkin slammed the door to FlabberGas Station #1.

Marson greeted him with a smile and a handshake. "Hi there, Thomas."

I did the same, explaining, "Frumpkin doesn't buy the adage that 'there's no such thing as bad publicity.' He saw this morning's *Register*."

Simms chuckled. "I was wondering how he'd react."

Marson asked him, "Is Gloria here?"

"Nah, wasn't interested. Dropped her off at home after church. Tommy, too. But me? It's a seven-day job."

I said, "Speaking of your job, we met your opponent—briefly."

"Yeah," said Simms, "he's something else."

Deputy Alex Kastle was indeed something else. It seemed impossible to imagine him stepping into the role of our good friend, whose mild manner and well-weighed words and sense of justice were such a credit to the entire community. Plus, there was a superficial but obvious distinction—Thomas Simms happened to be black, while Alex Kastle looked like a poster boy for a figmental Aryan master race.

Simms checked his watch. "About time to get this going, isn't it? Looks like everyone's here."

We glanced about the room, populated by most of the same people from Friday at Mary's. Walter Zakarian, the Karastan King, was working the edge of the crowd, pecking about with his walking stick, this one fashioned from gleaming ebony.

"Hold on," said Marson, joking. "Doc Phelps isn't here." He was referring to the veterinarian who'd walked out of the Friday presentation—in a bit of a huff.

With playful understatement, I suggested, "He may have lost interest in the 'investment opportunity.'"

Dahr bustled past, heading for the front door. He approached Deputy Kastle and apparently needed to check the list of attendees on the clipboard. Kastle gave him a hard time, and when he finally handed over the list—all but tossing it—he looked away with an expression of utter contempt.

Astonished, Marson said, "What an ass."

With a weary nod, Simms told us, "I guess he's no more fond of Muslims than he is of blacks."

Dahr returned in our direction and stopped near the door to the hallway, announcing, "Everyone? Your attention, please? Dr. Frumpkin is ready to begin the demonstration. Follow me, please."

Standing where we were, Marson, the sheriff, and I became first in line as everyone moved out of the waiting room and filed down the hall to FlabberGas Station #1. Stepping inside, we ended up in the prime position to witness what would follow. The room had not been built to accommodate an audience, so it quickly got crowded, with some of the guests remaining in the hall, watching through the doorway. Deputy Kastle brought up the rear and reported, "Everyone accounted for." Oh, brother.

Ready and waiting inside the room were Dr. Frumpkin; his daughter, Sarah; and her husband, Dr. Jason Ward, who wore green scrubs and black surgical Crocs. They were joined in front by Dahr Ahmadi, scanning through something on his tablet.

Also ready and waiting was the hyperbaric chamber itself. I wasn't sure what I'd expected—given its frivolous purpose in Frumpkin's crazy-sounding miracle fat-busting scheme—but the startling reality of seeing it there, of standing right next to it, was downright fearsome.

The entire contraption was at least eight feet long, about four feet wide, and five feet tall. A heavy metal frame, in a soothing shade of hospital blue, supported a huge, clear acrylic tube in which the patient would lie on a sliding gurney, which entered the end of the tube through a thick, round riveted door that resembled the hatch of a submarine. Along the side of the metal base, just below the tube, stretched a control panel containing switches, dials, gauges, readouts, and even a telephone handset. Atop the tube was a flat-screen TV aimed in toward the pillow for the patient's amusement. A tangle of plumbing, hoses, and gas lines dropped to the floor and disappeared through the back wall of the room.

Okay, I'm a sissy, but you couldn't have *paid* me to get inside that thing. And yet, Mary Questman had already done so—more than once.

"Welcome, my friends," said Dr. Frumpkin. "Today you'll witness a demonstration of the defining feature of our revolutionary FlabberGas process, which makes it unique among weight-loss programs. But first, I want to apologize for these cramped and sterile surroundings. We are standing, of course, in a section of a surgical suite. However, treatment rooms in the future FlabberGas clinics—which I *do* hope you'll want to join me in building—those will be spacious and inviting, even luxurious. In terms of general aesthetics, think of a spa."

And then, Glee Savage arrived. With a cheery yoo-hoo, she warbled from the lobby, "Where's the paaar-ty?" The sharp clack of her heels approached from the waiting room and progressed down the hall, landing her among the stragglers outside the door to FlabberGas Station #1, nose-to-nose with Deputy Alex Kastle.

Frumpkin froze. He eyed her through the door with an unbelieving stare. After a long, tense moment, he blustered, "How *dare* you show your face here?"

Glee answered, "Just trying to help, Francis. How about a little follow-up?"

"You won't be working long enough for *that*, if I have anything to say about it. Get out!"

"Now, *really*, Francis—"

"Deputy? Miss Savage is *not* allowed here. Please escort her *out*."

Kastle told Glee, "Okay, ma'am—let's go." His look was grim, but he must have enjoyed this development, earning his pay, flexing his stuff.

Glee warned him, "Don't you lay a *hand* on me."

"Then let's get moving." And he followed as she retreated. Seconds later, we could hear him noisily banging the metal-framed front door behind her.

Standing near me, Mary mumbled, "Oh, dear. Poor Glee."

Berta offered, "Want me to check on her?"

Mary nodded. Berta wended her way out.

"There now," said Frumpkin, pleasant as pie, "that's better."

Deputy Kastle returned—minus Berta and Glee.

We listened to too much technical gibberish from both Frumpkin and Sarah, who spoke at length about the traditional uses of hyperbaric oxygen therapy. A quarter hour later, she concluded, "Although the pressurized administration of oxygen is often associated with decompression sickness, serious infections, or the treatment of wounds that won't heal, a widely recognized side effect is that it induces a general feeling of good health, a pleasant sense of well-being. You'll remember Michael Jackson—or those oxygen bars that were trendy a few years ago."

"Aha," said someone. "No wonder Mary was so eager to be your guinea pig." Soft laughter rippled through the room.

"Actually," said Dr. Frumpkin, "we've had a slight change of plans." Without elaboration, he simply explained, "We decided to let Jason do the honors as today's guinea pig."

Frumpkin's son-in-law stepped forward and took a little bow. When I'd met him on Friday at Mary's, I was struck by how closely he fit my notion of a typical doctor—clean-cut, down to business, just the facts. Now, however, bowing comically in his scrubs, he looked more like a child who was ready for bed. He stepped out of his clogs.

Frumpkin opened the hatch at the end of the pressure chamber, Dahr slid out the gurney, and Jason hopped onto it, telling the crowd, "Good-bye, cruel world."

Sarah told us, "He's beginning to take after my father—that acute sense of theater."

Laughing, Frumpkin agreed, "I've trained him well."

Dahr slid the gurney into the transparent tube. Frumpkin closed the hatch. Jason plumped the pillow beneath his head.

When Dahr seated himself on a low stool at the control panel, Jason rapped on the inside of the tube. Dahr switched on the intercom. Jason said over the squawk box, "Don't tell me *you're* driving today." Even through the electronic crackle, there was something in his tone that conveyed dismay rather than humor.

Dahr picked up the handset and told him, "I *know* what I'm doing, Doctor."

Frumpkin told us, "Of course he does." He took the handset from Dahr, asking Jason, "Ready for blastoff?"

Jason gave a thumbs-up, and Dahr began tweaking the controls. A whirring of motors and pumps emerged from the hush of the room. Every now and then, the panel emitted a gentle sequence of beeps.

Sarah explained, "We're replacing the air in the chamber with pure oxygen. Room air contains only about twenty-one percent oxygen. We're also pressurizing the chamber, as they do in airplanes, which boosts the oxygen's healing powers. The beeping you hear indicates we've attained various levels of pressure."

Someone asked, "Doesn't it *hurt?*"

Sarah took the handset and asked Jason, "How's it going?"

"Just dandy." He gave another thumbs-up.

He looked so odd in there, our guinea pig. I thought of a lab specimen laid out in a giant test tube. And an eerier image sprang to mind: the pressure chamber resembled a futuristic coffin in some sci-fi space thriller.

Frumpkin told us, "These treatments can last about an hour, and patients often fall blissfully asleep." He asked into the handset, "Ready for a little shut-eye, Jason?"

Jason exaggerated a yawn and a stretch, then rolled onto his side, facing us with a smile, and closed his eyes.

Frumpkin continued, "We won't go the full hour today—you'll have the idea soon enough—but let's take some time for a few questions."

There were many. Frumpkin and Sarah took turns with their detailed answers. I tuned out. The churning of the oxygen chamber had a lulling effect. I lost track of the passing time. Twenty minutes? Thirty? The sight of Jason made me sleepy.

He seemed so peaceful ...

"Dr. Frumpkin?" said Dahr with a note of alarm.

Frumpkin and Sarah immediately joined him at the control panel, peering in at Jason, who hadn't moved.

Dahr said, "Something ... something isn't right."

Frumpkin ordered, "Begin decompression."

Looking horrified, Sarah moved back a few steps.

Instinctively, the crowd inched forward. Marson and I could see directly over Frumpkin's shoulder.

Sheriff Simms was right behind me. There was no masking the urgency in his voice as he asked Frumpkin, "Can't you just spring the hatch and get him *out* of there?"

Frumpkin tossed his arms. "That would *kill* him. Even *emergency* decompression takes about two minutes."

It was the longest, most frantic two minutes I'd ever lived

through. Everyone was mumbling and whining and milling as Frumpkin and Dahr took turns with the handset, shouting to Jason, who offered not the slightest response.

When at last the machine signaled the completion of its cycle, Frumpkin yanked the hatch open and Dahr slid the gurney out. They both went to work on Jason, trying to resuscitate him. Sarah, frozen where she stood, watched with disbelief. Others streamed forward, transfixed by the ghoulish curiosity of the moment.

An finally, Frumpkin made the pronouncement we all knew was coming: Dr. Jason Ward was dead.

Sheriff Simms suddenly had an investigation on his hands. "What happened?" he asked, stepping to the gurney.

Dr. Frumpkin's cheeks were streaked with tears. "Asphyxiation? Cardiac arrest? Impossible to tell—without an autopsy."

Dahr Ahmadi said, "I only noticed trouble because he looked unresponsive. All the settings were correct; readouts were normal. There's nothing wrong with the machine."

"We'll need to check that, of course." Simms started taking notes.

Mary Questman stepped over to comfort Sarah Frumpkin Ward, who had just lost her husband. She steadied the younger woman as they moved through the parting crowd and approached the gurney. Dr. Frumpkin hugged his daughter's shoulders.

Sarah wept as she reached to stroke Jason's hair. "It doesn't make *sense*."

Simms said, "I'm terribly sorry for your loss."

"But he was in perfect health. He's undergone these hyperbaric treatments several times before—with no problems at all."

Simms asked, "If you *had* to make a guess, what could have

caused this?"

Sarah exchanged bewildered glances with her father and with Dahr. "Well," she said, "if I *had* to guess, lacking any other explanation, I'd say he might have gotten something other than oxygen."

Frumpkin explained, "We store a number of medical gases here. Different procedures have different needs."

Simms asked, "Where are they stored?"

Sarah said, "There's a utility room—the gas closet. The tanks are there, also connections to the plumbing lines for the surgical suites. The closet opens to the outside, for deliveries. The door is always locked."

The sheriff asked, "Could the gas lines have been switched by mistake?"

Dahr said, "That's virtually impossible. The connections are all different—it's an important safeguard. Care to take a look?"

"You bet."

So Sarah stayed with her husband's body while Dahr went to find the key. Dr. Frumpkin led Simms out through the front of the building, with Marson and me at the sheriff's heels; everyone else fell in behind us as we passed.

Out in the parking lot, Frumpkin turned at the corner of the building. "It's right back here." He led us along a short service drive that ended at a gray metal utility door in the brick wall of the clinic.

And not twenty feet away, at the edge of the woods, Glee and Berta sat on a log, laughing their asses off, sharing a smoke—which smelled a lot like pot. When they saw the crowd approach, Berta dropped the joint and Glee stubbed it out with her shoe.

Frumpkin wondered aloud, "Where's Dahr with that key?"

Simms walked over to the door, took care not to disturb fingerprints by using both hands to turn the backside of the knob, and easily opened the door—without a key. Then he strolled back, writing notes on his pad.

I leaned to ask him, "What do you think?"

"I think it wasn't an accident," said the sheriff. "And if it wasn't an accident, it was a crime—a crime called murder."

PART TWO

Suspension of Disbelief

Mary Questman awoke from a fitful sleep on a chilly Monday morning, the day after Jason Ward's death. She checked the bedside clock—not quite seven. Though the October sun had yet to rise, the glow of twilight peeped around the edges of the closed curtains. She sat up, taking care not to disturb Mister Puss, who had nested on her pillow. He stirred, cracked an eye open. She leaned to touch noses with him.

Where's the fire?

"No rush," she told him, tracing a finger along his spine from neck to tail. "Go back to sleep."

He purred, stretched all fours, then buried his head in the pillow, falling silent. His belly rose and fell in contented slumber.

Downstairs in the kitchen, Mary switched on a light above the sink. She drew a pot of water for the coffeemaker and started it brewing. Then she stepped outside the back door to retrieve the morning paper.

Standing on the porch for a moment, she was struck by how different things were from the day when Mister Puss had landed on her doorstep, as if he'd dropped there out of nowhere. Back in May, birds were singing in the fragile spring foliage as the day began to warm to a nurturing sun. Today, though, the birds were quiet—had they flown south already? The leaves had turned. The gray sky was as cold as the house.

She hugged herself through a heavy chenille bathrobe (rusty orange for autumn, the color reminded her of Mister Puss's coat), then she stooped to pick up her rolled and bagged copy of the *Dumont Daily Register*.

Stepping indoors again, she set the paper on the table but was reluctant to open it. By the time the coffee was ready, the windows had brightened to the new day, so Mary switched off the light and carried the coffee to the table, where she tugged the paper out of its bag and let it flop open in front of her. The top story was no surprise.

Was it murder?

FlabberGas demo goes deadly in front of throng of investors

Compiled from *Register* staff reports
·

OCT. 11, DUMONT, WI—Dr. Jason Ward died early Sunday afternoon under suspicious circumstances while undergoing a hyperbaric oxygen treatment at Associated Surgery Center, owned by Dr. Francis Frumpkin.

The victim, a member of Dr. Frumpkin's staff, was participating in a demonstration of a novel weight-loss process being presented to a group of potential investors, who witnessed the fatal turn of events. An investigation is already under way by Sheriff Thomas Simms …

The lengthy story contained scant news that was not already known to Mary. What caught her eye, however, was a secondary story. She raised the page for a closer read.

Who was intended victim?

Mary Questman volunteered to take part in Sunday demo

·

OCT. 11, DUMONT, WI—Dumont County sheriff's deputy

Alex Kastle was off duty Sunday, but was hired to provide security at the investors' event where Dr. Jason Ward was killed in a hyperbaric oxygen chamber.

Kastle later told the *Register*, "Everyone was surprised when they announced that Dr. Ward was taking Mary Questman's place as the guinea pig today."

Mary Questman, known to all Dumonters as the community's leading arts patron and philanthropist, had expressed interest in the FlabberGas enterprise and had volunteered to participate in the event. The reason for the last-minute switch was not immediately known.

Kastle asked a reporter, "Can you imagine what might've happened if Mrs. Questman went through with this, as planned? Now they're talking murder. It makes you wonder who the killer was really after."

Deputy Kastle is the only opponent seeking to unseat Sheriff Thomas Simms in next month's election. When asked if Kastle thought the suspicious death could have an impact on voting, he replied, "Well, the clock is now ticking, isn't it? The loss of Mrs. Questman would've been a terrible blow to the whole town. Sheriff Simms needs to get to the bottom of this. The election will be a referendum on his ability to wrap it up fast."

That's a tall order. Early voting begins two weeks from today.

When asked for comment from the *Register*'s editorial board, publisher emeritus Barret Logan replied by e-mail, saying, "While we make every effort to give all candidates equal consideration for our endorsement in local elections, we have been solidly impressed by the professionalism Sheriff Simms has brought to the office. That said, this disturbing development is indeed a new wrinkle that deserves ongoing scrutiny from the editorial board and voters alike."

"Incredible," Mary mumbled. "I can't believe it."

Believe it.

Mary lowered the newspaper. Mister Puss was sitting on the table. She said, "I thought you were sleeping in this morning."

It was a cat nap.

"Very funny."

And I'm hungry.

"Yes, Your Majesty." Mary had picked up his nickname from Berta.

Poor Berta, thought Mary as she rose from the table to prepare the cat's breakfast. Her housekeeper had Mondays off, but Mary had to wonder if Berta would appear as scheduled the next day—or would she be locked up somewhere, held as a suspect for killing Dr. Ward? The very notion was ridiculous, of course. Mary had known Berta for at least twenty years, and while she could be a bit difficult at times, they had seen each other through many rough patches, particularly when their husbands had died—first Mary's, then Berta's.

Mister Puss circled Mary's ankles, purring, while she stood at the counter, cutting up chunks of beef tenderloin, carefully arranging each morsel in the cat's bowl, just the way he liked it. This ritual always gave her pleasure, but she fretted over Berta's predicament. It certainly hadn't looked good yesterday when everyone found her just outside the unlocked door to the clinic's gas closet—smoking marijuana and having a gay old time with Glee Savage.

Poor Glee, thought Mary. Her byline didn't appear in that morning's paper; she wasn't even mentioned in the stories about the event that she had gone to cover. Was she now in trouble? Making things worse, Dr. Frumpkin had threatened to sue the

Register over her last story. Was her job in jeopardy? Mary considered Glee one of her closest friends. None of this would have happened if Mary hadn't been pushing "the FlabberGas enterprise," as the paper had called it.

Mister Puss watched with hungry eyes as Mary lowered the bowl to the floor. He then began devouring the bloody beef. Mary always enjoyed the rapture of his eating, the way his purr transformed to a soft, gurgling roar, but it brought her no pleasure that morning as she fretted over Sheriff Simms.

Poor Thomas, thought Mary. He was the kindest, most dedicated lawman she'd ever known in Dumont, and she'd been there her whole life, except the years she'd spent away at school. He deserved to be reelected. Of course he'd be reelected—or so everyone had thought until this mess developed, a mess partly of her own making.

While Mister Puss continued eating his breakfast, Mary sat at the table again and resumed her litany of woes.

Poor Sarah Frumpkin Ward, thought Mary. Widowed so young. And before her very eyes.

Poor little Olivia, thought Mary. Fatherless at such a tender age.

Poor Dr. Frumpkin, thought Mary. His FlabberGas dreams were surely doomed.

Poor *me*, thought Mary. Deputy Kastle had raised a point she hadn't considered. Was Dr. Ward's demise intended for Mary *herself*? Good heavens, she didn't have an enemy in the world. Did she?

Mister Puss ambled over from his empty bowl and looked up at Mary. She patted her knees. He jumped into her lap. She kneaded the back of his neck. Purring loudly, he stretched up to her shoulder, then brought his chin to her ear.

What's wrong?

"I'm just so worried. Worried about everyone." She told him what had happened at the clinic and detailed her concerns.

Who was there?

"Everyone who was here at the house on Friday. At least I think so." Mary paused. "No, actually, the little girl wasn't at the clinic yesterday. Olivia."

There's something wrong with that sasspot.

Mary chortled. "Tell me something I *don't* know."

She broke a glass and hid the pieces. Behind the big chair.

"Well, accidents happen. She's a child." Mary had no time to fret over broken glassware; she had murder on her mind. "Ughhh," she wondered aloud, "what am I going to do?"

Talk to your friend.

"Which friend?" She had hundreds.

Brody. Ask him to help.

"Of course," said Mary, raising her fingers to her lips—she'd just been *thinking* of Brody. A year earlier, her friend Walter Zakarian, the rug man who sometimes served as her escort at charity galas, had run into some trouble resulting in injuries that might have killed him. He was reluctant to pursue the matter, but Brody Norris stepped in and helped Sheriff Simms figure it out. And now, Brody was so close to everyone involved in the FlabberGas mess, he just might be able to help again.

Mary gave Mister Puss an adoring look—his suggestion was nothing short of brilliant. She thanked him with a hug, then set him on the floor.

Mister Puss sat watching, purring, as Mary stepped to the phone.

The phone rang. At home Monday morning, I was trying to ease into the week with a second cup of coffee, but perplexed by a story in the *Dumont Daily Register*.

"I'll get it, Brody," said Marson from across the great room of the loft.

"Thanks, sweets." I was in no mood for distraction, wanting to finish the story I was reading. And I couldn't *believe* my own eyes.

Deputy Alex Kastle, that conniving alt-right opportunist, had not only gone on record suggesting that someone had tried to kill Mary Questman, but had also gone nuclear on Sheriff Simms, reframing the election as a referendum on the sheriff's ability to bring someone to justice—in just two weeks. And the paper's doddering ex-publisher, speaking for the editorial board, had all but *agreed*.

Fuming, I smacked the *Register* down on the kitchen island and shoved it away from me, knocking my cup of coffee and sloshing half of it on the newsprint. As I grabbed a wad of paper towels, Marson headed toward me with the phone.

"Just a moment," he said into the handset. "I think you'd better ask him yourself." Passing it to me, he said, "It's Mary." Then he took over for me, cleaning up the coffee.

After greeting each other, I said to Mary, "I totally agree—it was horrible. I'm so sorry Kastle dragged you into this. And I'm appalled that he stooped to the 'gotcha' mentality of using this against Simms."

"On top of all that," Mary said through the phone, "I'm just *sick* with worry over Berta. And Glee, too." Then her tone brightened. "But Mister Puss just gave me the most *lovely* suggestion."

"Oh? Really?"

After we hung up, Marson asked, "What was that all about?"

I hesitated to tell him. "Mary thinks I should reprise my role as amateur sidekick to Sheriff Simms." With a sardonic grin, I added, "It was Mister Puss's idea."

Marson nodded gravely. "A clever animal, that one—wise beyond his years. I was about to suggest it myself."

Reluctantly, I phoned Simms.

He invited me to his office.

I drove downtown and parked near our Miles & Norris architectural firm on First Avenue. The sheriff's headquarters was only a few blocks away, adjacent to the county courthouse, so I left my car and walked. When I arrived outside Simms's office, a deputy said, "He's expecting you." She opened the door, then closed it behind me. Both Simms and a woman I didn't recognize stood to greet me as I entered.

"We were just getting started," said Simms. "Brody, I'd like you to meet Heather Vance, our coroner and medical examiner. And Heather, this is Brody Norris."

As we shook hands, she said, "Delighted to meet you, Brody. I've heard a lot about you." She winked at the sheriff.

I said, "My pleasure—is it *Dr.* Vance?"

"Yes, but Heather's fine." She was blond and pretty, surprisingly young, thirty or so. I would have expected someone who was not only older, but more wizened, less vibrant, perhaps wearing a black rubber apron. But Heather looked sharp and lively in a chipper yellow skirt and jacket.

Having spent most of my life in California, I didn't know much about medical examiners in Wisconsin, except that the office was independent of any police agency or hospital. I also knew they were responsible for investigating "reportable" deaths—and I had no doubt whatever that Jason Ward's untimely passing fell into that category.

Heather said to me, "According to Thomas, you're here to observe?"

"Uh, yeah," I said, feeling stupid, "I guess so."

Simms laughed and pulled an extra chair over to his desk. "This investigation has barely begun; it's still evolving. Have a seat, Brody."

I sat in front of the desk, next to Heather, as Simms returned to his desk chair. He suggested, "Maybe you should start over, Heather."

"Of course." She turned to face me. "Testing is still under way, and definitive results always take longer than we'd like, but I think we're on the right track. The victim died while undergoing a hyperbaric oxygen treatment, and there at the scene, immediately afterward, his wife floated the theory that some gas other than oxygen might have been introduced to the pressure chamber."

Simms said, "Right, I asked Sarah for her best guess as to what might have happened, and that's what she said."

"And it makes sense," agreed Heather. "The victim was thought to be in perfect health. He apparently had undergone previous oxygen treatments without incident. And there was no observed malfunction of the equipment itself. The switched-gas theory would be consistent with all of that."

I asked, "So if it wasn't oxygen, what was the gas that killed him?"

Heather all but glowed with the love of her work. She slid to the edge of her seat, explaining, "Don't know yet. But *my* bet? Nitrous oxide."

"Laughing gas," said the sheriff.

"Right. Nitrous oxide is a common medical gas, typically used as an analgesic and mild anesthetic in dentistry and surgery. Most any surgical clinic would have it on hand—and one of the regular practitioners at Associated Surgery Center is an oral surgeon."

I asked, "But is it poisonous?"

"Not in the classic 'literary' sense," said Heather. "It's nothing like, say, cyanide, which attacks the system within seconds and causes near-instant seizures, cardiac arrest, and death. However, if nitrous—or any gas, for that matter—completely replaces the oxygen you need to breathe, you die of asphyxiation."

"And I presume," said Simms, "the conditions in a small, closed, pressurized capsule would favor that outcome."

"Sounds like the perfect setup."

I asked, "But wouldn't the victim be aware that something awful was happening? I mean, yesterday, during the demonstration, Jason never showed the least sense of alarm. He looked just fine—until he didn't."

"Right," said Simms. "We saw it all. Jason was sort of clowning around in there, and then he went to sleep—with a smile on his face."

Heather reminded us, "Nitrous is very well known for its euphoric effect, hence the common parlance, 'laughing gas.' Plus, nitrous oxide is colorless and odorless, just like ordinary air. Combine that with the euphoria, and the victim probably wouldn't even notice anything was awry before passing out—and *then* suffocating."

"Good grief," I said, reflexively raising my hand to my throat.

"Poor Jason."

Simms opened a notebook and clicked his pen. "So then," he said, "as I see it, we're three steps away from knowing if Jason Ward was a victim of death by laughing gas. First, we need to determine if nitrous oxide was stored at the clinic; that's an easy yes-or-no, a matter of simple fact. Second, we need to find out if anything was tampered with in the clinic's gas closet; it was fully secured after yesterday's incident, and I have an evidence team heading over there even as we speak. Third and finally, we need to know if our theory is consistent with the cause of death as determined by the postmortem."

"Right," said Heather. "The postmortem is the clincher. If Jason Ward died of asphyxiation by nitrous oxide, that will be revealed by testing. As to how and why it was done"—she stood—"that's up to you guys."

Simms walked us out to the lobby. He thanked Heather for her insights and held the door for her as she left. He watched as she moved down to the street, then he turned to me, asking, "Got time for a little walk?"

"Sure, Thomas."

We stepped outside; Simms led the way. Rather than heading out to the street, we turned at a driveway that led along the side of the building to a garage and maintenance area in back. A clearing among a few straggly trees contained a couple of metal picnic tables that seemed intended for staffers on break. No one was there, but cigarette butts littered the matted, patchy grass.

Simms strolled to the farther table and gestured for me to sit. Then he sat next to me, looking up into the trees, as if studying something that I couldn't see. "Did you ever want something so bad you could taste it, Brody?"

"Many times." I had wanted to become an architect. I had

wanted to be accepted at a great school to prepare myself for that career. I had wanted my first marriage to bring us a lifetime of happiness, but that one didn't work out. And now I wanted the same thing in my shared life with Marson. I told Simms, "We all have dreams."

He still gazed into the trees. "Know what I always dreamed about?"

I didn't answer because I wasn't sure, but I had an idea.

He continued, "There were lots of dreams, I guess, but they had a common theme. Growing up black still has its challenges—big time—but forty years ago, it was way worse, even though that was more than a decade *after* the Civil Rights Act. So my dreams simply focused on getting *past* all that."

"Thomas." I touched his arm. "My first husband, back in California, he was black."

With a quizzical look, he said, "Really? I never knew that."

"Now you do. His name was Lloyd Washington. He was an architect. Still is."

"That part—I knew that."

"And before Lloyd and I went into business together, he'd had a long teaching career at UCLA."

"Sounds like a smart guy."

I told Simms, "So I don't mean to sound presumptuous, but in a sense, I know where you're coming from. Lloyd and I had many deep talks about this. And you're a lot like him—a consummate professional who started from square one, then had to prove himself every inch of the way."

With a soft laugh, Simms told me, "I guess you get it, then." He stood, looking into the trees, then turned to me. "May sound corny, but my dream? Just the basic 'American dream,' right? Terrific wife, great kid, upward mobility—don't have a dog yet."

"But you *are* the duly elected sheriff of Dumont County."

He gave me a slow, knowing nod. "And *that's* the part I always wanted so bad I could taste it. The office. The respect. The validation."

I studied him for a moment without speaking. He was dressed, as always, in a dark, dapper suit, immaculate white shirt, and a smart silk tie with just enough snap to convey his strong self-confidence; today's stripes were pink and gray. It would be easy to assume his clothes were merely a symbol of what he'd achieved. But if that were the case, he'd also be flaunting his gun and his badge, which were both tucked away. No, for my friend Sheriff Simms, the care with which he always presented himself said loud and clear, but simply, This is who I am.

And at the opposite end of the spectrum, I recalled, was Alex Kastle. For the ambitious deputy, it was *all* about the gun and the badge—even on his day off, on a Sunday while playing rent-a-cop for Dr. Frumpkin.

"And now," I told Simms, "someone's trying to kill your dream."

He ambled around to the far side of the picnic table and sat. As I turned to face him, he leaned forward on his elbows. "When I read this morning's paper, I nearly cried."

"Thomas—"

"But big boys don't cry, right? So I didn't. Instead, I took a more objective look at the election, and it became pretty clear—if it wasn't before—that the outcome is *not* in the bag. And I determined that there are two things I need to do."

"Great," I said. "What's the plan?"

"First, and most obvious, I need to start taking Deputy Kastle's threat much more seriously."

"What a prick," I said with a snort, then backed off. "I mean, sorry—he's your deputy."

"Not by *my* choice," Simms assured me. "He was already on the force when I joined the department. Those days, I never much liked him, so I didn't pay him any attention. But then, when I was promoted to detective, he didn't bother hiding his resentment."

"Well, after all"—I grinned—"you were uppity."

"Uh-huh. And then, when I ran for sheriff—and won—Kastle suddenly found himself working for me. *Not* what he had in mind. Later, when he applied for promotion to the rank of detective, I nixed it. That sealed our 'friendship.' And now? He must figure the only way to get promoted is to take my job."

"I can well understand why you don't *like* Kastle, but was there a particular reason for nixing his promotion?"

With a note of weariness, Simms explained, "He has a history of temperament issues, as well as some dangerous views, none of which belong in law enforcement. Not sure how he managed to pass the psychological evaluation when he was first hired, but he did. And now, without serious cause, it's hard to get rid of him. Plus, in the context of the election, if I even *tried* something like that, it would come across as shenanigans. So Kastle is just a fact of life—at least until this is over."

Mulling all this, I asked Simms, "What was Kastle's background—before he joined the department?"

"Glad you asked. I was never much curious—till I read that story this morning. So I did some digging in his files. Turns out, his time in the military involved a stint as a medic. And that training qualified him as an EMT when he got out. But I guess the ambulance work wasn't exciting enough for him, and that's when he switched to law-enforcement training."

I searched Simms's face for a clue to his thoughts about the information he'd just shared, but his expression was blank, as if waiting for my reaction. "Bottom line," I said, "is that Kastle has some medical background."

"Yes."

"And if the switched-gas theory holds up as the explanation for Jason Ward's death, whoever did it probably had at least *some* medical knowledge."

"Reasonable, yes."

"So," I asked, "what does this tell you? You said you had a two-part plan."

"Right. The first part was to take Kastle's election threat much more seriously, which I'm now doing. And the second part is not to allow Kastle to be in any way involved with this investigation. He's already tried to use a suspicious death to his political advantage, and now I've come to understand—at least in theory—that Kastle could have been more than just a chance witness to that death."

My eyes bugged. "You mean, you think—"

"I'm not going that far, Brody. Not yet. But meanwhile, I have ample evidence to conclude that Kastle can't be trusted." Simms paused. Looking me in the eye, he added, "But I can trust you. And I could use your help."

This was not what I'd expected. With a quiet laugh, I told Simms, "Earlier this morning, when Mary Questman all but *begged* me to insinuate myself into the investigation, I assumed you'd want no part of it."

"On the contrary," Simms assured me, "I think she had a fine idea."

"Her cat thought of it."

He grinned. "Be that as it may, I find the prospect of your involvement quite promising. First, you've done this before—with the Zakarian matter. And second, you've had a working relationship with both Frumpkin and his daughter—your insights into this whole FlabberGas scheme are *way* deeper than mine."

Good grief, I thought. Even the sheriff assumed that Frumpkin's proposed business venture boiled down to a scheme that verged on fraud.

"Do you have time for this?" Simms asked.

"I'll *make* time—of course."

"For instance," he said, "I wonder if you could pay a visit and do a little digging with both Glee Savage and Mary's housekeeper."

"Sure, great. Mary is sick with worry about Glee and Berta."

"Exactly. This needs to be handled with ... delicacy. If I called them in, it would appear far too intimidating, and I don't want to upset them—*or* Mary. Truth is, I have no serious suspicion of either Glee or Berta, but they sure *looked* suspicious yesterday, in front of a crowd of witnesses, so we need to address that."

"Understood," I said. "When do you want me to do this?"

"They're not a high priority. Anytime this week is fine. However, this afternoon—"

"Wow," I blurted, "you're not wasting any time, are you?"

"Can't. Kastle himself said it. He said it in print: 'the clock is now ticking.'"

That afternoon, Dr. Francis Frumpkin and his daughter, Sarah Frumpkin Ward, were scheduled to meet with Simms in his office. Simms asked if I could be there as well. I agreed to return after lunch.

So I ate lunch at my desk that day, catching up with some of the work I'd missed that morning. After dealing with a backlog of old e-mails, I sent a message to Glee Savage, asking if we might meet on Wednesday. She replied within seconds: "Of course, love. Anytime for you. Just let me know when and where."

Marson had driven to a neighboring town for lunch with prospective clients, but I was able to reach him in his car as I walked the few blocks from our office, on my way back to meet

Simms. I said into the phone, "This morning was all gung-ho adrenaline: Sure, Sheriff, sign me up, I'm in! But this afternoon, I'm feeling sorta queasy about it. I mean, Frumpkin and Sarah, they're dealing with a death in the family, a sudden death that looks like murder. And me? I'm just dealing with a puzzle. Maybe I've waded into something where I don't belong."

"Kiddo," said Marson, "trust Simms. Even if, at first, it feels like a game to you, Simms has the perspective of experience. He knows what he's doing—and he asked you to be there."

So I arrived at the county complex a few minutes before one-thirty, as requested. As before, the deputy outside the sheriff's office told me, "He's expecting you." She took me in, but the office was empty, and she led me through another door that opened into a conference room.

Simms brightened when he saw me and waved me in; the deputy left. Someone else—I assumed it was a police stenographer—was setting up a few feet away from the oblong conference table. The room had a high ceiling with tall windows and venetian blinds that were tilted to admit abundant sunlight but no view; perhaps there was nothing to see outside other than a brick wall of the jail. Opposite the windows was a wall of wooden bookcases, brown and varnished, containing miscellaneous volumes and cockeyed binders of whatnot that didn't appear to have been read, or dusted, in quite a while. On the wall behind Simms, who arranged a stack of file folders at the head of the table, hung a darkened old portrait, cracked by the passing of years, depicting a man with a horse and something that looked like a monkey. Simms saw me staring at it. With a shrug, he explained, "No one's got a clue—it's always been there."

The space was actually sort of pleasant, in an old-timey, comfy kind of way, bearing no resemblance whatever to the sterile, fluorescent interrogation rooms that pop up every night on cable.

I asked Simms, "Anything I should know before they get here?"

Simms sat at the head of the table and gestured for me to sit along the side, near him. "Brody," he said, "I want you to stay focused on motive. I expect the conversation will ramble; in fact, I want it to. But while we're dancing around with the details, keep in mind that if Jason Ward was murdered, the killer *had* to have: a motive to do it, the means to do it, and an opportunity to do it. Now, if the switched-gas theory holds up—and it's *just* a theory at this point—it makes sense that either Dr. Frumpkin or his daughter probably had both the means and the opportunity to set it up. They have the knowledge and the access. *But.* What about motive? So keep that in mind today."

I nodded. He made perfect sense.

The door opened. The deputy admitted Frumpkin and Sarah, then left.

Simms and I both stood and moved over to greet them.

Sarah looked like hell. Her husband was barely twenty-four hours dead, and the shock had taken its toll. Her eyes were swollen and bleary; her lips were crusty. Her hair looked as if she had just gotten out of bed, but it was evident she hadn't slept. Since meeting her only six days earlier, I had consistently noted her drab choice of wardrobe, which today seemed lamentably well suited to her mourning.

I wrapped her in a hug and blubbered condolences; she thanked me through teary sobs that left my cheeks wet, my lips salty.

Dr. Frumpkin, though upset and shaken, was far better put-together than his daughter. Even under such trying conditions, his flashy sense of style did not fail him, though he had the good taste to tone down the palette, with silks of muted gray and somber maroon.

When I offered a hand in sympathy, he opted instead for

a bear hug, clinging so tight and so long that I half-expected Sarah to tell him, Christ, Dad, get a room. But of course she did not.

And moments later, we were seated at the table, with Simms and me at our prior places and the new arrivals along the other side, across from me.

Simms told them, "I know how difficult it must be for you to be here today, under these awful circumstances. And I truly appreciate your willingness to help us lay out the facts. So I want to assure you that our meeting today is just a conversation, a discussion. Please don't consider it a questioning or interrogation."

Soothing words, indeed, but I couldn't help thinking that the microphone planted on the table, as well as the soft but audible keystrokes of the stenographer, sent a different message.

Dr. Frumpkin said, "Thank you, Sheriff. I know your only purpose is to get to the truth. Sarah and I want to assist you in any way we can. And I'm delighted to see our young friend Brody here today"—he winked at me—"but I must admit, I'm a bit surprised, as well."

I thought I'd better let Simms address that.

He said, "Brody was a prime witness yesterday, right up front—in front of me, in fact. I've also come to know him as a very … *visual*, observant sorta guy. I think he might be able to contribute to our conversation, so I asked him to join us."

"Excellent, Sheriff. I *couldn't* agree more." Frumpkin's tone was a little too flirtatious for comfort, especially in the grim context of sudden, unexpected death.

Sarah offered tepid agreement with her father, nodding with a weak smile. She had a faraway look that drifted beyond the sheriff's shoulder, as if staring into the vast unknown that had consumed her husband.

Frumpkin asked, "I know it's still early—in your investigation, I mean—but do you have any idea when they might release Jason's body? We'll need to arrange some sort of memorial, and I have to decide on a suitable mourning period for keeping the offices closed."

"Maybe a week for the coroner," said Simms.

Those logistics hadn't occurred to me. I asked Frumpkin, "You're shut down today, I presume?"

Frumpkin nodded. "Someone is there to answer phones and juggle appointments, but I doubt that we'll get back to normal soon, if ever. I mean, Jason's now *gone*, and *I've* been looking forward to retirement, and Sarah"—Frumpkin wrapped an arm around her—"poor baby, Sarah's just a mess."

She whimpered, still gazing into the void beyond Sheriff Simms. She said, "It's bad enough for me, but what about Olivia? She's so young. Maybe she doesn't fully understand what happened. She seemed surprised when I told her she wasn't going to school today. She'll go tomorrow, but I have no idea how her classmates might react to the news—or to Olivia herself. I'm afraid all the fuss could really disturb her."

As if the kid wasn't wacky enough already, I thought. But I reminded myself to take a more charitable view of the child, who had just lost her father. I asked, "If Olivia isn't in school, where is she today?"

"Dahr has her," said Frumpkin. "She seems to like him."

Sarah added, "He's good with her."

Simms said, "Let's talk about Dahr Ahmadi. I interviewed him at length yesterday afternoon at the clinic. Most accommodating—very thorough with his answers. It's apparent he has a complete working knowledge of the practice. How long has he been with you?"

"At least five years," said Frumpkin.

"Six," said Sarah.

Simms said, "Let me ask a blunt question. If, as it appears, Jason was murdered, do you have any suspicion at all that Dahr might have been responsible?"

"Preposterous," said Frumpkin, leaning into the table. "He's one of the sweetest, most affable young men I've ever met. I'd trust him with my business; I'd trust him with my life. And in fact, I'd like to *build* a life with him. To answer your question, Sheriff—Dahr would never harm a fly. It's unthinkable that he could ever concoct a sufficient reason to kill Jason."

"Yes," agreed Sarah, "unthinkable."

But I could think of a reason. Although I didn't believe Dahr might be a killer, I did recall Frumpkin telling me on Friday that there was enmity between Dahr and Jason, that Jason was jealous of Frumpkin's affection for Dahr and its possible consequences for the future of the practice and, by implication, Jason's legacy in the business. I myself witnessed the tension between them at Mary Questman's house, and I saw it again Sunday at the deadly demo.

Sheriff Simms had also noticed. "Yesterday, after Jason got into the pressure capsule, there was an odd moment, a testy exchange—when Jason realized that Dahr would be manning the controls. And Dahr responded to him, 'I *know* what I'm doing, Doctor.' In retrospect, doesn't that concern you?"

Frumpkin assured him, "Not at all, Sheriff. It's all a matter of context. And the context was *not* murder."

"Not at all," agreed Sarah, still gazing into the void beyond Simms. Then she sputtered a noise that sounded almost like laughter. "Is that … is that a *monkey?*"

"Good *heavens*," said Frumpkin, taking notice, then laughing so hard I thought he might slap his knee.

And from that point forward, the interrogation—or rather, our fact-finding "conversation"—went downhill.

When it seemed to be wrapping up, I was still troubled by the suspicion of Dahr that had been voiced by Simms. Perhaps he was only being thorough, considering every remote possibility, but I firmly believed he was on the wrong track. I suggested, "Maybe I could get together with Dahr. Have a talk. Sound him out."

"Fine with me," said Simms. "Go for it."

With a roguish grin, Frumpkin wagged a finger at me. "No poaching, Brody."

It was a ridiculous thing for him to say—and baldly inappropriate to the gravity of our meeting. Still, Frumpkin had picked up on something I found difficult to admit to myself. Certainly, I found Dahr attractive. Who wouldn't? Marson did. But that didn't mean I had any intention, even an inkling, to "poach" the guy Frumpkin was pursuing.

And yet, you bet, I was excited by the prospect of knowing Dahr better.

After Frumpkin and Sarah had left, Simms dismissed the stenographer and asked me to wait. Standing with me near the closed door, he asked, "Any reactions?"

I returned to the table and sat. "Frumpkin seemed a little too matter-of-fact, as if he was merely tending to the details of tidying up after a sloppy mishap. But maybe that's just his way of tamping down the emotion."

"Exactly," said Simms, joining me at the table. "Over the years, I've seen a lot of people in tragic situations, and believe me—they all have different ways of dealing with grief."

"And then," I said, "there's Sarah. While Frumpkin seemed to be underreacting, Sarah was taking it much harder than I would've thought. In the brief time I've known her, she's always been so down-to-business. But today, I saw some very raw emotions."

Simms nodded, repeating, "Different ways of dealing with grief."

"It shouldn't surprise me, I guess. Good God, to lose your husband like that, the person you love most—how awful."

Simms asked, "It was a good marriage?"

I shrugged. "Yeah. They seemed a little harried and busy, but who isn't? Other than that, they struck me as loving, equal partners—in both business and life."

"Okay, then," said Simms. "The big question: I asked you to focus on motive. We agreed that either Frumpkin or his daughter probably had the *means* and the *opportunity* to kill Jason—if they were so inclined—but did either have a plausible *motive* to do it?"

"None that I can think of."

"I agree"—Simms scribbled a note to himself—"at least for now. Why would either of them do something that poses such a distinct threat to the family business?"

Reluctantly, I asked, "Is that why you seemed to be zeroing in on Dahr?"

"I'm not 'zeroing in' on anyone, Brody. But looking at what we've got to work with right now, which isn't much, Dahr at least seems to have had a plausible motive."

I looked him in the eye, telling him, "I think you're wrong."

"Good. Prove it."

I paused in thought. "Hey. What if the bad guy's motive was *not* to kill Jason? What if Jason wasn't the intended victim?"

Simms asked, "You think the intended victim might have been Mary Questman?"

"Not really," I said, "but Deputy Kastle made a case for it in today's paper. Or, you could take that logic a step further. It was Mary who volunteered as the guinea pig, then cancelled at the last minute—supposedly on the advice of her cat. What if the whole setup was *her* idea?"

Simms looked stunned. Then we both laughed.

"Or," I said, "what if the intended victim wasn't either Jason *or* Mary? What if the background intent was to harm Dr. Frumpkin's business plans? Or swing the election?"

"You're asking all the right questions, Brody. So here's what we've got." Simms scanned his notes. "Dr. Frumpkin, daughter Sarah, reporter Glee Savage, housekeeper Berta, and Deputy Kastle are all possible suspects—but I think each one is a long shot, at best. Then there's Dahr Ahmadi, who checks most of the boxes—but your instincts tell you otherwise. Now, what are we missing? Anyone else?"

Something seemed stuck at the back of my consciousness. Yes, there was someone else. But who?

Simms jogged the stack of folders on the table.

Over his shoulder, the monkey danced.

CHAPTER

6

Tuesday was my day to catch up at the office, so I got an early start. While I could safely back-burner the FlabberGas design project for a while (probably for good, but I needed to hear that from Dr. Frumpkin), there were plenty of other jobs that needed my attention, as I had let them slide for nearly a week. Marson had come in early with me, and a few minutes later, he popped over from his office across the hall, asking, "Need any help, kiddo? If anything's urgent, I could pitch in." Though tempted by his offer, as well as grateful for it, I declined any help and hunkered down, determined to put in a productive day.

Shortly after nine, Simms phoned with some follow-up: "When Frumpkin and his daughter came to see us yesterday, I never got around to asking about nitrous oxide. Later, though, the evidence team reported back to me after inspecting the gas closet at the clinic. Remember, when we talked to the medical examiner, we decided we were three steps away from knowing if Jason Ward was a victim of death by laughing gas."

"Right," I said, recalling our meeting with Heather Vance. "First, we needed to determine if nitrous oxide was stored at the clinic. Second, we needed to find out if anything was tampered with in the gas closet. And third, we needed to know if that theory is consistent with Jason's postmortem."

"And now," said Simms, "we have answers to the first two questions: yes, and yes. There was nitrous on the premises, and the gas lines were tampered with."

I asked, "That's it, then. Right?"

"Not open-and-shut. Not yet. There's still the issue of circumventing the safeguards—the different connectors for different gases. We're still looking into that. And the postmortem, that's not concluded yet. Anyway, thought you'd want to know."

Of course I wanted to know, but the findings reported by Simms gave me more questions than answers as I contemplated the "friendly visit" I'd set up with Glee Savage for the following day.

Wednesday afternoon, I parked at the curb in front of Glee's cozy Craftsman bungalow, as I had done the prior Thursday, when we had driven out to look at the building site of the perfect house—when I had inadvertently tipped her off to the Flabber-Gas story, which started a chain of events that now made people wonder if she'd killed Dr. Jason Ward. Last Thursday, she had eagerly decked herself out for a photo safari and had been waiting for me at the front gate.

Today, though, she was not waiting at the gate. Was she stewing? Or would I find her to be glib as ever, unfazed by the perplexities of suspected murder?

I passed through the gate and along her front sidewalk, stepping up to the porch amid the potted geraniums. When I poised my hand to knock, the door swung open before my knuckles made contact. "Brody, love!" she gushed. No, she was not stewing.

She was baking. "Cookies later," she promised. The rich, layered smell was crazy-making, perhaps peanut butter, definitely chocolate.

We settled in the sunny inglenook of her living room and sat across from each other in front of the dark fireplace. Between us, on a low maple table, were two decorative bowls. One was heaped with an assortment of plump, flawless nuts, which made me all the hungrier for the cookies; the other contained a mound of Glee's swirl-patterned castor beans, which were most decidedly not for eating.

With mock formality, Glee asked, "May I inquire as to the nature of this visit, Mr. Norris?"

I replied in kind, "Does one need an excuse to indulge in the pleasure of such effervescent company, Miss Savage?"

She let out a hoot of a laugh. "You are *so* full of it."

I got serious. "I was hoping we could talk about ... Flabber-Gas."

"Meaning," she guessed, "the FlabberGas incident that left Jason Ward dead."

I nodded.

She nodded. "Have a nut."

I plucked from the bowl a colossal cashew the size of a thumb. "Thomas Simms asked me to sound you out about it."

"The sheriff sent you?"

"Uh-huh." I chewed the nut and swallowed.

"So this is like"—she whirled a hand—"an interrogation?"

"Sorta. But I left the rubber hose in the car."

She smirked.

I continued, "Mary's worried about you—afraid you might be in trouble—so she asked me to intercede. To my surprise, Simms welcomed my involvement. He didn't want to alarm you—or Mary—by 'asking you downtown,' so he sent me to nose around instead. I'll tell you this: he does *not* consider you a serious suspect."

She huffed a little sigh. "That's a relief, I suppose. But just the same, I get it—it didn't look good—sitting there with Bert, doing a little weed, sassing off at the wrong moment, in front of the whole world."

I had to laugh. "It was quite a performance."

"Christ."

"So," I said, "may I ask a few questions?"

"Fire away, sir."

I felt silly, out of my league, pulling a notebook from my jacket pocket, but I would need to report to Simms. I asked, "While you were back there with Berta, did you see anyone enter or leave the gas closet through the gray utility door?"

"No. We were just a few feet from the door, so we'd have noticed. The whole time, there was no one there but us."

Which left a more important question, the one I hadn't wanted to ask first: "And neither you nor Berta used that door at any time?" I waited. "Correct?"

Glee tapped her chin with a finger. "May I answer with a hypothetical?"

I set the notepad on my knee. "Why not?"

"I understand the subtext of your question. Essentially, you're asking me if I 'did it.' So let's suppose—merely for the sake of discussion, mind you—that I *was* responsible for what happened. Let's say that I sneaked in and jiggered the oxygen—"

"Wait," I said. I had never told her about the switched-gas theory that Simms was exploring. I asked her, "Is that how it happened—Jason Ward died because someone jiggered the oxygen?"

"Sure," she said with an innocent shrug. "Mary told me. While I was outside with Bert, Mary was inside, watching the demo with you and all the others. According to Mary, when Jason died, Sheriff Simms asked Frumpkin and his daughter for a guess as to what went wrong. The daughter thought Jason might've gotten something other than oxygen. And that's why everyone came rushing out to the gas closet. Right?"

"Right," I admitted. "That's just how it went."

"So," continued Glee, "suppose I did it. Suppose I was the killer. And the killer switched the gas. Problem is, I didn't know what I was doing. I didn't know the first thing about which gas would or wouldn't kill Jason. So, if I did it, maybe I wasn't trying to *kill* Jason—or anyone else. Maybe I was just trying to screw up Frumpkin's demo."

With a cautious tone, I asked, "Why ... would you do that?"

Glee flipped her hands. "Simple. Frumpkin is a big-ass gas-bag of a bully, a grifter who needs to be taken down a notch. I'm a reporter doing my job, and he treats me like the enemy. He threatens to sue the *Register*, which could cost me my job, which I not only love, but *need*. Nothing's resolved yet; I haven't had a byline since Sunday. And it *still* has me scared."

This was not a turn I had expected our conversation to take.

Ending an awkward lull, Glee said with a laugh, "But of *course* I didn't do it."

I rephrased my original question, which she had not yet answered: "So you were never in the gas closet?"

"Brody, love—don't be silly."

Ding. A timer went off in the kitchen.

Glee stood. "Need to pull the cookies out to cool. Don't want 'em to burn." Her heels pecked the hardwood floor as she stepped out of the room, but then she turned back to me. "Can I get you something to drink?"

"No, thanks. I'm fine."

She suggested, "Maybe milk? Good with cookies."

It had been at least twenty years since I'd had a glass of milk. My mother wasn't very domestic, not in any traditional sense, but she'd insisted on milk while I was growing up. And yes, now and then, there were cookies. "You know," I told Glee, "that sounds pretty good."

"Won't be a minute." And she was gone.

I had no idea what to make of Glee's "hypotheticals." On the one hand, she had flatly denied having any involvement in deadly mischief, but on the other hand, she had painted a highly plausible motive for taking revenge on Frumpkin after chancing upon the unlocked gas closet. If that's what actually happened, she also had a motive for lying to me about it. Simms had told me to focus on motive—or was I reading too much into this?

Then I recalled the story Marson once told me about long-ago suspicions that Glee had been responsible for the death of a foe, a woman named Gillian Reece, who fell from the balcony of her lavish new house. "Nothing was ever proven," he had told me. "But she was never flat-out exonerated, either."

Pondering this now, seated in the closeted confines of the inglenook adjacent to Glee's living room, I listened as she puttered in the kitchen.

"Brody?" she called to me. "Too nice to be stuck indoors— let's go out back."

"Great idea," I said. Picking up the bowl of nuts, I joined her in the kitchen, which gleamed with pink and gray tile and classic white appliances so pristine I thought they must be reproductions. She suggested I leave my sport coat, so I hung it on the back of a chrome dinette chair. She picked up a tray with the cookies and milk, then led me through the back door to the porch.

The backyard was filled with flowers, fruit trees, and a manicured vegetable patch extending the length of a side fence. The opposite fence backed a tall stand of more castor plants in a colorful range of species, with little tags spiked in the ground at the base of each. At the back of the property stood a large shed attached to a vine-covered carport, under which was parked Glee's ancient fuchsia hatchback.

As I surveyed all this from the porch, Glee arranged on a low table the nuts, a pitcher of milk, two tumblers, which she filled, and the plate of cookies—brown, warm, and gooey, with melted chocolate chips glistening in the afternoon sun, plus a few of the giant cashews erupting through the dough. "Please, Brody, get comfortable," she said, indicating I should sit on the cushioned glider bench. She sat across from it in a deep Adirondack chair, placing her glass of milk on one of its broad wooden arms.

I settled onto the glider, stretched a languid arm along the back cushion, and with my other hand, nibbled a cookie—ah, the rush of sense memories. It took but the slightest flex of my foot on the porch floor to set the glider in motion. Lulled by the rocking, I heard sounds emerge from the quietude of the afternoon. From beneath me came the slow, gentle squeak of the glider. Out in the yard, on a low branch of a fruit tree, a robin warbled, puffing his ruddy breast, wondering, perhaps, if it was time to plan his winter getaway. Next door, beyond the fence, the flutter of a push mower's blades made halting progress, harvesting the season's last crop of thick turf. From somewhere down the back alley, a basketball pinged on the asphalt. And overhead, the faraway, muted roar of a high-flying jet drew my gaze to the cloudless autumn sky, where a tiny glint of metal led a long, straight vapor trail from west to east.

"Did you know I grew up with Inez?"

Glee's question yanked me from my reverie. Silence—birds, lawn mower, basketball—nothing. I flinched, snapping back to the moment. Turning to Glee, bringing her words into focus, I asked, "You're *from* here?"

"Born and raised. And I went to college—at Madison—with Inez."

"You know my *mother*?"

"Not anymore, Brody. But back then? Thick as thieves." The

trace of a smile faded from Glee's face. She reached for her milk and drank, then cleared her throat.

I recalled, "She's never said much about college. I knew she went to Madison, but that's about it."

Glee lolled in her chair, eyes adrift. "I was in journalism, which is all I ever wanted to do. Inez majored in women's studies, which was the latest thing. Those were times of huge social change—Vietnam, civil rights, women's lib—and we were both staunch progressives, but for her, it wasn't just politics. It was her life. Once I called her a bra-burner, just joking, and she thought it was funny, but not long after that, she went to a rally and *did* it. I wrote it up, and the story made the front page of the campus paper. She loved it."

"That sounds like Mom," I said. "She hasn't changed much."

Glee looked me in the eye. "May I make a pointed observation?"

"Please do."

"Your mother was a lesbian."

"Still is, mostly." I leaned to whisper to Glee, "But I was not immaculately conceived."

"No kidding?" said Glee with a wry expression. "That's just my point. Inez was a *feminist* lesbian—it was a *political* statement as much as a sexual preference. But now and then, let me tell you, she got the itch. She had no problem making occasional whoopee with the right man."

I began to ask, "Were you ... ," but I hesitated.

Glee moved from her chair to sit next to me on the glider. Resting the fingertips of one hand on my knee, she said, "What would you like to know?"

"You said that you and Mom were thick—thick as thieves. Were you lovers?"

"No, sweetie. I'm not gay, never was. I've never *married*, either, which sets some folks to wondering. But I did come close once. It didn't work out."

"Sorry."

"So am I. But that was *very* long ago." Her hand left my knee and reached for a cookie. Gazing out toward the wall of castor plants, she ate it. She paused, squinting, her features twisted in thought. Then she turned back to me, asking, "Do you ever talk to your mother?"

"Of course. All the time."

"Of course you do. Gosh, we haven't spoken since she left college and took off for California."

Astonished, I asked, "What *happened* between you two? That was more than forty years ago."

"Yes, it was," she said with a pensive sigh. "Could you maybe tell her I said hello?"

"Happy to do it."

"Awww, thank you, sweetie. But she never knew me as Glee Savage—she wouldn't know that name."

"Aha. It's your pen name, right? I had a hunch. I mean, who would name a kid Glee Savage?"

She countered, "Who would name a kid Glee *Buttles*? I'll tell you who—Mr. and Mrs. Russell Buttles. God, isn't it *awful*?"

I thought it judicious not to answer.

She saved me the trouble. "As a little girl, I couldn't stand that name. You can imagine the jokes. But at least, growing up in the fifties, I had the comfort of knowing that a Prince Charming would come along to rescue me with some other name. Smith, Jones, Johnson—it didn't matter which prince, so long as it wasn't Prince Buttles. But things didn't go as planned. So when I got my first job out of school, right here with the *Dumont Daily Register*, the paper's founder, Barret Logan, asked me, 'And what byline will you be using?' That's all it took. And to this day, I have happily been known as Glee Savage."

"You tiger, you." I growled.

"That played into it, I admit. Back then, reporting was *still* dominated by men, so I felt it would be to my advantage to juice up my byline. And you know what, Brody?"

"What?"

"It made me more aggressive—as if I were living up to the name."

What's in a name? Sitting there on the back porch, I pondered the power of Glee's chosen surname, Savage. It had made her more aggressive, she said, and yet, there she sat, the picture of civility and style, tidying up after our tête-à-tête, returning cookies and milk to a painted tôle tray that sported huge, pink, ladylike peonies. I wondered, though—was there darkness deeper in her soul?

"There, now," she said, standing and lifting the tray. As she led me back into the kitchen, she asked, "Can I wrap these up for you and Marson?"

I held the screen door for her. "A couple, sure—thanks."

While she fussed at the counter, ripping off a long sheet of waxed paper, I retrieved my jacket and shrugged into it. She asked, "Can you stay a minute, Brody?"

"Happily." I sat at the little round dinette table.

She turned to ask over her shoulder, "Inez raised you alone, correct?"

"You bet. She bragged about being a *proudly* single mother. She was born a Norris, and by God, so was I."

Glee laughed and came to the table, sitting near me. She plunked down a package of two or three dozen cookies, heavy as a brick. "You two, eat these—they're good."

"They're great."

"So," said Glee, "when you were growing up, was it difficult, not having a father?"

With the slightest grin, I reminded her, "I may have my mother's name, but I also had a father—even though he was never acknowledged. Inez referred to him as 'the sperm donor.'"

"That's *so* Inez," said Glee, returning my grin. "I meant: Was it difficult not having a father *around?*"

"The only life I knew was the one I had, so I can't say whether it was difficult or not. It didn't *seem* bad at all—I had a happy childhood."

Through a wide smile, she said, "That's wonderful, Brody. So glad to hear that."

"It's sweet of you to be so concerned."

"Guess I can't help it."

Her comment struck me as strange, which must have shown on my face.

"Did you ever meet him?" asked Glee. "Your father."

"Oh, sure. I saw a lot of him. But I didn't know he was my father. He was sort of an uncle figure."

"Nosy me." Glee's hand drifted to a stray wisp of hair. "May I ask his name?"

"My father? Gordon Harper."

Glee's eyelids fluttered, then closed.

I explained, "Gordon died about ten years ago. I didn't learn he was my dad until later."

Glee opened her eyes and peered into mine. "I'm sorry you never knew your father—*as* your father."

I said, "He was an astronomer."

She corrected me: "An astrophysicist."

"Ah, that's right, of course." I blinked. "You *knew* him?"

She rolled her eyes. "You look just like him."

I asked Glee, "You knew *Gordon*—back in Madison?"

"That's right."

And bang. It all made sense: Glee had told me she'd once found her Prince Charming, but it hadn't worked out. That was Gordon Harper. And Glee's best friend, the radical lesbian Inez, stole him on a whim, ran off to California with him, and although they never married, she bore his child. And now, here I was. And here sat Glee—sixty-something, single, and childless.

With a pained sigh, I said, "I'm sorry for what Inez did to you."

"Oh, sweetie"—Glee shook her head—"don't be crazy. If she hadn't done that, you wouldn't be here. And wouldn't that be a tragedy?" Glee reached to wrap me in a tight embrace, having recognized in me the long shadow of the guy that got away.

And I understood she loved me, truly loved me, as the son she never had.

I hadn't talked to Mom in over a week, so I phoned her in California the next day. "By the way," I mentioned after the usual pleasantries, "a woman here, a Miss Savage, asked me to say hello to you."

The line went silent for a moment. "Who?"

"Oops," I said, playing along, "that's right—she changed her name. You'd have known her as Glee Buttles."

The line went silent again, longer. "Glee is *there*? She ended up back in *Dumont*?"

"She's worked for the local paper since she got out of college. You didn't know?"

"I guess we lost track of each other."

"She said you two were pretty close."

"We were. But I made the move to California after my junior year."

"And you never followed up with her?"

"Never." Mom paused before adding, "She wanted to kill me."

With an uncertain laugh, I asked, "That's a figure of speech, right? Hyperbole?"

But Inez Norris changed the subject: "Good news, Brody. That mountain conservancy? We've just managed to protect another twenty square miles as bighorn habitat."

Taken by itself, my mother's contention that Glee Savage "wanted to kill her" was easily dismissed. In light of what Inez had done, it was understandable that Glee might have *wanted* to avenge the betrayal by her once best friend; she might have even *said* it. Clearly, though, Glee had never *acted* on the threat, buried now by the sands of time.

But there was more. Other considerations were piling up that made me question my initial assumption that Glee was merely a long shot as a suspect in the FlabberGas calamity. There was the cold-case mystery of Gillian Reece, shoved to her death from a balcony. There was Glee's unabashed claim that her pen name, Savage, had made her more aggressive. There was even her fascination with deadly castor beans—what was *that* all about? But most important, there was the hypothetical scenario she had laid out for me, detailing credible motives for sinking Dr. Frumpkin's business plans.

Combine all of this with heavy new emotional baggage—knowing that Glee did not simply think of me as a friend, but loved me like a son—and I found myself in a serious quandary.

How would I report these findings to Sheriff Simms?

CHAPTER

7

On Wednesday, after visiting Glee, I had decided to postpone reporting to Sheriff Simms until I'd had a chance to talk to my mother.

On Thursday, after phoning my mother, I again decided to postpone my report, needing more time to mull what I'd learned.

On Friday morning, though, Simms phoned me at the office, so dithering was no longer an option. He got down to business: "Just checking in, Brody. Have you been able to spend some time with Glee or Berta yet?"

The last of Glee's cookies, just one, sat on a plate on my desk. Marson and I had been passing them around the office, and they didn't last long. I fingered a crumb and lifted it to my tongue.

"As a matter of fact," I told Simms, "I'm scheduled to meet with Berta later this morning. I checked with Mary Questman first, since Berta works for her, and asked if I could drop by during her shift. Mary was thrilled to 'donate' some of her housekeeping time toward my effort to clear Berta."

Simms said, "But you'll be able to remain objective—right, Brody?"

"Sure, Thomas. Absolutely." But I wondered if I'd already allowed my instincts to cloud my objectivity.

"Great. Glad to hear that's moving forward. And how about Glee Savage?"

I hesitated. "I've already met with Glee. We had a good conversation—very direct, even heartfelt at times. But it did seem to ramble, and I'm still trying to resolve some details. Can I ask you something?"

"Of course, Brody. Shoot."

"About the gas closet. On Sunday, after Jason died, we all went outside to the closet door, and you found it unlocked. As I see it, that presents two possibilities. First, someone with a legitimate reason to be inside the gas closet might have left it unlocked by mistake, and then the killer chanced on the opportunity to do some deadly mischief. The other possibility is that the killer himself—or herself—*deliberately* left the closet unlocked in order to spread suspicion beyond the keyholders who had access. This has an important bearing on how seriously we should consider Glee as a possible suspect. In fact, same goes for Berta."

"Yeah," said Simms, "I get it. So what's your question?"

"I have several, all related: Can we find out the last time the surgery center's gas supplier made deliveries? Does the supplier have a key? And who at the surgery center has a key—or access to one?"

"Regarding the supplier," said Simms, "sure, we can look into that. As for those with access to the key *within* the surgery center, we already know the answer. Dr. Frumpkin owns the facility, so he has all the keys. And the core members of his staff also had access to the keys: Dr. Jason Ward, Sarah Frumpkin Ward, and Dahr Ahmadi."

I said, "That's helpful, Thomas. Thanks."

"Isn't there something else you want to ask me about?" He paused, chuckled. "Fingerprints?"

I thumped my head. "Sorry. I'm new at this. What about fingerprints?"

"Inside the gas closet, it gets complicated—we're still analyzing all that. But the door? Specifically the outside handle? We secured that whole area immediately after finding the door unlocked, and the knob was dusted that same afternoon. Result? No prints at all, other than my own on the back of the knob. It had been wiped clean."

"That's huge," I said.

"It doesn't *prove* anything, but it points to intent. It's an added bit of circumstantial evidence that what happened was *not* an accident. Keep me posted, okay?"

I assured him, "I'll do that, Thomas."

But I never did tell him that my quirky interview with Glee had raised unexpected suspicions that I was struggling to reconcile with my feelings for the woman who now thought of me as a surrogate son.

Nor did I tell him that I'd made plans to meet that weekend with Dahr Ahmadi, whom Simms had already extensively interviewed.

Instead, I hung up the phone and ate the last of Glee's cookies. Then I moseyed into the office kitchen to see if we had any milk. Alas, we did not.

At ten o'clock, I drove over to Prairie Street, to Mary Questman's house, for the purpose of interviewing her housekeeper, Berta. Two days earlier, when I arrived in front of Glee Savage's bungalow, I'd expected to make easy work of clearing my reporter friend of any suspicion in the FlabberGas matter, but it hadn't worked out that way. Now, arriving in front of the Questman mansion, I was more than prepared to shift that suspicion to Berta, who had always struck me as odd at best.

Marson had never bothered to conceal from me his distaste for the woman. He'd known her far longer than I had, so perhaps his opinions had played an outsized role in shaping my own thinking. While walking from the car to the front door, I reminded myself that I had promised Simms that I would remain objective.

When Berta answered the door, she said quietly, "Morning, Mr. Norris. Mary said you were coming." Berta's voice had always sounded unpleasant to me—nasal and harsh—but today there was a softness to it that I hadn't heard before. Was it muted by apprehension?

Stepping inside, I asked, "Is Mary here?"

"No, she went to run some errands, but I think she just wanted to leave us alone." Mister Puss traipsed down the wide staircase and paused on the landing to see who had arrived. "Except," Berta added, "no one's ever really 'alone' here anymore."

"Awww," I said, "your little helper."

Berta gave me a starched smile. Then, indicating a side parlor off the main hall, she said, "We can talk in here."

I followed her into the room. Mister Puss followed me and settled near my chair as Berta and I seated ourselves. It was a small, intimate space, intended for conversation, but its large swagged window on the front wall of the house, combined with the high ceiling and elaborate cornice, lent a note of cultured formality—a stiffness—that was not conducive to a friendly chat.

I said, "Thanks for making time for me, Berta."

With a listless shrug, she noted, "It's Mary's nickel."

During the uncomfortable lull that followed, I took some time to really *look* at Berta. She had always been in the background, slipping into and out of the scene, which was never focused on her, but on Mary. Today, though, she had my singular attention. I didn't know her age, but guessed she had passed her fifties. She was a tall woman, lean, even bony, but strong-looking—probably a hard worker. Many people, not just Marson, described her as stern, but there was something in her plain face, behind her creased features, suggesting a life that had known a measure of pain. Her hair was neat but drab. She wore a gray uniform and sturdy service shoes.

She asked, "Can I get you anything? Something to drink?"

"No, thanks." But then I reconsidered. "I don't suppose you have any ... milk?"

Stifling a laugh, she said, "Since His Majesty moved in, you bet. It's whole milk, homogenized—that okay?"

"That's all I drank as a kid. Anything else—skim milk, God forbid—it tastes so watered-down."

Berta made a hideous face. "Awful, ain't it?" She brightened, stood. "Be right back."

"Don't bother," I said, standing. "I'll go with you."

"Suit yourself."

So I followed her to the kitchen. As before, Mister Puss followed me.

I'd always liked Mary's kitchen. Bright and inviting, the room did not convey the hushed elegance of the rest of the house; rather, it extolled the primal spirit of food and warmth and nurturing. What's more, it put Berta in a setting more natural to her. The moment we entered the room, I sensed that our conversation would be less strained.

An elegant old fixture of hobnail glass hung low over a big center table of pale oak. I pulled out a chair and sat. Mister Puss hopped up to the chair next to mine. Berta clanged around in the refrigerator, asking over her shoulder, "Mind if I join you?"

"I'd be embarrassed if you didn't."

She brought me a tall glass of milk and set another across the table for herself. Stepping back to the counter, she said, "Can't have milk without cookies," and then returned to the table with a plateful, which she set between us with a couple of paper napkins.

I said, "Thank you, Berta. This is nice." Eyeing the cookies, I thought they looked just like the ones Glee Savage had sent home with me. A few giant cashews mingled with the chocolate chips. I asked, "Did you make these?"

"No," she said, sitting, "these are from Glee. We trade back and forth. She's a pretty good cook, considering."

I had to ask, "Considering what?"

"I taught her. We weren't really palsy till a few years ago, after Snook died."

"Snook?" I took a sip of milk. Mister Puss was watching. I dipped a finger in the glass and let him lick it.

Berta explained, "Snook was my husband. His last name was Snook—well, mine too, of course."

I never knew that.

She continued, "He hated Fred—that was his first name—so everyone just called him Snook. So did I. We both worked for the Questmans, long time. I did the cleaning, most of the cooking, still do. Snook was the handyman, did the gardening, some fussing with the cars. But something sorta snapped. He got— what's the word? Senile. Demented. Started doing crazy stuff. One day, your friend Marson was here having lunch with Mary, and he saw Snook outside digging in the yard—eating *worms*."

I cringed, grabbed a napkin, and wiped my mouth, gone suddenly dry.

"He got to be an awful handful, poor thing. No family, no kids to help take care of him. It was hard to remember the way he *was*, and then to watch, every day, what happened to him. Awful hard. It makes you scared. I mean, we're all getting older."

"I'm sorry you went through that," I said. "Were you around when Mary's husband died?"

"Quincy died a few years before Snook. He never lost his marbles, like Snook. No, Quincy just got real *old*—way older than Mary. Mean, too. Don't get me wrong. He loved Mary, and Mary loved him. But God forgive me, she's better off without him."

While Marson would have judged Berta's last comment as another sign of her impertinence, I thought she was probably right. In fact, Mary herself sometimes openly marveled at the turn her life had taken—for the better—after learning to embrace the independence of widowhood. That said, she happened to be the richest woman in the county, which made it relatively easy for her to forge ahead. I assumed Berta, on the other hand, was struggling with issues more pragmatic than weepy memories.

And those pragmatic issues—finances—had previously prompted Marson to speculate that Berta was up to no good, scheming to set herself up for a fat inheritance from her longtime employer, the kindly and unsuspecting Mary Questman. Consistent with Marson's theory, as recently as Friday, one week earlier at Frumpkin's pitch session right there in Mary's home, Berta had confided to me, with a measure of bitterness, that she had eaten the cat's "leftovers," his rejected ground sirloin.

I asked Berta, "On Sunday, when you came with Mary to the FlabberGas demo, did you know she had decided *not* to be Dr. Frumpkin's guinea pig?"

"Oh, sure. Mary told me that the day before."

I thought, okay, if that's true, it rules out Berta as having a motive for what happened at the clinic, at least if an inheritance scheme was contemplated.

I asked her, "Did Mary tell you why she was backing out?"

"Uh-huh." She eyed the cat. "His Majesty warned her not to go through with it."

I patted my knees. Mister Puss jumped over from his chair to my lap. I asked Berta, "When Mary told you that, what did you think?"

"I thought, good idea. But I also thought, I hope to God she isn't *losing* it—losing her mind, like Snook did."

Purring, the cat pawed my chest and worked his chin up the side of my face. The soft fur of his chin tickled my ear. I twiddled his cheeks and tugged him down, asking Berta, "Have you ever heard a conversation between Mary and Mister Puss?"

"Sure"—Berta laughed—"lots of times, but Mary does all the talking."

And yet, I thought, Mary has often—and lucidly—maintained that the cat communicates with her.

I slipped the notepad out of my jacket, set it on the table, and helped myself to a cookie, holding it with my left hand. With my right hand, I clicked a ballpoint and began jotting some notes. Mister Puss swatted at the wiggling pen as I asked Berta, "Can you tell me more about Glee Savage? You taught her to cook?"

"Right. She's been to lots of Mary's parties, and now and then she'd wander through the kitchen and compliment the food. And she'd say, 'One of these days, Bert, you'll have to teach me how to cook'—sorta joking. Well, after Snook was gone, I had some time and wanted to get my mind off things, so I asked if she was still interested. I didn't really think she'd take me up on it. I mean, she's an office gal—nice clothes and such—but she really took to it. Now she's got this big garden. She bakes. She's even taught *me* a few things. She does 'research.' I just cook what I know."

Cute story, I thought. Sweet. And they made such an unlikely pair of friends. I'd certainly been surprised to see them yukking it up together outside the gas closet.

Breaking off a bit of cookie for Mister Puss, I asked Berta, "Can you tell me more about last Sunday at the clinic? When Glee showed up, Dr. Frumpkin had her thrown out. Then you went to look after her. What happened out there?"

"Well, first I had to get past Deputy Prick—pardon my French. He's horsing around, locking the front door so Glee can't get in again, and I tell him I want out. And he's all hassled and giving me mouth, so I tell him, 'If it's such a big deal, I'll just go get the sheriff.' And that does it—he opens the door, tells me to have a nice day, but real snotty-like, then bangs it shut and locks *me* out."

"He's a charmer, all right," I told Berta while making a note: *Deputy Prick.*

Berta continued, "So by the time I get outside, Glee's gone. But then I notice her crazy pink car, still in the parking lot, so I go looking. And around the corner, back where you found us, she's stomping around, mad as hell, yelling at a *squirrel,* if you can believe it. And I tell her, 'Calm down, honey. Ain't the end of the world,' and she's like, 'That bastard, that asshole,' or whatever, and I ask, 'The deputy?' and she says, 'No—*Frumpkin.* He's trying to get me fired.' And I'm thinking, Glee's probably right, but I tell her, 'Now, now, you'll think of *something.*' And she gets quiet."

I prompted Berta: "And …"

"And Glee finally asks me, sorta secret-like, 'Any *ideas?*' And I tell her, 'Yeah, I have an idea: I think we need a joint.' And Glee starts laughing, and she's like, 'Amen, sister!' and then"—Berta crossed her arms—"that's what we did."

I laughed at the memory of spotting the two of them sitting on the log. "Well," I conceded, "it certainly calmed her down."

Mister Puss yawned. I put a drop of milk on his nose and watched him stretch his tongue to lick it. I kneaded his spine near the base of his tail; he started purring.

"And the rest," said Berta, "you saw the rest, when Sheriff Simms came out and tried that closet door."

While scratching a few more notes, I asked, "You yourself

never tried the door or entered the gas closet?"

"Of course not. Why would I?"

"And neither did Glee?"

Berta shook her head. "Not while I was with her."

"And you were with her from the time you found her out there until the time when everyone else came out?"

"Well, *no*. I had to go get the pot."

Mister Puss shot me a look.

I asked Berta, "So you left Glee alone for a while? How long?"

Berta explained, "I was gone maybe twenty minutes, ten minutes each way. We keep a teensy stash here at the house. Mary likes a little hit now and then."

Sounding perhaps too incredulous, I asked, "Mary does *pot*?"

Berta reminded me, "She also did FlabberGas. But I think she's kicked that one." Touché.

I struggled to gather my thoughts. "So ... when you returned to the clinic, you found Glee where you'd left her, correct?"

"No. When I got back, I went around to the side of the building, but she wasn't there. I thought maybe she'd managed to get indoors again, so I walked back to the front and tried the door, but it was locked, like before. Her car was still there, so I returned to the side of the building, and there she was, walking over toward the log."

I asked carefully, "She was walking toward the log ... from *where*?"

"Well, at first I thought she *must* have come from that metal door back there—nothing else made sense. But I pestered till she told me. Nature called."

I winced. "That's what she told you—'nature called'?"

"No, Mr. Norris. She said she had to take a leak. And I said it made a pretty picture—her in those fancy heels and Sunday dress, tromping around in the back woods, sprinkling the pinecones. That's when the laughing jag started; the pot kept it going."

Mister Puss seemed to enjoy the story, purring merrily.

But I was anything but amused.

My quandary regarding Glee Savage had worsened. When I had visited her on Wednesday, my intention was to neatly dispatch any suspicions of her possible guilt, but by the end of that visit, she had left me with a convincing hypothetical argument that she might have actually done the deadly deed.

Today, visiting Berta, I'd been inclined to be swayed by a different hypothetical, the notion that an impertinent housekeeper, struggling with finances, could be capable of scheming to murder a rich, childless widow and then becoming the new lady of the Questman mansion. But now, sitting across from Berta in the kitchen, I was all but certain she had not been responsible for such devilry.

Logistically, it didn't make sense that Berta would stoop to Sunday's crime when she'd learned the day before that Mary had bowed out of the gas treatment. Plus, today's conversation left me with a more informed view of Berta and her relationship with Mary: Berta was not only Mary's cook and housekeeper, but since the death of their husbands, Berta and Mary had become companions, perhaps even pot buddies, in their adjustment to a later life that no longer included the security they had known in marriage.

However, the most significant takeaway from my conversation with Berta was the detail she'd supplied regarding her Sunday-afternoon encounter with Glee Savage outside the clinic, which further fueled my mounting suspicion of Glee. When Berta lost track of Glee that day, had Glee been responding to nature's call? Or had she been responding to a different call, the call to vengeful mischief against Dr. Frumpkin, not in the woods, but in the gas closet?

Mary waltzed in through the back door. "Well, just *look* at you two," she twittered, "having a cozy conversation in the kitchen." She laid her purse on the table and set a shopping bag on one of the chairs. Mister Puss hopped onto the table and stepped over to the open bag, poking his head into it.

I stood. "Welcome back, Mary. This has really been helpful." I gave her a kiss.

"Can I then assume that Sheriff Simms *won't* be locking Berta up?"

"Highly doubtful," I said.

"That's nice." She reached for one of the cookies and took a bite. With a subtle turn to Berta, she arched an inquisitive brow, which seemed to ask, Anything *in* these? Berta answered with the slightest shake of her head. Mary shrugged and continued eating.

Berta asked, "Would you like some milk with that, Mary?"

"No, dear. I'm fine, thanks."

"Then I'd better get some work done," said Berta. She cleared the milk from the table, thanked me for making time for her, and left the room.

Mary swooped up Mister Puss and sat at the table.

I sat again. "May I ask you something—about Berta?"

"Of *course*, Brody. Happy to be of help."

"When Berta drove you to the surgery center last Sunday, did she already know that you'd decided *not* to be Dr. Frumpkin's guinea pig?"

"I'm sure of it. Saturday afternoon, I was having trouble reaching Dr. Frumpkin, and I had to go out, so I asked Berta to try phoning him with my decision."

Good, I thought—that confirms what Berta told me, and it eliminates any conceivable motive for Berta to have caused what happened. I asked Mary, "Did you tell Berta *why* you were backing out?"

"I told her Mister Puss warned me not to go." She rubbed the scruff of the cat's neck.

Good—that, too, was consistent with Berta's narrative. I took the questioning one step further: "When Mister Puss advised you to back out, what reason did he give?"

She smiled down at Mister Puss, who purred. "He said it was just a feeling."

Her explanation made me wonder if in fact it was Mary herself who'd had the feeling she should back out. Had she been projecting her own reservations about the gas treatment onto her cat? Or did she really have, as she claimed, some sort of psychic connection with the animal? Not that I believed—even for argument's sake—that there was any possibility Mister Puss could actively, independently communicate with her.

She said, "Can I ask you a big favor, Brody?"

"Anything, Mary."

"This coming Monday, I need to be in Appleton that afternoon. I'm on the women's league of one of the university councils, and they're having a little program, a tea or something, honoring me for something—I forget what—and it's a bit of a drive, so Berta's going to take me. We'll be away for several hours, and even though Mister Puss can look after himself pretty well, I'd rather not leave him alone that long. So I was wondering if you'd mind having some company that afternoon." Mary gave me a sweet, pleading smile. So did her cat.

"I wouldn't mind at all," I told them. In fact, I welcomed the opportunity to spend some one-on-one time with the chatty Mister Puss. And I was eager to get an earful.

Yeah, right.

8

I asked Marson, "Did you actually see Berta's husband eat worms?"

Marson was sampling one of the appetizers he'd prepared for our Saturday dinner at the loft with Dahr Ahmadi. He grimaced, swallowed, and set down the remaining half of a large pesto-stuffed mushroom. "Did you have to bring that up *now?*"

"Sorry, bad timing." I reached for the mushroom and finished it off.

"Yes," said Marson, wiping his oily fingers on a kitchen towel he had tucked through his belt, "I saw it happen, about four years ago. I was at Mary's home one morning, giving her a private presentation of my proposed plans for Questman Center. She *loved* everything, so I was on cloud *nine*, and then she asked me to stay for lunch, which turned out to be a heavenly carrot soup prepared by none other than surly Berta herself. While I was enjoying another spoonful—so warm and rich, with an aggressive spark of nutmeg—I glanced through the window to the front lawn, and that's when I saw it … *happen*." Marson gagged and lifted a hand to his throat, as if reliving a horrid sense memory. Recovering, he said, "I think his name was Snook, of all things."

"Right, he went by his last name, Snook. Which is Berta's name, too."

Marson crossed his arms and gave me an unbelieving look. "Berta Snook?"

I assured him, "I was a bit floored, myself."

Getting back to business, Marson asked, "How are the mushrooms?"

"They're great. They'll be perfect with cocktails."

"I just had a thought." Marson looked stricken. "What if Dahr doesn't drink? Sarah said he's Iranian. Sheriff Simms implied he was Muslim. I think they don't drink."

"Most don't," I agreed. "But I'm pretty sure he had a glass of champagne at Mary's last week."

"But it could have been ginger ale."

With a laugh, I reminded my husband, "We *have* ginger ale." I found it not only funny, but also endearing, that Marson seemed a tad nervous about hosting Dahr Ahmadi in our home. And in truth, I shared a sense of uncertain expectations. The dinner date was my idea. But why, exactly, had I wanted to do this?

At the most obvious level, Dahr was a handsome, professional, middle-aged gay man—a sparse commodity in small-town Dumont—so both Marson and I were inclined to know him better and perhaps draw him into our circle of friends.

At a baser level, I had to admit (to myself, if not to Marson) that Dahr's physical attractiveness had an erotic edge, as if his bodily presence transmitted a secret signal, a coded query, wondering if I was interested. We each knew that the other was off limits, as I was married to Marson, while Dahr had apparently reached some level of understanding, if not outright commitment, with Dr. Frumpkin. Nonetheless, in the brief, limited interaction I'd had with Dahr, there had been a spontaneous energy, an undertone of something that felt a lot like temptation. Even Frumpkin himself had tuned in to it, as demonstrated when he playfully warned me, "No poaching, Brody," which only intensified Dahr's allure as forbidden fruit. To be clear: I was not "looking." I was not open to seduction. But flirtation was a subtle game that offered a harmless lift with little risk of fallout.

And finally, at a higher and more pragmatic level, I had wanted to invite Dahr to dinner because he was still an undefined but active cipher in the mystery of Jason Ward's death. Dr. Frumpkin had insisted that Dahr would "never harm a fly," but Sheriff Simms had expressed his doubts and challenged me to prove him wrong. The clock was ticking. The past week had slipped away with scant investigative progress, and it was now only nine days until early voting would begin in Dumont County.

While planning our dinner for three, Marson—ever the supportive spouse—had suggested, "I'll cook, Sherlock. You'll have your hands full with the suspect."

Grrring.

Now, at seven on Saturday, the sputtering old bell at the loft's street door announced the arrival of our guest. "That must be your suspect," said Marson, doffing his oven mitts.

"Stop that," I told him, pecking his cheek, as we crossed from the kitchen to the door together.

Marson swung the door wide. "Dahr! Good evening! Come on in!"

Stepping inside, Dahr presented a gift bag containing a bottle of good champagne.

Marson and I shared a grin—no ginger ale tonight. We shook hands with our guest, then hugged him.

"This is so *great* of you guys, having me over," said Dahr. "And look at this place—wow—who'd have thought, in *Dumont?*"

My initial reaction to him was reconfirmed: what a swell guy. I'm easy.

When I had phoned to invite Dahr on Thursday, I reached him at home on his cell number, as Dr. Frumpkin's office was still closed in the aftermath of Jason Ward's death. Dahr answered at once and, from the lilt of his voice, seemed delighted to hear from me. But I was concerned—in fact, fretting—that the dinner invitation from Marson and me, a couple, might be interpreted by Dahr to include Frumpkin, who would then totally dominate our evening together, which would spoil its purpose.

To my boundless relief, Dahr said, "Saturday is perfect for me. Francis is a wreck, poor guy, and he mentioned something about spending that evening with Sarah. Anyway, I could use a night out." I asked if he was okay with beef—you just never know these days—and he said he looked forward to it.

In closing, he asked what he could bring, and I told him, perhaps with a tinge of something unintended, "Just yourself."

And now, there he stood.

I watched him from the kitchen as Marson pointed out a few features of the loft. I had seen Dahr only twice before—when we met at Mary's the previous Friday, during the pitch session, and then again on Sunday, the day of the fateful demo. On Friday, he had dressed nicely in casual office attire, having come from his duties in Frumpkin's practice. Then, Sunday, on the job as nurse practitioner at the clinic, he'd dressed smartly for that role in a crisp white lab coat, accessorized with his stethoscope.

Tonight, though, he sported a different look altogether. On this Saturday evening, visiting the home of two gay men, well away from the job—and away from his boss—Dahr wore all black. Tight slacks. Silky shirt. Leather blazer. Plus the tasteful punch of some silver bling, including a heavy chain bracelet. Combined with his dark hair and tan complexion, the total package was a jaw-dropper. When I first met him, I'd instantly recognized a pleasing hint of the exotic in his features and bearing, but tonight, he'd amped it up. Tonight, by the way he presented himself, by the way he walked, without even saying a word, he projected a teasing aura of danger. Not a physical, threatening danger—but a sexual tension that was palpable.

Marson sensed it, too. He almost giggled when asking Dahr if he'd care to see the sleeping loft on the mezzanine.

"Well, *yeah*," Dahr answered, "I'd love to see it."

And up the spiral stairs they went. Marson led the way. I watched from below, enjoying the view too much as Dahr followed.

While they gabbed up there—Marson was showing him my large rendering of "the perfect house" that hung near our bed—I busied myself arranging the tray of appetizers on a massive low table that anchored the conversation area of the main room. I called up to Dahr, "Do you want me to open the champagne?"

He stepped over to the edge of the mezzanine and looked down at me. Great smile. "No, Brody," he said, "that's for you and Marson to enjoy later."

I told him, "We'll be having red wine with dinner. What would you like now?"

"Surprise me." He winked.

Oh, honey.

I surprised him with a basic Scotch on the rocks, splash of soda, twist. The colder weather always sent a signal for me to switch to darker cocktails, so I poured Scotch for myself as well. Marson's taste in such matters knew no season, however, and he began the evening with his usual martini.

Dahr was saying, "The new house will be fantastic, Brody. I can't wait to see it."

"It ought to be presentable soon—in a year or so," I quipped.

Marson said, "We'll invite you to the housewarming."

"I'll mark my calendar," said Dahr.

We were seated around the low table at the front of the loft, with Marson and me across from each other on a pair of love-seats; Dahr sat perpendicular to us on a tufted leather bench, looking across the table toward the wall of windows on the street.

Between the two center windows, a three-foot section of brick wall rose from the floor to the twenty-foot ceiling, resembling a chimney, so Marson had designed a minimalist mantel and surround of feathered slate, resembling a fireplace—baldly artificial, yet wonderfully evocative. It contained several tiered rows of fluttering pillar candles, also fakes, but forgivably theatrical. Atop the mantel were a few homey curios, including a clear apothecary jar containing a pound or two of intricately patterned castor beans, courtesy of Glee Savage. Above the mantel hung a tall antique mirror. From the ceiling, centered over the low table, hung a huge Mexican chandelier of punched tin, casting playful starlight about the room. And beyond the windows, streetlights glared in the black October night.

The total effect was urban and trendy and—mixed with Dahr's sultry presence—achingly romantic.

Marson broke the lull. "Lucky me," he said. "I've got the best view in the house. You two look great together."

Perhaps we did. Perhaps we had a yin-and-yang thing happening—Dahr's dark hair and clothes, contrasted with my sandy hair and Anglo features. Perhaps Marson truly did enjoy the view. But it made me uneasy that he had linked me with Dahr in a context that had such steamy overtones—at least to me, it did. Or had my imagination shifted into overdrive?

"That's kind of you, Marson," said Dahr, "but *I've* got the best view in the house. You guys are the best."

Okay, I thought, that's better, that's the right comeback, that gets us all on track—if only he hadn't winked at me. Again.

Attempting to divert my thoughts from Dahr's hotness, I

said, "Sarah mentioned to us that you're Iranian, but I'm guessing you've been here a long time."

He nodded. "I was born there, yes. But I came here as an infant, and I've been a citizen since I was a kid. I have no memories of Iran. This is home."

Marson said, "Most Americans, we're all immigrants—at least by descent. But you actually made the journey. You *left* somewhere to be here."

"My parents did." Dahr shrugged. "I happened to be with them."

I said, "Do you mind my asking—why did they bring you here?"

"It was in the early eighties, after the revolution. I was a baby, and my parents were both university students, in medicine. Like many others at the time, they opposed Khomeini and the new theocracy, so they left in the wave of emigration that followed. They were both accepted at Madison, came here on student visas, and were granted permanent resident status. Naturalization came later."

Marson asked, "Where are they now?"

"Dad died a few years ago, too young, but Mom is still going strong. She's a doctor of philosophy in nursing, teaching in Milwaukee. Just a few years now till she retires. All said," he summarized, "my family found a good life here."

"Plus," I noted, "you're gay."

"And as we all know," said Dahr with a tone of heavy understatement, "that might have been a serious wrinkle, a deadly wrinkle, in the 'old country.'" He picked up his cocktail and took a goodly sip.

"Obviously," noted Marson, "you drink alcohol. I apologize for my ignorance of these things, but ... are you a Muslim?"

Dahr set down his glass and waggled his hand in a mezzo-

mezzo gesture. "I was born Muslim, certainly. And at some level, I still think of myself as a 'cultural Muslim,' in that I came from those traditions and hold a certain respect for them, up to a point. My parents were skeptics all along, intellectuals—I guess you'd say freethinkers. Once we were here, they found the freedom to let go of their heritage and never forced it on me. Bottom line: I have no religion. I don't pray. I don't even believe."

Freethinking. For me it was a concept so self-evident, so taken for granted, that I had never seriously questioned why anyone would object to it, let alone find it offensive. Or punishable. But for Dahr's parents—who had seen their country taken over by fundamentalists, coming from a place where they could *die* for not believing—the concept of freethinking had been evasive enough and powerful enough to justify the uprooting of everything they had known, then starting over, a world away.

Marson chuckled. "Sorry if I seem to be making light of a heavy topic, but I just happened to think of Mister Puss."

Dahr chuckled, too. "Are you talking about Mary Questman's cat? Francis told me about their, uh, *special* relationship."

"Exactly," said Marson. "According to Mary, she had an epiphany last spring, shortly after Mister Puss arrived, when he told her, and I quote: 'God is a myth.'"

I added, "She hasn't gone to church since."

"I think she'd already been tapering off for a while," said Marson. "Funny, though—it makes you marvel at her ability to embrace new ideas that she might've once thought unimaginable."

I didn't consider it quite the right time to inform Marson that Mary had taken to another new idea, as well—toking up with the help.

Marson continued, "Anyway, Dahr, thanks for sharing the story of your family's exodus. And more to the point: we're glad you're here."

Dahr responded not to Marson, but to me, "So am I."

And *again* the wink. Or was it maybe just a tic?

My mother raised me as a heathen. Her word.

I grew up in California, and a few days after I started going to school, I came home one day and asked Inez, "What am I?"

She hunkered down, smiling, to ask me in return, "What do you mean, Brody?"

"Some of the kids at school say they're this-or-that. Like"—I struggled with the words—"like Catholic or Methodist, so what are *we*?"

With a grin, she tapped my nose, explaining, "We're heathens, dear. It's nobody's business, but if anyone asks, just tell them you're a heathen. And be proud of it."

Inez was like that, a true iconoclast: feminist lesbian, political activist, single mother, and yes, freethinker. By the age of six, I understood that we were different, and following her advice, I was proud of it. Still am.

Marson's upbringing, here in Dumont, was far more conventional. He was raised in one of those mainstream Protestant congregations—sociable, colorless, fungible—that instilled in him its traditions and its fables, but no religious fervor or commitment to doctrine. He told me that he'd "lost God in college," meaning, he'd simply stopped thinking about it. The belief was gone, and that was that.

His career has now brought him a good measure of later-life fame as a designer of magnificent public buildings, and one night over dinner, I asked if he had ever designed a church—or would even consider such a commission.

He sat back at the table to gather his thoughts, then answered, "Le Corbusier was an avowed atheist, but he designed the chapel at Ronchamp and managed to inspire generations of believers. No, I've never designed a church, but I *have* designed theaters, and if you think about it, churches and theaters share an uncanny similarity of purpose, scale, and effect. To answer your question, then—of course I'd consider such a commission." With a laugh, he added, "Not that I'm expecting one."

Tonight, at that same table, Marson said to our guest, Dahr Ahmadi, "I hope you'll enjoy the tenderloin." We had finished our gabby cocktail hour and moved to the loft's dining area for the main event. Marson continued, "Out here in the sticks, we're not much known for 'cuisine,' but the beef is reliable."

"It's perfect," said Dahr. "My compliments. And wow, this Bordeaux." Raising his glass, he added, "To my gracious hosts— and new friends." He winked at me. I think.

"I'll drink to that," said Marson as we all touched glasses.

Marson and I sat across from each other, similar to our earlier configuration for cocktails, with Dahr between us, looking out toward the front of the loft. The table was big enough for six, which left ample room for a lavish grouping of candles. Though their flames were fake, the mood was plenty real. Candlelight danced through the deep red lenses formed by the wine in our glasses.

While Dahr quizzed Marson on the particulars of preparing the tenderloin—seared under the broiler before roasting with the baby potatoes—I made a mental note to put aside a slab of the meat for Mister Puss, who would be entrusted to my care on Monday afternoon. I recalled the rapture with which he had gobbled Berta's bloody-rare tenderloin appetizers.

Earlier that evening, Dahr had enlightened us with details of his family background. Just now, he and Marson had covered the requisite chitchat about food. So the time had come to address my underlying purpose in bringing us together that night.

"Dahr," I said, perhaps sounding a shade too solemn, "since you arrived, there's something we haven't even mentioned yet."

He heaved a sigh while setting down his fork. "Jason's death."

"Of course. I'm sorry to put a damper on things."

"Don't apologize, Brody—I completely understand. In fact, Francis told me I could expect to hear from you, so I assumed tonight would *not* be just a friendly visit."

Marson interjected, "But it's definitely that as well."

"Absolutely," I said. But I was thinking of the afternoon meeting in Sheriff Simms's conference room, where Dr. Francis Frumpkin had assured us that Dahr was incapable of murder, which I wanted to believe—then, and now. I asked him, "What do you think happened last Sunday?"

Marson caught my eye and gave me a subtle but approving nod, as if to say, Good move. Don't lead. Just get him talking about it.

Dahr said, "I'm not sure what happened, although there's talk that the gas lines might've been switched, which would at least explain the 'mechanics' of how Jason died. As to *why* it happened—accident or murder, and if so, who did it—I have no idea. It's baffling. But something *else* happened that afternoon, which is no mystery at all." He paused.

I decided to follow Marson's muse, decided not to lead, not to question. Instead, I waited.

And Dahr resumed, unprompted. "Jason died that day, yes, but so did the dreams that Francis wanted to pursue in his retirement. I'm not sure, but his reputation may have died that day, too. At the very least, his professional stature was dealt a serious setback. So Jason is dead, and FlabberGas is dead. The question remains: Will this also kill the existing practice? No secret, Francis has done *very* well, so he could just call it quits, but that's not the way he'd want it to end. And what about Sarah? She's not wealthy, and she's lost her husband. If the practice closed, how would *she* pick up the pieces? And me? I have even fewer options. Everyone who works there—we're scared. And *that's* what happened that day." Dahr stopped speaking, glanced to the ceiling, then reached for a sip of wine.

Marson shot me another silent signal, seeming to ask, Well, what do you think?

Off the top of my head, I thought that Dahr had just made a highly reasonable argument for dismissing everyone connected with Dr. Frumpkin's practice as possible suspects in the death and likely murder of Jason Ward.

Taking those thoughts a step deeper, though, one niggling detail had raised a flag. Dahr had just said that if the practice were to close, he would have "even fewer options" than Sarah for financial security. But he'd neglected to consider, or at least to say, that he still had the option of Dr. Frumpkin's affections as the ultimate lifeline. Dahr could do a lot worse than hitching his wagon to a successful, retiring doctor who seemed crazy for him. Dahr may not have found that lifeline attractive or ethical, but it was, in fact, an option. Had he merely overlooked it in the woe-is-me spirit of a heartfelt narrative? Or had he consciously brushed that detail aside, unmentioned, while hoping it would go unnoticed?

Although I had tried to refrain from questioning Dahr, there was one matter that had to be addressed. I asked him, "What did you think of Jason Ward?"

"I think he was a skilled and compassionate physician. I think he was a loving husband and a doting father. I think he was completely dedicated to the practice and was looking forward to taking over the family business with his wife. And most important, Brody, I think Jason Ward did not deserve to die."

Marson closed his eyes, as if he understood what I needed to say next.

I asked Dahr, "But did you *like* Jason? He seemed to have some issues … with you."

"Ah. Well. That." Dahr leaned on his elbows to tell me, "Early on, for those first few years after I was hired, Jason and I were great together. We respected each other professionally, and we enjoyed each other as friends. But later, when Francis began to be more open about his 'interest' in me, things started to change. Jason was fine with me when I was just another underling, when I was just the hired help. But as soon as there was even a *hint* that Francis wanted to bring me into the family—and by extension, into the family *business*—Jason got cold, even combative. He started putting me down, dissing me, first in front of staff, then in front of patients. It felt like a campaign to run me out."

I said, "But Francis would have no part of that, I assume."

"Not at *all*. He made it clear that, one way or the other, I would always be part of the picture. Which made Jason's resentment all the worse. It was pretty childish—as if he felt that Francis was taking sides." Considering this for a moment, Dahr added, "In a sense, I guess he was."

Marson gave me a look that asked, May I jump in?

I responded in kind, Be my guest.

He said to Dahr, "This is terribly personal, but do you mind if I ask: What is the nature of your relationship with Francis Frumpkin?"

Good God, I thought, I would never have gone there. But I was glad Marson did.

Dahr was disarmingly candid as he lolled back in his chair, swirling his wine. With a soft laugh, he said to Marson, "The nature of our relationship? That's a good question. As far as Francis is concerned, it's the real deal—courtship intended to lead to marriage. And it's way more than sweet talk. We do have sex—as recently as last Saturday, a week ago tonight, but there's been a dry spell since Jason's death. Naturally."

I reached to fill his glass and keep him talking. I asked, "Do you love him?"

"Yes," said Dahr, "I do. Maybe not in a gung-ho, passionate kinda way, though the sex is fine. For me, the relationship is more of an emotional thing. I love Francis for the love he's shown *me*. I've *learned* to love him. He fulfills a certain need in my life—and I don't mean, for lack of a better word, money."

Interesting, I thought. Dahr and I were about the same age, and so were Marson and Dr. Frumpkin, which seemed to suggest a parallel. However, I interpreted the subtext of Dahr's words to mean that he loved Frumpkin as something of a father figure, which was not at all the basis of my commitment to Marson. We were equal partners in love and in our shared life. We were drawn to each other not as father and son, not as mentor and pupil, not *because* of our age difference, but in spite of it.

Marson said to Dahr, "It sounds as if you and Francis have a lot to offer each other. And I know that Francis truly wants to build a life with you; he said so. But you're just not interested?"

Dahr weighed his words before replying, "Let's say I have reservations. For one thing, with Francis, it's all business, all the time. I realize he's an entrepreneur and a promoter—as well as a doctor—which has brought him great success. But he can never let go of it, never turn it off. Last Saturday night: an intimate dinner for two at his place, getting cozy afterward, getting in the mood, then Sarah calls, and he *can't* send it to voice mail, and suddenly he's in a dither because Mary Questman won't be the guinea pig the next day, and he doesn't know how to explain to the crowd why Jason is stepping in. And on and on. After he hung up, it took a full *hour* to hit 'reset' and get us back on track—if you know what I mean."

Marson laughed. "Oh, I know what you mean."

I rolled my eyes.

"But our *main* issue," Dahr continued, "is children."

Marson nodded. "You want kids. He doesn't."

"Right. He's already been there, paid his dues, and likes being a granddad, with zero interest in the day-to-day messiness of raising a family. But I've never had that. And I *crave* that. I mean, kids are so great. Look at little Olivia ..."

Little Olivia, I thought, would not have been *my* choice as an example of the rewards of child-rearing.

"Olivia," he continued, "sure, she's been a challenge lately. And now, with the sudden death of her dad, I expected her to have a complete meltdown. But know what? She's taking it pretty well, much better than you'd think. And then there's Sarah—my God, she's just a total mess, no surprise. It's almost as if Olivia has stepped in and gathered the strength her mother has lost. Kids can be remarkably resilient."

From the moment when I had first heard mention of Dahr—the night at the restaurant when I met Dr. Frumpkin and his daughter and heard their plans for FlabberGas—I'd been intrigued by this exotic-sounding creature, Dariush, who now sat in my home, within easy reach if I were so inclined. Soon after, upon meeting him at Mary's and then again at the clinic, I'd found him not only attractive and seductive, but also a source of continuous surprise. Tonight's conversations had included an array of unexpected tidbits, from his Muslim apostasy to his frank appraisal of sex with Dr. Frumpkin. But the greatest revelation was the depth of his affection for kids and his empathy for the ordeals of childhood. I must admit, his concern for Olivia's troubling situation—and his willingness to understand her problems on *her* terms—made me ashamed of the harsh judgment I had rushed to impose on the girl, which was based on little more than one unfortunate outburst. That, and a tacky princess dress. Was I really that shallow?

Our dinner conversation at the loft moseyed on in this vein, returning to Jason's death now and then, but with no persuasive insights regarding who bore the guilt. From the outset, I had been willing to abide by the strictures set down by Lady Justice and presume Dahr's innocence. I had also wanted to believe Dr. Frumpkin's contention that Dahr would never harm a fly, let alone murder a colleague, and I was relieved to have heard nothing at dinner that would dissuade me from that conclusion.

And yet: It was difficult to ignore, impossible to forget, what Dahr had said as he manned the controls of the hyperbaric chamber, telling Jason Ward, "I *know* what I'm doing, Doctor."

I'd heard it clearly. Sheriff Simms had, too.

Some three hours after Dahr arrived at the loft, our evening together came to a close. A wonderful time, as they say, was had by all. Marson had charmed Dahr with his cooking and his small talk and his considerable skills as a gracious host. Dahr had charmed both Marson and me with his stories and his magnetism and his winks. Or were they tics? And apparently, I, Brody Norris, had all but charmed the pants off Dahr Ahmadi. It was not my intent to create an atmosphere of flirtation—I had simply tried to be amiable and welcoming—but Dahr must have tuned in to a more primal vibe.

When he arrived that night, we had greeted each other with handshakes and tentative hugs. Upon parting, however, we had cemented our friendship, so we forwent the handshakes altogether and hugged in earnest. And then, after the thank-yous and good-nights, Dahr offered kisses.

"May I, Mr. Miles?" he asked Marson outside the front door, leaning near for a smooch.

"With pleasure," said my husband, and they exchanged a chaste peck.

"And Mr. Norris?" he said to me.

"Of course, Dahr." We pecked.

Marson said, "Hope to see you again soon, Dahr. Good night." And he turned inside to begin cleanup. It was *not* in his nature to leave things till morning.

Dahr asked me, "Walk me to my car?"

First Avenue was dead quiet—Saturday night, and our tiny town had "rolled up the sidewalks" already. A bit of evening drizzle had left the street dark and shiny. Yellow leaves glistened and dripped in the warm glow of a streetlamp. The soles of our shoes kissed the damp pavement. Then the man in black turned, and once again, he kissed me.

This was no tic. This was no ritual observation of some ancient parting custom handed down by Dahr's Persian forebears. No, this was a kiss that meant business. This was a kiss that shot through me, that left me speechless and woozy and open to the unknown.

But then, without a word, he turned and left.

Shambling back to the loft, I wondered, What the hell was *that*? Was he making a statement? Was he challenging me? Daring me to fall for him?

Or was Dahr just using his wiles—buttering me up for a good report to Sheriff Simms?

When I stepped inside and closed the door, Marson looked up from the kitchen sink, merrily rinsing his way through a stack of dishes. "He's such a sweet guy—what a great evening."

Still a bit dazed, I confessed, "He kissed me."

"He kissed me, too, kiddo."

"I mean, he kissed me again, outside."

"I've said it before, Brody: you're an attractive man, desired by many."

I took my explanation a step further. "I mean, he *really* kissed me."

Marson gave a playful growl. "Yikes. Was it good?"

"Marson"—I moved toward him in the kitchen—"aren't you … *jealous?*"

He set down his sponge. "Jealous? I'm complimented! Besides—" And he broke into laughter.

"Besides what?"

Marson grinned. "He's not *old* enough for you."

"Or"—I grinned—"he could be just the exception that proves the rule."

CHAPTER

9

Truth is, there were no rules, etched in stone or otherwise.

True, when I was fourteen, I had developed an abiding attraction to older, creative men. True, my first marriage had been to an older, creative man, an architect in California named Lloyd Washington. True, my current marriage was to an older, creative man, a Wisconsin architect named Marson Miles. True, this seemed to denote a pattern. But there were no rules.

True, Dahr Ahmadi was perhaps two or three years older than I was, but this did not qualify him as an "older man." In the generational scope of things, we were contemporaries. Dahr was a certified nurse practitioner, a respected professional with a noble and humane calling, but this did not qualify him as a "creative man." He was a man of science. So it was easy to understand Marson's confident assumption that, in my eyes, Dahr could never measure up. But there were no rules.

True, Marson and I were married. The conventions of marriage—of conventional, heterosexual marriage—demand a lifelong commitment of body, soul, and desire, frequently sworn in vows at the altar, which can lend poignancy to a fairytale ceremony. But even the most earnest exchange of vows offers no guarantee that reality will not evolve and intervene. And the truth is, for us—for any gay couple, married or not—there were no rules, other than those we were content to define for ourselves.

True, Marson and I had written "vows" and delivered them at our tidy civil ceremony, but they were sworn to no god. They focused on an abiding love, which sprang from friendship, and a commitment to "be there" for each other in a joining of forces till death do us part. But they made no reference to carnal fidelity, which struck us both as an irrelevant hangover from some medieval obsession with procreation. So for us, in the matter of Dahr Ahmadi, there were no rules.

True, we had a shadowy understanding that indiscretion could be hurtful to each other and therefore harmful to "us." Did such an understanding therefore imply that any contemplated indiscretion should simply be replaced by discretion, by the venerable bromide that what you don't know can't hurt you?

I don't know.

What I *do* know is that the memory of Dahr's kiss—the second one, out on the street, under the drizzle in the yellow lamplight—vexed me and excited me and consumed my thoughts from the moment I stepped back into the loft on Saturday night. It followed me up the winding staircase as I prepared for bed. It stirred beneath the blankets as I cuddled with my husband, who drifted off, exhausted by his efforts to stage the perfect dinner party. It staved off my own sleep, and when at last I slumbered, the memory of the kiss peppered my dreams with possibilities. This was temptation, pure and raw and simple.

Sunday morning, unrested and bleary-eyed, I finally snapped free of this obsession when I poured a mug of coffee, sat down with Marson at the center island in the kitchen, and opened the front section of the *Dumont Daily Register*.

Clock is ticking on FlabberGas fiasco

*Lack of progress in suspected murder case
may dominate closing arguments in election*

Compiled from *Register* staff reports

•

OCT. 17, DUMONT, WI—One week from tomorrow, voters

in Dumont County will begin heading to the polls for early voting in the election that will either award a second term to Sheriff Thomas Simms or, in an upset, turn the office over to his opponent, Deputy Alex Kastle.

The drama began last Sunday afternoon, when Dr. Jason Ward died under suspicious circumstances during the demonstration of a novel weight-loss technique, Flabber-Gas, presented by its inventor, Dr. Francis Frumpkin. A group of potential investors witnessed the tragedy, now being investigated by Sheriff Simms as a likely murder.

When questioned by e-mail on Friday about progress with the case, Simms offered no particulars. He replied, "An investigation of this nature requires time and diligence. We are still in the early stages of collecting the known facts and determining what directions to pursue as follow-up. There is nothing to report at this time."

The *Register* asked the sheriff's election opponent for comment. After reading the statement from Simms, Deputy Kastle said, "Obviously, the guy's got nothing. He's dragging his feet, brushing this under the rug till after the election. But voters won't buy it. They're plenty mad that the victim of this killing could have been our beloved Mary Questman. So it's time for Simms to deliver."

Kastle may be right. We sent a reporting team to ask Dumonters about the case during a busy Saturday morning at the local Walmart. Among those planning to vote, we found broad skepticism that Sheriff Simms would be able to solve the case quickly, if at all. Some expressed anger.

Mother of three and volunteer librarian Janet Stanley said, "It sends a terrible message that something like this can happen in Dumont. Then nothing? We need answers. We deserve better."

Others were more blunt. Harvey Boller of Harvey's Heating told us …

"Oh, boy," I said to Marson, who'd already read the story. "This is *not* looking good. And that jackass Kastle is just stirring the pot, having a ball."

Marson gave his head a woeful shake. "It's just *unthinkable* that the voters in this town would even consider such an ignorant, bigoted, unqualified candidate. They're not that dumb."

I said, "Wisconsin sent you-know-who to Washington."

"Christ, don't remind me."

My phone rang. I glanced at the screen, then answered, "Good morning, Thomas."

"Hi, Brody. Not sure how good a morning it is."

I asked, "You've read it, huh?"

"Right. Sorry to call so early on a Sunday, but I'd like to nail down a meeting tomorrow with the medical examiner. Nine o'clock at Heather Vance's office. She has a report and some updates. Can you be there?"

"You bet. Just try and stop me."

"Thanks, Brody. Gotta run now—taking the family to church."

The medical examiner's office was located downtown in the complex of county buildings, but not in the courthouse or the sheriff's headquarters, so I was on new turf that Monday morning. I walked past the main entrance to the jail, then down a street that resembled an alley, heading toward a smaller, inconspicuous building tucked in at the rear of the grounds. Most of the county buildings were limestone, classically ornamented, but this one was plain red brick, designed for a strictly utilitarian purpose—such as a garage or dispatch center. And it had an uncommonly stout smokestack. From a distance, I couldn't read the signage, so I paused, wondering if I'd gotten the wrong directions.

"Hey, Brody." It was Sheriff Simms, approaching me from around the side of the jail. He was impeccably dressed, as always, but there was no bounce in his step, no broad smile to brighten his handsome features.

I gestured toward the brick building. "Is that it?"

"Yeah." And he fell in beside me, not speaking another word, as we walked the remaining distance. It wasn't far, but the awkward silence made the trek seem arduous.

I stopped to ask him, "Is something wrong?"

He stopped and turned to me. He checked his watch; we were a few minutes early. He said, "Wanna sit down?"

"Sure." One of the county's shabby metal picnic tables sat off to the side of the building's entrance under a tree that had dropped slender golden leaves among the cigarette butts on the ground. We sat across from each other.

"Yesterday," said Simms, "I took Gloria and Tommy to church at St. Alban's. Have you been there?"

I shook my head.

"It's a pretty little church, very old and established, Episcopalian. When we moved here, Gloria and I shopped around awhile, and we settled on St. Alban's because it seemed like the right environment for bringing up Tommy. And we've made a lot of friends there—including Sarah and Jason Ward—their daughter knows Tommy in school. So all of that, it's great."

I had a sinking feeling. "What happened, Thomas?"

"Not so fast," he said with a trace of a grin. "As you might guess, there aren't too many black Episcopalians, not in Wisconsin. St. Alban's has no *other* black families, but they've welcomed us warmly. Point is, it's a small congregation, so everyone knows who I am."

I asked, "Was Sarah there yesterday?"

"No. I was hoping she would be—wanted to give her some encouragement—but I guess she just wasn't up to it, which is understandable. But I *was* there, of course, and frankly, needing a little brotherhood—this last week hasn't been easy on *me*, either. I mean, that's what churches are *about*, right?"

I couldn't answer that one.

"The whole ordeal—arriving there, then the service itself, and the mingling afterward—it was all kinda grim. Sure, emotions were still raw. The congregation had just lost a member, quite possibly to murder. And naturally, the sermon was all about Jason, but it was also, to use the rector's words, a 'call to justice.' See where this is heading? This may sound nutty, but I was made to feel that the problem wasn't so much Jason's death as it was *my* inability to wrap it up fast."

I asked, "Did anyone actually *say* that?"

"No. Maybe I was just being paranoid, maybe not. But the whole time we were there, not a soul would even look me in the eye to say hello. I'm sure they'd all read the morning paper. I don't know if it was the story that started giving them ideas—or if the story just confirmed what they'd been thinking all along."

I wasn't sure what to say. "Don't read too much into this, Thomas. People are confused and hurt, especially, I imagine, at St. Alban's."

"Oh," said Simms, adding another detail, "and it wasn't just Jason being mourned—you could read it between the lines. There was also the speculation that Mary Questman could have been at risk, that she could have been taken from them. The Questman family helped *build* that parish."

"Was Mary there?"

"No, I haven't noticed her at church in quite a while—maybe last Easter."

God is a myth, I recalled. Mary said her cat had enlightened her. Or was she tripping?

After we talked, Simms seemed better. The cold shoulder he'd gotten at church must have felt less chilling after I'd lent him a more sympathetic shoulder to lean on—an outcome that struck me as odd, but at the same time, gladdening. After all, he was the strong one, the enforcer, the guy with the badge; I was the gay guy, the creative one, just trying to help. And although we had always been chummy, I sensed we had now become friends.

When we entered the brick building together, I didn't know what to expect and was feeling apprehensive—morgue, bodies, autopsies, chimney—but Simms led the way, and I drew confidence from his experience, which seemed to be telling me, This is no big deal. We entered a lobby of sorts, with a clerk behind a window who greeted Simms and said to go in. We bypassed a pair of hospital-style double doors (thank God) and breezed into the medical examiner's office, which was perfectly pleasant: Sunny window, potted plants, a framed degree or two. No hanging skeletons, no ghoulish display of crime-scene photos, no spleens in jars.

Heather Vance stood and crossed the room to welcome us with a smile. She wore a cheery autumn dress of nubby silk, the color of squash soup, set off with a wide cream-colored belt. "Come in," she said, "sit down."

As Simms and I settled in, Heather resumed her seat behind the desk, telling the sheriff, "I was so sorry to read that your deputy's been grandstanding again. It's not only dirty politics—it could hurt the investigation. If it were up to me, he'd be disciplined."

"There's nothing I'd like better," said Simms, "but Kastle and his supporters would simply turn that against me, claiming I was using my office to 'impede his free speech' or whatever. They'd be accusing *me* of dirty politics. So I think the best approach is to ignore him—and not even dignify his remarks as being worthy of a response."

"I hope you're right," said Heather.

I hoped so, too. It was a risky gambit, but in the new political atmosphere of alternate truths and upside-down logic, Simms's reasoning made sense.

"Anyway," said Heather, "I have the results you've been waiting for, and we're releasing the victim's body to the family today. So you should now be able to shift the investigation into high gear."

"Okay," said Simms, not bothering to suppress his smile, "let's have it."

Heather opened a folder on her desk but didn't need to read from it as she told us, "Our autopsy and subsequent testing revealed that Jason Ward's *cause* of death was, as we surmised, asphyxiation by nitrous oxide."

Simms nodded. "And *manner* of death?"

With a wry expression, Heather said, "There are only four possibilities, so let's run through them. First, Jason Ward's manner of death was not 'natural causes' because factors such as old age or illness played no role in what happened; he was a robustly healthy middle-aged man. Second, the manner of death was not 'accidental' because the gas lines to the hyperbaric chamber were switched, correct?"

"Correct," said Simms. "The physical evidence collected and observed in the clinic's gas closet proves that someone went to considerable effort to switch the gas feeds, which required circumventing the standard connectors. Those connections are unique to each gas and specifically designed as a safeguard against mix-ups. Accomplishing this had to be a deliberate, intentional act—not an accident."

"So," said Heather, "running down the list, the only remaining possibilities for manner of death are suicide or homicide. If this was a suicide, it was beyond bizarre. Aside from the pure zaniness of killing yourself in public by such contorted means, we found nothing in Jason's medical records indicating depression or concealed illness or any of the other factors associated with suicide. There was no note. There were no reported patterns of suicidal talk. No, Jason Ward didn't kill himself."

"Which leaves only homicide," said Simms.

"Murder," I mumbled.

Jason Ward was now known to be a victim of *murder*. Murder by laughing gas. That assumption had been in the air since the afternoon of his death, but hearing the word from my own lips, hearing the step-by-step reasoning articulated by both the medical examiner and the sheriff, hearing that Jason had left his wife without a husband and left his daughter without a father—as the result of deadly mischief *intended* to kill him—all of this brought into perspective not only the importance, but also the urgency, of naming his killer.

Simms turned to me. "As you suggested, Brody, we checked the clinic's supplier of medical gases, and they had made no recent deliveries—none in the three weeks preceding Jason's death. So the possibility that their driver left the closet door unlocked is very remote; it would have been discovered and then locked again by any clinic staffer with routine access."

I asked, "So you think the suspects are limited to the clinic staff?"

"No, not necessarily. Any of the staffers might have accidentally left the gas closet unlocked, affording some motivated individual the opportunity to rig the lines. Or another possibility:

a knowledgeable outsider could have *picked* the lock at a time of his or her choosing."

Heather tossed her hands. "Then it could've been just about *anybody.*"

"Anybody," said Simms, "with sufficient knowledge of medical gases—and sufficient motive to kill."

I said to him, "You mentioned that switching the gas feeds took considerable effort because the connectors are designed to prevent mix-ups. How would someone manage to circumvent that safeguard?"

"The killer constructed a pair of adapters, one of them oxygen-to-nitrous, the other vice versa. It's not exactly rocket science, but it does require knowledge of the connectors and a few basic tools. The killer also needed enough time to install the adapters and switch the lines—it's not the sort of thing you could do quickly, on a moment's notice. And by the way, in case you were wondering, the killer left no fingerprints on the adapters."

"Naturally," said Heather.

I said, "In other words, the setup for the murder was pretty complicated, so it could *not* have happened that Sunday, on impulse, the day of the demo."

Simms thought for a moment, shook his head. "That now strikes me as impossible."

"So in *other* words," I said, "the killer wasn't Glee Savage, and the killer wasn't Berta Snook."

The sheriff and the medical examiner asked in unison, *"Snook?"*

"Yeah," I said, "who knew?"

Simms again thought for a moment. "Safe to say—both Glee and Berta are clear."

I was of course relieved. I also knew that Mary Questman would be thrilled, since it was her concern for Glee and Berta that had first nudged me into the investigation.

Heather was saying, "Then the most likely time for the set-up would have been Saturday night. Any earlier wouldn't have worked; the clinic had a full schedule that day, and the gases were in use."

"So where are we?" said Simms. He took out his notebook and started drawing a grid. "As I see it, this murder puzzle is like any other, in that the answer ultimately boils down to motive. But *unlike* most other murders, this one still has us confused about the intended victim—Jason Ward or Mary Questman." Simms drew an X in one of the boxes on his grid. "If the intended victim was Jason, not Mary, the killer would have needed to know, the night before the demo, that Jason was replacing Mary as the guinea pig on Sunday." Simms drew another X. "And if the intended victim had been Mary, God forbid, the killer could *not* have know, the night before, that Mary was backing out."

"Remember," I said, "there are at least two other possibilities. For starters, what if the intended victim was neither Jason *nor* Mary? What if the motive was not to kill a particular individual, but simply to screw up Dr. Frumpkin's demo and hurt his business or his reputation?"

Simms arched his brows and drew another X. "Good one, Brody."

"Or"—I hesitated—"what if the intended victim was none of the above? What if the victim was meant to be *you*, Thomas? In the election."

Simms blew a low whistle. "That's crossed my mind, more than once. But I find it hard to believe that Alex Kastle, a sworn officer of the law, would stoop to murder for a lousy job promotion. Still, I must admit, Kastle checks all the boxes—motive, medical knowledge, plus, working for Frumpkin as a rent-a-cop, he might very well have had access and opportunity." Then

Simms drew an *X* in each remaining square.

He looked up from his notebook. "What are we missing? Anyone else?"

He had asked me this once before, in the conference room adjacent to his office, after we had interviewed Dr. Frumpkin and his daughter. At the time, I felt I'd forgotten something or someone. And now, I felt it again.

My head was spinning—there were just too many intertwined possibilities, including one that I didn't want to raise. I didn't want to remind Simms that we both had clearly heard Dahr Ahmadi tell the victim, "I *know* what I'm doing, Doctor."

My head was spinning, all right—not only with the puzzle, but once again, with the memory of Dahr's stolen whopper of a kiss.

10

Later that morning, while working downtown at our Miles & Norris offices, I received an e-mail from the practice of Dr. Francis Frumpkin, sent as a group message to an undisclosed list of recipients. It bore the subject line: Funeral Announcement.

Dear Friends, Neighbors, and Colleagues,

We have been gratified beyond measure by your outpouring of sympathy and support following the tragic death of our loved one and colleague, Dr. Jason Ward. Many of you have inquired regarding funeral arrangements, which were left pending due to the needs of the medical examiner's office.

We have just learned that Jason's body will be released today, and arrangements have been secured for funeral services tomorrow morning, October 19, at St. Alban's Episcopal Church, beginning at 10 o'clock. If you are free to attend on such short notice, you will be most welcome.

Please also join us at a reception in the church hall following the service, as we shall not only mourn Jason's passing, but celebrate his life.

With our loving thoughts,

Sarah Frumpkin Ward, wife of the deceased
Dr. Francis Frumpkin, father-in-law

Marson stepped into my office from across the hall. "I assume you got word of the funeral tomorrow?"

I nodded. "And I assume you want to go with me—reception, too?" When he nodded in return, I clicked the link and responded that we would attend.

Marson said, "You've seemed a little distracted, kiddo. Anything wrong?"

"Nah." I stood and hugged him. "There's a lot on my mind right now—that's all."

"Got it," he said, whisking a hand through my hair. "Murder, funeral, election."

"Not only *that*."

"What?" he asked with a note of concern.

"I promised to cat-sit Mister Puss this afternoon."

Mary needed to leave for Appleton around one o'clock, and she had offered to drop off Mister Puss at the office—in a cat carrier so he wouldn't be a nuisance. But I figured, If I were a cat, I wouldn't like spending half the day in a cage. So I told Mary I would work at home that afternoon, where Mister Puss could have the run of the place.

I was standing in the kitchen, tidying up after a simple lunch of leftover chicken casserole—it had been frozen, but it was really time to throw the remainder out, so I did—when the rusty old ringer sounded from the loft's street door. Wiping my hands, I carried the towel to the door and greeted both Mary and Berta, who stepped inside while the Buick idled at the curb.

Mary set down the carrier. She sing-songed, "Here's the livestock, Brody," and she pecked my cheek.

"And *here*," said Berta, sounding much less jovial, "here are His Majesty's supplies." She carried his spanking-clean litter box, which also contained a small can of cat food and a couple of stuffed toys. "Where do you want this?"

I laughed. "Anywhere's fine, Berta. Just set it down."

Checking her watch, Mary bubbled, "We really *must* dash off, love. Back by six."

As they hustled out to the street, I called from the doorway, "Have a great time, ladies." I was tempted to add, No smoking in the car—but what the hell, that was their business, not mine. Mary buckled up, Berta shifted into gear, and they lurched into traffic. I waved and watched them zip away.

Stepping inside, I closed the door.

Meow.

"What's the matter, Mister Puss? They'll be back." I lifted the carrier and set it on the tufted leather bench in the sitting area. Perching on the low table, I hunched forward to look through the wire grating at the cat, who peered out past me at his new surroundings. I opened the grate. "Wanna take a look around?"

Cautious—but plenty curious—Mister Puss stretched his head out for a quick one-eighty. Soon, he stepped out onto the bench for the full three-sixty.

"Make yourself at home," I told him. "It's just you and me for a while."

He paced the bench, glancing about, eyeing the high ceiling, taking everything in. Then he hopped down to the floor, stepped over to his litter box, and sniffed it. That seemed to be in order, so he set about exploring the loft.

I remained seated on the low table, watching but not intruding as he made the rounds. He skirted the spiral metal staircase several times, drifting away from it as if he didn't quite know what to make of it. Finally, he approached it head-on, then sat on the floor in front of the first step, twisting his neck as his gaze followed the upward turns.

Meow?

I stepped over to him and crouched to rub his shoulders. He began to purr. "Come on," I said, lifting the cat and setting him on one of the steps, where he could face me nose-to-nose.

He stretched for a nose kiss, purring, then peered about the room, taking it in from the higher perspective. But he stayed put, as if unsure what to do next.

I sat down on the floor cross-legged at the foot of the stairs and patted my knees. "Here, Mister Puss."

He hesitated. I'd seen him use the carpeted grand staircase in Mary's house, but this contraption, with its curves and wedge-shaped stairs and open metalwork, presented a different sort of challenge altogether. So he took the more direct route and simply jumped to the floor, an easy leap.

I stood, scooped him up, and began climbing the stairs, telling him, "Now, pay attention." Arriving at the top, still carrying him, I showed him around the bedroom, then took him to the edge of the mezzanine, where he could look out over the entire loft. Still, he purred. A few moments later, I carried him down the stairs.

When we arrived on the main floor, I asked, "Got it?" Putting him to the test, I reached to place him on a step about six feet high. Then I moved to the base of the stairs, saying, "Here, Mister Puss." And he trotted down the spiral, easy as pie.

I tucked the litter box out of the way, where I couldn't see it but the cat could easily find it. I put the can of food on the kitchen island, set out some water, and tossed the stuffed toys on the floor. Mister Puss batted them around once or twice before strolling over to the sitting area, near the faux fireplace, where he hopped onto a loveseat and curled up for a nap in the shaft of sunlight that angled in from one of the street windows.

With my guest contentedly acclimated and accounted for, I

decided to clock a bit of office time, so I settled in at the computer desk we had hidden behind folding doors along a side wall of the loft, near the dining area of the main room.

Earlier that morning, we, Miles & Norris, had received by e-mail a "call for entries" to a design competition for the new wing of an important contemporary art museum in Chicago. "Now, *that* looks interesting," Marson had said as I prepared to leave the office during the lunch hour. The high-stakes competition was by invitation only, so we were honored to be asked. Now, with some quiet time at home, I was determined to study the lengthy, detailed prerequisites for the design entries, as well as the mechanics of the contest itself. The deeper I delved into it, the more excited I became about pitting our Miles & Norris design brand against dozens of other firms that were recognized as the best in the business.

Incoming e-mails were a distraction that I had learned to tune out while I was creatively engaged in my work, but the soft chimes often managed to pull my eye to the alerts in the corner of the screen, where I could see who'd sent the new message. That afternoon, none had mattered. And then, *ping*, I saw one arrive from Dahr Ahmadi.

I slid from the museum screen to the e-mail program and clicked the message from Dahr. It was sent to both Marson and me, with the subject line: My sincere thanks.

Dear Marson and Brody,

You are perfect hosts, and I am delighted to consider you wonderful new friends. A million thanks for Saturday evening, for opening your home to me, for reaching out and bringing me into your shared life. I hope you'll allow me to reciprocate your many kindnesses sometime soon.

Life in Dumont can be a bit suffocating at times, but

meeting you has been a much needed breath of fresh air. I'm truly happy to know you.

Please forgive this informal communication in place of a more proper, handwritten note, but these are hectic days, and I did not want you to think me ungrateful.

Fondly,

Dahr

And then, *ping*, a brief response from Marson arrived, copied to me: Dear Dahr, the pleasure was all ours. Brody and I had a ball. Let's do it again soon. —Marson.

Figuring I'd better stay in the loop, I, too, sent a response, copied to Marson: Dahr, let me second Marson's reply. Enjoyed our evening together. Looking forward to the next time. —Brody.

Within seconds, *ping*, a follow-up from Dahr. But this one was not copied to Marson. The message was succinct and pointed: When? xoxox.

I froze. My first reaction was to write back at once, to defuse it, to inject a note of humor and sidestep the electricity. Instead, I chose to interpret his question "When?" as a mere hypothetical, the equivalent of "whenever," rather than a request to pin me down for a time and date to get clandestine. And I would simply ignore the "xoxox" as a friendly sign-off, rather than a literal reference to hugs and—God help me—kisses.

I would let this slide. I would not respond. The e-mail thread would end right there.

Returning my attention to the museum's call for entries, I opened a blank document next to the contest website and began typing notes.

Immersed in these thoughts, I lost track of the time and had filled nearly four pages when I was startled by something beneath the desktop, touching my shins.

Of course. It was Mister Puss, risen from his nap and seeking attention. It was nearly three o'clock.

I pushed back the chair and patted my knees. The cat hopped up to my lap and nuzzled my chest. When I rubbed behind his ears, he broke into a rumbling purr and slid his head up to my neck, burrowing his face beneath my chin. "Awww," I said, "aren't we affectionate?" As I stroked the length of his spine, his purring intensified, and he worked his snout toward my ear. I felt the cool spot of his nose trace over my lobe; his purr now thundered. I could hear his breathing, the gurgle in his throat, the beat of his heart, which had a curiously soothing effect on me. My hands dropped to my sides as I surrendered to it.

Starved, his purr seemed to say.

"Okay," I said with a laugh, snapping out of it. "I got the message."

He plopped down to the floor as I rose from the chair and crossed to the kitchen. He followed, tail erect, on full alert, as I opened a cupboard to find a small bowl, then took it to the center island, where the little can awaited my finger in the ring of its pop-top. Before zipping it open, however, I paused to glance over the ingredients. With a grimace, I asked the cat, "You *eat* this stuff?"

Mister Puss circled my ankles, still purring.

Then I remembered—that slab of tenderloin I'd put aside for him on Saturday night. I took the bowl over to the cutting board, next to the sink, and opened the refrigerator to retrieve the foiled packet of leftover beef. When I unfolded the foil on the square of butcher block, Mister Puss instantly picked up the scent. He purred and chattered. He circled and circled. He practically danced as I diced the meat and then gathered the bloody blob with both hands to place it in the bowl.

Mister Puss couldn't—didn't—wait. As I leaned over the

sink, rinsing my fingers, he pounced up to the countertop and helped himself. Drying my hands, I watched with a smile as he neatly devoured my offering.

This was rapture. This was bliss. His needs were so basic, his instincts so primal—and I had managed to satisfy both with a modest, though decidedly elegant, helping of table scraps. I returned to the cutting board and leaned on my elbows, watching as he finished. When he had licked the bowl and then licked his chops, he returned my gaze and pussyfooted toward me, touching my nose with a kiss of thanks. Nice.

I asked, "Did His Majesty approve?"

Purring—he didn't seem to have stopped, even to eat—Mister Puss rubbed cheeks with me and, once again, made his way to my ear.

My eyes drifted shut as I listened to his breathing and the beat of his heart—a rudimental, ageless beat, the sound of life itself. And through the drone of his purr, other sounds began to emerge. A rustling. A rippling. And rising above it all—gibberish—the babble of an ancient marketplace.

Hair fire.

I blinked my eyes open. Removing my elbows from the countertop, I stood erect and backed off a step. With a laugh, I told Mister Puss, I told Mary Questman in Appleton, I told the universe, "Well, *that* didn't quite make sense, did it?"

Mister Puss stretched toward me from the edge of the counter.

I leaned in again. Other than the cat's purr, all was quiet.

Then the rusty racket of the door ringer shot through the loft. Mister Puss jumped to the floor and followed me. Crossing the main room, I wondered who had arrived. It couldn't be Mary; she wasn't due until six, and it was now a few minutes past three. It couldn't be Marson; he would use his key or come in from the back. Was it maybe—just *possibly*—Dahr?

I swung the door open. "Sarah," I said, "what a pleasant surprise. Do come in."

Sarah Frumpkin Ward, widow of Dr. Jason Ward, stepped inside the loft, followed by little Olivia. The girl wore a variation of her princess dress, this one bright green; she looked a bit like Tinkerbell, plus tights, minus the wand and the wings. I wondered what she'd wear tomorrow—to her father's funeral.

Mister Puss wasn't purring anymore. At the sight of the child, he slunk backwards a few steps, then turned to retreat to the rear of the loft, where he tiptoed up the stairs to the mezzanine. Olivia watched him with a devilish stare, like some demon-baby in a bad movie. I could hear the background screech of violins, shrill and ominous—it was a fertile afternoon for hearing things.

Sarah didn't look well. I hugged her, saying, "I know it's been rough. How are you holding up?"

"Each day seems to get a little better—a *little*, for a while— and then everything comes rushing back. It doesn't seem real, like being adrift in a bad dream."

"*KITTY?*" yelled Olivia, moving a few steps toward the spiral stairs.

"Honey," said Sarah, "please bring it down a notch." Turning to me, she explained, "Since Jason died, everything's been such a mess. I've been trying to figure out a new routine for Olivia's after-school hours, before the clinic closes. It may sound like a minor item, but trust me, it's just another iron in the fire." Her head snapped to the girl: "Stay away from those stairs." Then to me: "I apologize for bringing her along, but I just picked her up at school, and there's something I need to discuss with you."

"She's welcome here anytime," I lied, closing the front door. Then I led Sarah over to the dining table and pulled out a chair for her. "Can I get you anything?"

She shook her head.

So I sat across from her, asking, "What's on your mind, Sarah?" I watched her daughter poking around, nosing into this and that.

"It's about the clinic," she said.

"The surgical clinic—where it happened?"

"No, Brody. The FlabberGas clinic, which you're designing. If you've been wondering if those plans have now been derailed, the answer is yes. I talked to Dad about it last night, and he agrees—we're pulling the plug."

"I guess I'm not surprised." In fact, I was relieved. From the corner of my eye, however, I spied Olivia approaching the staircase. She then sat on the bottom step, watching us.

Sarah continued, "So I wanted to make it official: you can close the file on *that* bright idea. FlabberGas—what were we thinking? When you have a chance, figure out your time, send us your bill, and we'll make it right."

With a shrug, I told her, "I worked on it for only a couple of days, and I had fun with it. I truly did. So let's just call it even."

She reached across the table to pat my hand. "That's too generous. But thank you."

"If I can give you one less thing to worry about, I'm happy to do it." I glanced toward the staircase again and saw Olivia traipse up a few steps. When she saw me looking, she stopped. I didn't want her going up there, so I caught Sarah's eye and jerked my head toward her daughter.

Sarah fired a warning shot: "Behave, honey."

Olivia struck a casual pose, lolling against the railing, just passing the time of day.

Sarah sat back, exhaling a weary sigh. "Tomorrow's the funeral—getting that behind us, maybe that'll help."

"I understand. Closure."

"Sure, that—but also being done with the coroner and the uncertain timing—that should help restore some sense of normalcy, or at least the 'new normalcy.' One way or another, we need to get the practice up and running again."

"You'll get there, Sarah. It'll take time, though. Everyone's rooting for you."

"Thank you." With a quiet laugh, she added, "It seems I keep thanking you—you've been great, Brody."

"You and your dad showed plenty of faith in me, with your project. The least I can do now is lend some moral support." I heard the patter of someone's little feet climbing a few more of the metal stairs.

Sarah said, "You've given *way* more than moral support. Sheriff Simms tells us you've been helpful in moving the investigation along."

"I've tried. But he's the pro. And now that things are wrapped up with the medical examiner, the investigation should proceed more quickly." I heard Olivia's voice from the mezzanine, jabbering softly to the cat, as I told Sarah, "Just this morning, Simms began focusing on a new lead—he says it 'checks all the boxes.'"

"Really?" She seemed distracted. "I hadn't heard."

I waffled, telling her, "It's still a theory, but a strong one. It could have been someone who was right there when it happened." I didn't want to go so far as to name Deputy Kastle— loose lips could sink more than ships—and in fact, I was not yet sold on Kastle's guilt. So I concluded, "Simms has a lot riding on this. He'll figure it out. He's getting close."

Sarah had listened with evident consternation, which blossomed into an expression of full panic as her gaze drifted up beyond my shoulder to the heights of the loft. "Olivia!" she shouted. "What do you think you're *doing*?"

I spun in my chair and looked up.

"Nine lives—nine lives—nine lives," chanted Olivia as she dangled Mister Puss out over the mezzanine's railing. If he

squirmed, or if she simply let go, he'd fall a good sixteen feet to the polished concrete floor. Although I knew cats were perceived as highly resilient, I was sure they weren't designed for *that* kind of abuse.

Sarah stood. "That's just a saying, honey. Cats don't have nine lives. You wouldn't want to *hurt* him, would you?"

The brat shook her head strongly. Mister Puss swung like a pendulum. He eyed me with a frozen, glassy stare that seemed to ask, Well, aren't you going to *do* something?

I stood. "Olivia? I think you should hold on to Mister Puss and—very carefully—just back away from the railing, and then set him down nicely on the bed, where it's soft, so he can take his afternoon nap."

She glared at me with suspicion.

Sarah told her daughter, "Honey, please listen to Brody and do what he says—please put the cat on the bed." The panic in her voice, the *pleading*, must have gotten through to the kid more effectively than my sweet talk; Olivia backed safely away.

Sarah and I stepped to each other and threw our arms around each other, shaken and trembling.

Having delivered her message that there would be no worldwide chain of FlabberGas clinics—or even a fabulous butterfly-roofed prototype—and having averted a crisis stemming from her daughter's fascination with Mister Puss's mortality, Sarah Frumpkin Ward hustled her hellion out to the street, pausing in the doorway to tell me, "I'm so sorry, Brody. She's *such* a handful—but she's been much better lately, believe it or not."

I had my doubts. "No harm done," I said.

Tinkerbell stomped her green shoes on the pavement. "But he tried to *bite* me." She showed us the back of her hand, supposedly wounded, but I saw no blood, no marks. If Mister Puss had nipped her, she had surely been too rough with him.

Sarah and I hugged good-bye. Then they left.

Stepping inside, I closed the door and strolled toward the kitchen, keeping an eye on the stairs, wondering when the cat might reappear.

I rinsed the bowl that had held the tenderloin and tucked it away in the dishwasher, leaving no evidence for Marson that I had allowed Mister Puss to eat his meal on the countertop, which would have prompted an obsessive round of sanitizing. Then I tidied up around the sink, put away the towel, and turned away from the kitchen, stepping toward the computer.

And there was Mister Puss, sitting near my chair, looking up at me as I approached.

I took him in my arms and set him in my lap as I sat. "Poor little guy," I said, rubbing his cheeks, which caused the instant eruption of a deep, loud purr. "Such a scare you had. But you were brave."

He nuzzled my chest, then stretched his head toward my face. His nose touched mine for a moment before the soft fur of his chin slid to the opening of my ear. The drone of his purr evoked a distant time, a drowsy place, somewhere far away. My pulse relaxed. My tensions faded. I said, "She's gone. She won't hurt you."

There's something wrong with that sasspot.

I laughed. Taking our imagined dialogue one step further, I asked, "Did you try to bite her?"

She tried to put her finger in me.

Whoa—I shook my head—I did *not* need to hear that.

"You didn't hear a thing," I reminded myself aloud while setting Mister Puss on the floor.

11

Tuesdays always strike me as a "nothing" kind of day, far from Friday, let alone Saturday, stuck in the shank of the work week—nose to the grindstone, all business. But that Tuesday in late October was anything but typical. Everyone we knew, it seemed, would find little time for work that morning because we all would attend Dr. Jason Ward's funeral, which began at ten. And hours before that, when Marson and I awoke at the loft and poured a first cup of coffee, our surreal Tuesday began with an added surprise, a distressing turn. Opening the *Dumont Daily Register*, we were greeted by yet another salvo in the drumbeat of Deputy Kastle's nonsensical election rhetoric.

Only six days until early voting

*Deputy Kastle gaining momentum
against silent Sheriff Simms*

Compiled from *Register* staff reports

•

OCT. 19, DUMONT, WI—Within a week, voters in Dumont County will have begun voting in a sheriff's election that was previously thought an easy win for incumbent Thomas Simms.

Many observers have been surprised, however, by the recent surge of support toward his opponent, Deputy Alex Kastle. At a rally on Sunday evening, Kastle tried a new pitch on an enthusiastic crowd, telling them, "I will never lie to you. Let me be your voice."

On Monday, the *Register* sent its reporting team back to the local Walmart to sample the mood of shoppers in the aisles. Again and again, likely voters said of Kastle, "He tells it like it is."

When Simms was reached by the *Register* and asked for a response to the campaign's increasingly populist rhetoric, the sitting sheriff offered no comment, stating only, "I have a job to do. We have a murder to solve."

Ironically, it was the October 10 death of Dr. Jason Ward, now being investigated as a homicide, that may dash the sheriff's reelection hopes ...

Marson flicked the paper aside with quiet restraint. After pouring us both another cup of coffee, he set down the pot. "This election story is starting to stink. I could use some fresh air. How about you, kiddo?"

So we put ourselves together and spiffed ourselves up and left the loft about an hour before the funeral. Marson got behind the wheel of his Range Rover, driving us not to church, but out past the edge of town, where our dreams for the perfect house had just begun to take shape above an isolated stream in a grove of birches.

There had been some construction activity the prior week, mostly pilings and a retaining wall below the upper plateau of the waterfall. It didn't yet resemble a house, or even a structure, but it represented a sturdy foundation—concrete and steel— that would anchor not only our home, but our joined lives.

Marson switched off the engine. We lowered the windows, admitting the cool morning air, which still carried the dusty, limy scent of setting cement. The building site was too muddy for us to be tramping around in our funeral clothes, so we just sat there in the SUV, where we could gaze out at the view while enjoying the rustle and chatter of the birds. We didn't speak much, as there was little to say. We held hands for a while. And then, feeling refreshed by the quietude and secure in our future, we knew it was time to return to the precarious reality of the day.

Marson revved up the Range Rover and drove us back to town, to the aftermath of a murder.

St. Alban's Episcopal Church fronted the historic downtown commons, across the park from Dumont's handsome neoclassical Carnegie library. While the library was foursquare and stone, hunkering solidly to the earth, the church was more modest, of weathered yellow brick, with neo-Gothic arches and a steeple reaching for the vivid October sky. Its double doors were painted brightest crimson, which glowed that morning amid a golden flutter of foliage from the surrounding trees.

I had never been inside the church, and I didn't know much about the parish, except that it was well over a hundred years old and that the Questman family—the family of Mary's deceased husband, Quincy Questman—had been among its founding members.

As Marson and I walked the two blocks from where we'd parked (we hadn't even bothered to try the church lot, which was jammed beyond capacity), he explained, "St. Alban's has always been known as Dumont's 'society' church, but the moneyed class has been dying off, and so has the membership. It's a lovely old building, but it's seen better days."

A hearse was parked at the curb in front of the church, but otherwise, parking on that side of the street had been blocked off with police signs. As we joined the flow of mourners who filed toward the entrance, the sounds of a choir drifted on the crisp autumn breeze with a subtle tang of incense. Mounting the front steps, I noticed that their limestone treads had been worn shallow by a second century of passing feet. Above the doors, an arched window of stained glass depicted the church's patron saint. Who, I wondered, was St. Alban? He wore a red cape and carried a dagger. Or was it a crucifix?

Having been raised a heathen, I was now on shaky ground.

When we stepped inside, I paused to close my eyes and let them adjust to the dim light of the vestibule. When I opened them, they stung from the incense, which had been laid on thick in anticipation of the requiem rites. The choir was in full voice, belting out another verse of some proper English hymn. To my ear, they all sounded alike, filled with sheep and glory and "Thou"s and "Thine"s.

We moved through the swinging doors and into the nave, past the holy water stoup, and because the church was nearly filled, we decided to grab seats off to the side, in a back pew.

Settling in, I glanced about and got my bearings. I saw Dr. Francis Frumpkin, Sarah Frumpkin Ward, little Olivia, and presumably some other family members, unknown to me, in a front pew. I wondered what Olivia had worn that day, but couldn't tell from my vantage point. Across the center aisle from them, Mary Questman sat in the first pew with Berta. I whispered to Marson, "Look, there's Mary—she got a front-row seat."

Marson whispered back, "I assume the Questmans popped for a family pew eons ago. When St. Alban's needs a new boiler, they know where their bread is buttered."

The choir was assembled in a stall to the side of the altar, led by a tall man in a lacy white surplice. Even from a distance, he struck me as uncommonly good-looking, no older than thirty. His flowing sleeves wagged as he directed the choir, mostly children, all of them in shorter surplices worn over red cassocks. It was easy to spot little Tommy Simms among them, conspicuous among his Waspish brethren. I also spotted Tommy's parents, the sheriff and his wife, who sat a few rows behind Mary.

I nudged Marson. "Hey, who's the choir guy?"

"You noticed, eh? Not a clue. Maybe we'll run into him later."

"I just have a hunch …"

Marson suppressed a sputter of a laugh. Feigning shock, he whispered, "Keep your salacious thoughts to yourself, young man. This is a house of worship."

Sitting at the end of the pew, I felt someone rudely bump my shoulder from the aisle. I turned to discover the hip of Glee Savage. Looking up, I told her, "Morning, doll. Need a place to sit?"

"Thanks, sweetie. Shove over." She slid in next to us, giving me a smooch and then leaning across me to peck Marson. I had to duck away from the swooping brim of her enormous black hat. She took a steno pad out of her purse and began writing notes.

I said, "It seems you're back in good graces at the *Register*."

"Hope so. I had a column this morning. But *this*"—she indicated the throng assembled in the church—"this could be *the* social event of the year."

"Good to see you in your element again," I said, "even at a funeral."

She paused to touch my arm. "I can't thank you enough, Brody—setting everything right with Sheriff Simms. It's ridiculous to think I'd ever stoop to *murder*. And I feel just awful for poor Sarah and little Olivia." Glee then leaned close to tell me from the side of her mouth, "Although I *can't* say I feel much sympathy for Dr. Frumpkin. What a pompous blowhard—he deserved a bit of humbling."

I *really* wished that she would stop qualifying her statements about what had happened. I was perfectly content to accept her expressions of innocence, but then, each time, she had a habit of tacking on an afterthought that made me question my charitable conclusions. Now, though, those doubts had ended—she was in the clear. I hoped.

The church got quiet. The organ began heaving through a dirge as everyone stood to watch the processional, led by an aged priest who had difficulty walking. Glee told me, "That's Charles Sterling, rector of St. Alban's. He's been here forever—hope he makes it through the next hour."

He was accompanied by a phalanx of clerics who carried assorted liturgical whatnot. One of them swung a smoking censer in showy cartwheels, further gassing the crowd, who responded with a wheezing chorus of coughs.

Bringing up the rear was Dr. Jason Ward himself, or rather, his casket, draped in white. Dahr Ahmadi was one of the pallbearers, representing Dr. Frumpkin's practice. I didn't know the others; perhaps they were members of Jason's extended family.

When the casket was in position at the head of the aisle and the clerics had taken their places in the sanctuary, the congregation sat. The service began. And I tuned out.

We all had our reasons for being there that day. Some truly mourned the loss of Jason, as their lives had been forever changed by his death. Others may not have felt the loss directly, but they were there to support and respect those who grieved. Still others may have had no connection to those touched by the tragedy, but they were drawn there by the news, as members of an affected community. Others, just curious onlookers.

Plus, there was someone else. I was fairly certain that—for whatever perverse reason—Jason's killer was there among us. Perhaps the guilty one simply *had* to be there; if it was someone close to the deceased, by blood or by association, their absence would be deemed strange or even suspicious. But the guilty one may have had little or no connection to the victim, other than the crime itself, and may have been there that day for the sport of it, for the thrill of witnessing communal grief. And if so, what did that imply about the many nameless others in the crowd? Was each a potential killer?

The organ moaned. The choir wailed.

The Reverend Charles Sterling, rector of the parish, shepherd of his flock, hobbled to the pulpit, a fanciful structure of wrought iron that had been tortured into the likeness of a bird of prey, with its spread wings supporting the lectern and a red leather Bible of operatic proportions.

"My dear friends in Christ," said Father Sterling, "St. Alban's weeps today as we lay to rest our dear brother Jason. And yet, as Christians, we rejoice in knowing that Jason now lies resplendent in the arms of our Lord ..." Patchy sobs arose from the congregation as the priest pattered through his eulogy, plugging Jason's name into the blanks that peppered his dog-eared script.

My eyes drifted to the ceiling, where the crusty beams and stained plaster revealed a history of water damage older than the priest. Candles and the smoke of ages had grimed the elaborate niches and arches of the main altar. When I shifted my weight where I sat, the pew creaked, as if the dark mahogany was ready to split and snap beneath the weight of countless coats of yellowed, sticky varnish. I sensed that the floor itself might soon collapse, plunging all of us—hundreds of lost souls—not into the labyrinths of hell, but into a dank cellar of disrepair.

"... in jubilation with the angels and all the blessed saints ..."

My eyes drifted through the crowd. I saw someone in a khaki police uniform, and although I couldn't be certain from behind, I thought it might be our man of the moment, upstart Deputy

Alex Kastle, emerging leader of a groundswell, a zombie movement in this little town, my adopted hometown—which I found absolutely frightening. Kastle was just warped enough, just self-absorbed enough, to find political opportunity in a murder and to take advantage of the victim's funeral, which he would attempt to reframe as a campaign event. Worse yet, if Sheriff Simms was correct in his calculus that Kastle checked all the boxes on his suspect list, the town could be poised to elect a killer, an actual murderer, as the county's top lawman.

"… cleansed by the blood of the lamb, redeemed by the blood of our Savior …"

My eyes drifted to the front pew, where Dr. Frumpkin sat with his daughter, Sarah. Between them sat the troubled little Olivia. Both Frumpkin and Sarah leaned to the girl, holding her in a tangle of arms and shoulders as they listened to the words of the priest. Was Frumpkin taking comfort from the crowd, from the outpouring of sympathy, from the poetry of psalms and the silver-tongued oratory? Or was he, in fact, not grieving at all? Sarah had often spoken of the man's "acute sense of theater." Was this an act? Had he seized on a chance opportunity to rid his life of the conflict, the perceived rivalry, between his son-in-law and his lover? Had he made the ultimate choice between Jason and Dahr?

And what of Dahr himself? After fulfilling his duties as pall-bearer, he had joined Frumpkin, Sarah, and Olivia in the front pew, sitting right next to Frumpkin—just like family, as if he and Frumpkin were already a committed couple, which Frumpkin had wanted all along, but which Dahr had coyly resisted. Had he been playing a deadly game?

I didn't want to admit it—and had avoided discussing it with Sheriff Simms—but Dahr checked most, if not all, of the boxes. Whether it was true or not, there had been a growing perception that he was the rival of the man now being eulogized, which gave Dahr a plausible motive for what had happened. And yet, I had gone out of my way to steer clear of that conclusion, or even consider it. Why? I had the worst possible reason for shielding Dahr: I found him attractive. I had enjoyed his masterful kiss. I felt a growing lust for something forbidden.

And I felt remorsefully ashamed of myself. Seated at my side was the man who had changed my life, who had given me his ring, who had held my hand that morning as we envisioned the walls of our future home, taking stock of our shared life, offering silent recommitment. Now, in the church, I slipped my hand over to his leg. He glanced at me with a soft smile and covered my hand with his.

"He can wrap it up anytime," said Glee, whispering too loudly, prompting a few snickers. But the priest didn't hear it. Clueless, he yammered on.

Again I had to wonder, And what about Glee?

Stop it, I told myself. Stop relitigating the issues of her motive, means, and opportunity. Stop anguishing over her rocky past with your mother, years before you were born. Stop feeling guilty for giving Glee a pass. Just stop it—Simms has cleared her of all suspicion.

And that's when I noticed Walter Zakarian. Seated across the aisle from Glee, a few rows ahead, the Karastan King poked the floor with the tip of his swank walking stick, as if restless with the sermon, trying to prod the priest along. Twice, while reviewing the case with Simms, the sheriff had asked me, "What are we missing? Anyone else?" And both times, I'd thought we *had* overlooked someone or something that I couldn't remember. And now, there he sat, big as life, wearing one of his custom-tailored topcoats—black for this occasion, probably cashmere.

During Dr. Frumpkin's pitch session at Mary's house two

days before the murder, Zakarian and I had gabbed briefly before the presentation. When I asked if he was thinking of investing in FlabberGas, he replied, "I just don't like him—Francis Frumpkin. We've had issues." He gave no further explanation, but warned me, "So be careful with him."

Were Zakarian's "issues" with Dr. Frumpkin significant enough to earn the rug merchant a square on the sheriff's suspect grid?

"My brothers and sisters," said Father Sterling, "the family has asked me to remind everyone that Jason's burial will be private, later this afternoon. But you are invited to gather in the church hall for refreshment and fellowship at the conclusion of this morning's service."

The conclusion of the service was a long time coming. Though the sermon was over, we sat through a good deal more of the music and the incense and the ceremony that were meant to clear the way for Jason Ward's send-off to paradise.

When at last we were sprung, some simply fled, but most of us dutifully, somberly left the church and crossed the grounds to the parish hall, which appeared to have once been a gymnasium. After we were inside, the mood lightened.

"Gotta love that old-time religion," said Glee, hoisting her first glass of champagne. "When it comes to putting on a show, Episcopalians do it right."

"Now, now," said Marson, "many people take comfort in ritual. I'm sure the family appreciated it."

A tall, handsome man stepped into our conversation. "We do our best."

It clicked. I told him, "You're the choir director." He'd ditched the cassock and surplice.

"Guilty," he said, extending his hand. "David Lovell."

We all introduced ourselves. I said, "You sounded great today."

"Thanks, very generous of you. We work with what we've got. It's a small parish."

Glee gave me a grin that seemed to ask, Is he hot or what?

He was indeed hot, and his manner left little doubt that he was gay. Things were perking up in sleepy little Dumont. In the space of eleven days, I'd broadened my circle of acquaintances with two of the town's previously hidden assets, each distinctly different from the other. While Dahr Ahmadi was dark, exotic, and left-brained, David Lovell was blond, corn-fed, and arty to the max.

Sheriff Simms barreled toward us—broad smile—along with his wife, Gloria, and Tommy, who'd also ditched his choir duds, looking cute as ever in a natty little suit and a bow tie. Simms greeted David, "Congrats, choirmaster! They've never sounded better."

David almost blushed. "Thank you, Thomas. We love what we do."

Gloria chimed in. "Tommy certainly does, thanks to you, David. He even looks forward to *practice*."

David patted Tommy's shoulder. "He's got a strong voice—perfect pitch and timing—he'll be a *real* singer someday."

Tommy beamed.

Father Sterling was wending his way through the crowd—tippling his champagne, gabbing here and there, shaking hands—but mostly tippling.

Sarah Frumpkin Ward stepped over to us with little Olivia. Sarah wore basic black and looked no better than she had since Jason died—the pain in her eyes said it all—but she'd found some sustenance in her champagne flute, which was nearly empty. Olivia, to my surprise, had forgone her storybook costumes and was dressed appropriately in a gray flannel pinafore with a frilly white blouse and black patent Mary Janes. Her hair was nicely done in an asymmetrical swoop, set off with a black barrette. She looked like a little lady.

As they approached, we opened our circle to welcome them with hugs and condolences. Someone raised a glass: "To Jason's memory." We toasted in respectful silence, and Sarah finished off her champagne. "Well," she said, "that makes it official—I'm a *widow*." Clearly, she didn't like the word.

Gloria Simms took Sarah's hand and peered into her eyes. "Awww, I know it's rough, honey. It'll take time, but it'll get better—trust me."

"Thank you, Gloria. Everyone's been so sweet. I'm still having a rough time … *adjusting*. I mean, the emotions, sure. But all the day-to-day stuff—everything's different. And hard."

"How can I help? Really."

Sarah hesitated. "Afternoons are worst, after school. We're trying to get the office back on a regular schedule. We're closed today, of course, but tomorrow? It's back to the salt mine."

"Look," said Gloria, "let me pick up Olivia at school tomorrow—I'm there every day for Tommy anyway. She can come over for an afternoon 'play date,' and you can swing by later, whenever you're ready."

Sarah heaved a deep sigh of gratitude. "That would be perfect, Gloria."

Tommy, the model child, had watched this exchange with wary skepticism. As Olivia's classmate, he'd doubtless witnessed a good deal of her hellish behavior.

I said to Sarah, "There now. Things are looking up, right? A little?"

She managed a weak smile. "A little." Then a thought crossed her face. "Olivia owes you an apology, Brody. You and Mister Puss."

The others standing there—the Simmses, David, and Glee, as well as Marson—exchanged curious glances, as they had no idea what Sarah was talking about. She patted the little girl toward me.

"Mr. Norris?" said Olivia. "I'm sorry I was bad yesterday. I would *never* hurt the kitty—he's nice. I've been so confused lately."

I crouched to hug her. "Thank you, Olivia. I accept your apology—and I'll pass it along to Mister Puss. You'll feel better soon. Don't worry."

She smiled at me. She looked as if she believed me, as if she'd awoken from the nightmare of the past two weeks. She looked like a normal little girl.

"Come on, sweetie," said Sarah, still in the depths of her nightmare. "Let's find Grampa."

As they were taking their leave, Sheriff Simms said, "Sarah? This is starting to move fast now. Brody's been a huge help. We're getting to the bottom of everything—and believe me, you'll be the first to know."

I wish I had your confidence, I thought.

Looking miserable, Sarah thanked Simms. Then she took Olivia's hand and led her into the crowd.

Marson excused himself, wanting to graze the buffet. Gloria Simms and Tommy went with him, as the boy was getting hungry. David Lovell drifted away to mingle with some of the choir parents. Glee said she needed to round up quotes for her story, but she made a beeline toward Berta, and a moment later, they were yukking it up.

Which left me alone with Sheriff Simms. We watched Dr. Frumpkin with Dahr Ahmadi across the room, huddling in conversation. Now and then Dahr looked in our direction, and then

I thought he winked at me. But the second time he did it, no, I decided it was just a tic.

The man I'd spotted in church wearing a khaki uniform was indeed Alex Kastle. Simms and I watched him making the rounds, doing a bit of retail politicking, shaking hands, patting backs. I even saw someone pass him some folded cash.

"Thomas," I said, "during the service, I thought of something important."

Simms asked, "About Kastle?"

"Sorry, no. Remember how you've asked me if we've been overlooking any possibilities? And I couldn't think of any? Well—how about Walter Zakarian?" I gestured toward him hobnobbing with Mary Questman at the fringes of the crowd. He carried his walking stick in one hand, a champagne flute in the other.

Intrigued, Simms asked, "What about him?"

I recounted what Walter had told me—that he didn't like Frumpkin, that they'd "had issues," that I should "be careful" with Frumpkin.

Simms shrugged. "Interesting, I guess. But is that a motive to kill? And even if it were, how would Zakarian pull it off? As far as we know, he has zero knowledge of medical gases—or how to rig the connections."

"Oh." I paused, feeling stupid. "I'm sorry, Thomas. My head is just spinning with all this."

Simms chuckled. "Don't sell yourself short, Brody. You keep having ideas, and you keep asking questions. Without those, we'd get nowhere. A few blind alleys? We chalk them off. And *then* we get down to the final problem-solving."

"Oh, *Thomas?*" trilled Mary, trundling up behind him.

He turned with a smile. "Morning, Miss Mary."

She leaned into him with a hand on his arm, speaking low:

"Do you have any idea what that *awful* deputy of yours is up to?"

"I think so, Mary."

"And *here,* of all places. No shame, no decency whatever."

"He's a piece of work, all right," said Simms. I'd have phrased it differently, but not in front of Mary. Simms added, "Elections aren't as clean as they used to be."

Mary said, "We just *can't* let him get away with this, Thomas. I want to write you another check, and I know you'll need it quickly. Can you stop by tomorrow?"

He hesitated. "Sure, Miss Mary. Thank you. Noon hour okay?"

"Perfect." She tweaked his cheek, tweaked my cheek, and left.

Simms checked his watch. "Speaking of noon, I'd better get down to headquarters. Talk soon."

I watched as he went over to tell his wife he was leaving. He kissed Gloria, stooped to kiss his son's forehead, and then made his way through the crowded room, walking out through the glass doors to the parking lot.

Just inside the doors, he'd passed by a man I recognized but couldn't quite place. Seeing him, I thought of Mister Puss for some reason. Odd. Then, aha: that was the veterinarian, Jim Phelps. I'd met him two Fridays ago at Mary's house, at the pitch session. And I realized that it was *he* I'd been overlooking, not Walter Zakarian.

Jim Phelps had referred to FlabberGas as "nonsense" and "nuts." He'd referred to Dr. Frumpkin as a "huckster." Regarding the investment proposal, he'd told me, "It's a fraud. Frankly, it should be stopped."

Plus: Dr. Jim Phelps surely had a working knowledge of medical gases.

CHAPTER

12

Wednesday morning, I left the office shortly after eleven, drove to the outskirts of town, and found the county road that led to the office of veterinarian James Phelps. I had phoned the prior afternoon after the funeral, asking to make an appointment. The receptionist asked for information on my "furbaby," and I explained that the animal in question was not mine, but the cat owned by a friend, Mary Questman.

"I see …," said the young lady on the phone, sounding thoroughly flummoxed. "Will Mrs. Questman be coming in with you?"

"I doubt it. Do you have any openings tomorrow? It's rather important."

"If it's urgent, I can squeeze you in at eleven-thirty. That's the last appointment of the morning."

"That'll be just fine," I said.

So there I was, driving along the rustic road without another vehicle in sight, wondering how I would explain my solo arrival—without Mary or a cat or any other semblance of a furbaby.

It had been a cold night, with frost, but no hard freeze yet, and the day had dawned clear and crisp. By late morning, the frost had dried off, and the bucolic landscape of fields and fence posts whisked past me under a crystalline autumn sky. It was still cold; the car's heater lent its soft background whoosh to a bit of Vivaldi that rippled from the radio.

Up ahead, a folksy wooden sign with bent-twig lettering announced that I'd arrived at the practice of James Phelps, DVM, so I slowed the car and entered the gravel parking lot. Only one other car was parked there—the appointment before mine, no doubt—and a narrow gravel drive led around to the back of the building, where I assumed the staff had parked. A split-rail fence separated the front lot from a small wild-looking lawn, with a path down the middle leading to the quaint offices, which were clad in shake shingles, weathered long ago to a silvery gray.

A bell on a spring heralded my arrival as I stepped inside carrying a small zippered portfolio, in case I needed to take notes. The receptionist glanced at her computer, asking, "Mr. Norris?" She was not dressed like a nurse, but wore corduroys and a bulky sweater. "Dr. Jim will be just a minute. Have a seat."

I picked a chair near the window, next to a pile of magazines, and studied my surroundings, including an aquarium, which was soothing, and a parrot in a cage, which was annoying, and a lethargic snake in a terrarium, which creeped me out.

The receptionist peeped over the countertop at me. "No cat?"

"Actually, I just need to *talk* to Dr. Phelps."

"I see…," she said. "Then we'll bill this as a consultation."

After we'd passed my credit card back and forth, she led me down a short hall, opened a door for me, and said, "Dr. Jim will be right with you." I stepped inside, and she closed the door.

I sat, drumming my fingers on the portfolio in my lap. The cramped room was dominated by a stainless steel exam table. The paraphernalia filling an adjacent counter included medical instruments, sell-cards for pet medicines, and a baby scale. The walls were decorated with a couple of faded Currier and Ives prints, as well as charts showing the innards of dogs and cats. Bright fluorescent lighting competed with the blades of sunshine angling in from venetian blinds. Dogs barked from somewhere in back, where there must have been a kennel.

I heard a door open and close in the hall, a bit of farewell conversation, footfalls retreating toward the front, and then the turn of the knob as Dr. Phelps walked in to greet me. "Hi there, Brody. What a surprise to see you on the schedule this morning."

I stood to return his greeting and to volley a few pleasantries, but he seemed distracted, looking about the room. After a pause, he asked, "Where's Mister Puss? I thought—"

"Sorry for the confusion," I said. "I just wanted to talk to you about—"

"Is something wrong with the cat? Is Mary okay?"

"Everything's fine," I assured him. "But I need to discuss something with you."

He shrugged. "Sure, Brody. More comfortable in my office. Over here." And he led me across the hall.

His office was roomier, less sterile, and far more inviting. There was even a small, classic Chesterfield sofa of tufted brown leather. He took off his lab coat and hung it on a wooden peg behind the door, then put on the corduroy sport coat with knotted-leather buttons he'd worn to the pitch session at Mary's. He gestured for me to sit on the sofa. "Now," he said, sitting across from me in a maple captain's chair, "what's this about?"

A rap at the door interrupted us. The receptionist poked her head inside. "Thought I'd duck out for lunch and stop at the post office, Jim. Next appointment's at one-fifteen. Phones are switched to the service." When he thanked her, she left.

So we were alone. The room had the persnickety-sweet smell of cherry pipe tobacco.

"This is awkward," I said, not knowing how to broach my intended topic. Was there a tactful way to ask him if he had killed Jason Ward?

"Yeah," he said slowly, scratching behind an ear, "it's awkward.

You're concerned about Mary? And her talking cat?"

"I am." It was a convenient sidestep, but I was, in fact, concerned.

"Consider this, Brody. As children, we've all talked with animals, dolls, or imaginary friends—a normal exercise in creativity. At the time, those conversations seem very real, but *we* put the words in the *other* party's mouth." He went on to explain that the process was a sort of mental loop, not unlike déjà vu.

I reminded him, "But Mary's no child." Opening my portfolio, I jotted a few notes.

"Of course not. And I'm fairly sure she's not feeble-minded, either. But the lessons of childish play can often be adapted to later-life struggles. That's the purpose of play—it equips us with the foundations we'll need to navigate the larger world."

I tossed my arms. "But she's told me, and I assume she's told you, that she truly, literally, hears Mister Puss speak to her." And only two days earlier, I'd gotten an earful myself. Or so it seemed.

"But"—Phelps raised a finger—"Mary said the cat spoke to her *through his purr*."

Yup, I thought. That fit my experience, as well.

Phelps continued, "She said it was like being in a trance."

Check.

Phelps asked, "That leaves a lot of wiggle room, doesn't it?"

Did it?

"So," said the doctor, "I look at it this way. My best theory is that Mary has simply been 'channeling' through the cat to clarify her own thinking. I'm sure Mister Puss could never tell her something she doesn't already know."

I wasn't so sure about that.

Phelps concluded, "Bottom line, Brody: cats can't talk." He let out a hearty laugh.

That much, I had to agree with. I joined him in laughing.

Still, I felt compelled to add, "At least, cats can't talk ... in a *conventional* sense."

"Fine," said the vet, smiling.

So we were back to square one. I still had no idea what to make of my tête-à-tête with Mister Puss. And I had yet to touch on the purpose of my visit with Dr. Phelps.

He gave me my opening when he changed the subject, saying, "Mary seemed in good spirits yesterday. I was afraid that the murder, not to mention that morbid funeral service, might have upset her—or worse."

"Plus," I noted, "that nut-job deputy, Alex Kastle, keeps pushing the theory that the intended victim was Mary herself."

"That, too," Phelps agreed.

"It's odd, though," I told him. "From the start, Mary's biggest worry was that Glee Savage, or even her own housekeeper, might end up being accused of the killing. Now that *they're* off the hook, Mary seems content to let the investigation take its course."

Phelps nodded. "I've been following it in the paper—who hasn't? But that angle with the reporter and the housekeeper, that never made sense to me. How could *they* be involved with it?"

With a soft laugh, I explained, "Guess you had to be there. Believe me, when it happened, they *both* came across as plenty suspicious." I paused, then noted, "But you weren't there, Jim. Correct?"

"Nah, wasn't interested."

"I'm not surprised. At the pitch session, you told me Frumpkin was a huckster and FlabberGas was a fraud."

Phelps studied me for a moment. "I also recall telling you that I thought Frumpkin should be stopped. Is that why you're here?"

I played dumb.

He continued, "I understand you've been doing a bit of 'background' work for Sheriff Simms. So you're checking me out?"

I couldn't look him in the eye as I responded, "I guess so."

"Look, I've been half-expecting to hear from *one* of you all along. Would you care to hear what I was doing at the time of the murder?"

I felt like such a jerk. "Sure, Jim."

"You see, first of all, I didn't even *know* about the Sunday demo, because I left Friday's pitch session early, before Frumpkin announced the details. And second of all, like I told you, I wasn't interested in FlabberGas as an investment, so even if I'd known about the demo, I wouldn't have gone—unless, of course, I was up to some deadly plot, correct?"

"Yes," I said so quietly that I myself couldn't hear it.

"Which brings us to point number three, Brody. And here's the corker: Even if I'd *known* about the demo, and even if I'd *wanted* to go, I couldn't have. Why?" He grinned. "Because at the time of the murder that Sunday, I was in Green Bay—giving a speech to a roomful of cranky old veterinarians."

I couldn't help smiling. *"Really?"*

"Yes, my young friend. Really."

I hesitated to ask, "And … the night before that?" I didn't want to explain that Simms had already concluded that the set-up for the crime had taken place on Saturday night.

"Green Bay," said Phelps as I dashed off some more notes. He elaborated: "It was a short weekend conference of our regional vets' association. I drove up there early Saturday morning and drove back on Sunday afternoon. The final session was a Sunday brunch, and they'd invited me to deliver some closing remarks. The topic I proposed was 'The Vanishing One-Man Practice,' but someone on the board said it was sexist, so I changed it to 'The Vanishing One-Doc Shop.' Clever, huh?"

"Yeah, I like it."

"So did they. Ate it up. I think there were maybe sixty of us dinosaurs, including a couple dozen ladies. Excuse me: women. Times are changing. Did you know that in vet schools, there are now way more women than men?"

"I didn't know that—guess I never thought about it."

He pondered this briefly, then helped me with my notes, giving me the name of his association and the details of the conference hotel, adding, "Check those out."

"That won't be necessary," I told him, closing the portfolio. But we would indeed check his story. If there were sixty witnesses who'd spent the weekend with Dr. James Phelps in Green Bay while Dr. Jason Ward was being set up for death by laughing gas in Dumont, Phelps would be safely in the clear. And although that would represent yet another of the "blind alleys" Sheriff Simms had referred to, I remembered his encouraging words: "*Then* we get down to the final problem-solving."

Phelps and I chatted amiably for a few more minutes, touching on the election and the new county museum and the colder weather, but soon, there was nothing left to say. He asked, "Anything else I can do for you, Brody?"

I was about to say no, but reconsidered. "Could you maybe show me what's in back? I heard dogs. Is there a kennel?"

"Not really a boarding kennel. Oh, sure, sometimes I'll look after a client's pet for a few days, but mostly the kennels—cages—are simply for holding animals before or after a procedure. Happy to give you a look." He stood. "Come on."

So I followed him out of his office, then down the hall to the back of the building and through a door into a sizable room, where I was instantly struck by a hospital smell of medicines and disinfectants, overlaid by a kennel smell of fur and dog breath and accidents.

The space was white and utilitarian, serving multiple purposes. There was an operating area with tables, lights, sinks, and such. One of the corners served as an office, with a metal desk, file cabinets, computer, and printer. Along one wall there were two rows of cages, large and small, containing a few hapless patients; a couple of them were bandaged and groggy, recovering, while the others panted and yapped, wagging their tails, ignorantly awaiting the knife. Huge padded gloves hung nearby for handling the frightened or uncooperative. On the opposite wall was a door with a window that led outside. And next to it—bingo—just what I was looking for, a row of cylinders, half a dozen, resembling scuba tanks. Some were painted metal, the others stainless steel, all of them topped with valves and gauges, which were connected to a tangle of hoses and plumbing that climbed the wall and crossed the ceiling to the surgical area.

Phelps was checking on a dog that had been fitted with one of those Elizabethan-looking cone collars—"How ya doin' there, buddy?"—while I stepped over to give the tanks a casual inspection. I spotted several tanks of oxygen at once. The other one I recognized was labeled N_2O. Buddy, it seemed, was a little loopy on nitrous oxide. Who knew?

"Jim," I said, "what's the nitrous for?"

"Works on these guys about the same way it does on people." He patted the dog's belly and closed the cage. "It helps stabilize an animal during and after procedures. If it's a surgery involving other anesthetics, nitrous speeds their induction and then helps the animal recover faster. Lots of vets have switched entirely to injectable anesthesia, but I'm happy with the way things were."

I took a closer look at the tanks. The different gases did indeed have different fittings.

"You know," said Phelps, sounding wistful, crossing his arms as he leaned his weight against the edge of a countertop, "I'm getting old now, and starting to feel my age, and sometimes, it's hard not to look back and wonder what you might have done different, or better. I'm a country doctor—an *animal* doctor—and some folks might tell you, 'Sure, that's real nice, real noble,' but instead, you know they're really asking, 'What's that hick actually *done* with his life?' But animals are so innocent and pure. Just being entrusted with their care, by the people who love them, I'm telling you, Brody, it's a reward not known by many men." With a grin, he added, "Or women."

This guy did *not* strike me as capable of murder. I said, "We're grateful to have you here, Jim. And no talk of retirement—Mister Puss needs you."

"Oh, I plan to be around awhile."

"Great. Well, I won't waste any more of your time. Thanks so much." I shook his hand, a gesture that morphed into a hug. I told him, "I can find my way out."

"Bah," he said, "just go out the back. It's quicker, and the front's locked up."

So I stepped to the back door. But as I reached for the knob, a piercing, hideous scream reached our ears from the parrot in the waiting room. Only half joking, I said, "Hope the snake didn't get loose."

Phelps laughed. "She just gets lonely out there."

Outside, I pulled the door closed behind me and noticed a few gas canisters, presumably empties, sticking up from a crate against the wall. The only vehicle in the gravel parking area behind the building was a big old station wagon with Dr. Phelps's name and phone number—seven digits—painted in faded gold lettering on the door. A second parking space was unoccupied; I assumed it had been vacated by the receptionist. A shingled outbuilding stood at the far side of the lot, looking as if it might once have been a stable, but its current use was not apparent;

it may have been abandoned. Beyond it, juxtaposed with the angles of the shed, stretched a dry, harvested field—a scene that could have inspired an Andrew Wyeth painting. A crow cawed in the stillness.

My shoes crunched at the gravel as I followed the curving driveway to the front parking lot, where my car was now alone. Shortly past noon, the breeze still carried a biting chill—a mere hint of things to come—so I quickened my pace, opened the car, and got in. Thumping the door closed, I started the engine. The heater automatically switched to a high roar, rushing to counteract the cold interior. The radio blared Mozart, a piano concerto, played so loudly that the piano's notes sounded harsh and distorted. Had I really been listening to the radio cranked that high when I arrived? Whatever. I turned it down several notches till it was barely audible above the noise of the heater.

Sitting there in the lot, I decided to call Sheriff Simms and report on my meeting with Dr. Phelps while it was fresh in my mind. I took out my phone and tapped his cell number.

He answered at once. "Hey, Brody. What's up?"

"Is this a good time, Thomas?"

"Perfect timing," he said. "Mary Questman asked me to drop by. Just got here—outside at the curb."

I told him I'd met with Jim Phelps, which he hadn't known I was planning to do. I explained, "After you left the church hall yesterday, I had another brain wave, which shifted my suspicion from the rug guy, Zakarian, to Phelps, the vet. So I made an appointment and talked to him. Looks like another blind alley, though—he seems to have an airtight alibi." I paused, astonished. Was I, a mild-mannered architect, now acquiring an everyday lexicon that included such terms as *airtight alibi*?

Simms asked, "Where was Phelps at the time of the murder?"

I gave him all the details: Green Bay, the conference, the

speech, the hotel.

"Okay, Brody, we'll look into it. If it's just a blind alley, fine—we'll cross one more person off the list."

After hanging up with Simms, I checked e-mails and found that more than a dozen had piled up since I'd left the office. Scrolling through them, I found nothing urgent. Nothing from Marson. Nothing that even caught my interest. Then, *pow*, the last one on the list. From: Dahr Ahmadi. His message was brief: So sorry we weren't able to connect yesterday. The funeral left Francis completely drained. Needs lots of attention. Soon, though. xoxox.

I had no idea how to respond—or even if I *should* respond. I sat there awhile, mulling this. Then I put the car in gear and set the phone on the passenger seat, next to my portfolio and the morning paper, which I'd tossed there earlier on my way to work. The front-page stories were getting monotonous, as well as foreboding. Peeping above the fold was a headline to the daily follow-up: FIVE DAYS TILL EARLY VOTING.

Turning my gaze from the newspaper, I looked out the windshield and toed the accelerator, easing the car out of the gravel lot and onto the smooth pavement of the quiet county road.

Gaining speed, my tires thrummed on the asphalt, joining the persistent rhythm streaming from the radio and the whoosh of the warm, recirculated air that filled the car. I focused straight ahead as fence posts flicked past on either side of the road like alternating strobes, strung together by barbed wire in my peripheral vision. The dashes of the stripe down the center of the two-lane blacktop flashed white-and-black, white-and-black, as trees rushed to the side of the road, then retreated into the fields and disappeared. Here and there, concrete embankments pinched the highway where corrugated drainpipes slipped beneath the intersections of remote and rustic side roads. Out in the middle of nowhere, the stone pylon of a historical marker appeared, tall and phallic, commemorating what? Perhaps an Indian battle. Or a settlers' trail. Or a long-gone schoolhouse that had taken a stand in the wilderness, a stand against the wilderness itself.

The car was getting hot. The music was getting modern, loud, and strident. For some reason, I felt curiously detached from my surroundings.

I turned off the heat. I turned off the radio.

And in the relative silence, I heard a different sound, a sound I hadn't noticed before. It was a hiss—not an organic sound, not like the voice of a snake, but a steady, high-pitched pneumatic sound, like leaking air.

I lightened my foot on the accelerator, slowing the car, wondering if that would cause a change in the hiss, but it did not. In fact, as the car slowed to a crawl, the hiss seemed all the louder. Without the road noise to mask it, the hiss seemed to come from the backseat.

Glancing over my shoulder, I noticed the sporty little plaid jacket I sometimes wore while bumming around, running weekend errands, and I recalled tossing it back there, on the seat. But now it was on the floor—or rather, it appeared to be covering something on the floor. Feeling short of breath, I reached back to grab the jacket, and as I dragged it away, its zipper clanged along the length of a metal tank that it had concealed. The hiss, no longer muffled, seemed to shriek within the confines of the car.

Steering drunkenly, I pulled over to the shoulder of the road, hit the brake, and shifted into park. Then I turned in my seat and lifted the head of the tank to rest on the center hump. It was labeled N_2O. With one hand, I fumbled to close the valve; with the other hand, I worked the buttons to open all of the car windows.

The hissing stopped. Cold air filled the car. My head began to clear, but my thoughts raced.

I got out of the car and paced a few steps up the roadway and back again, repeating this a few times until I regained my equilibrium. Not a single vehicle passed in either direction as I struggled to comprehend what had just happened—and how it could have ended.

Seated in the car again, I shifted into gear and continued the drive back to Dumont. I had covered only several hundred yards when, up ahead, from a clump of shrubbery near a hidden inter-section, I saw emerge the front end of a tricked-out police cruiser from the sheriff's department. I slowed to let it turn out ahead of me, affording me an unobstructed view of Deputy Alex Kastle.

Watching as the rear of his car sped off toward the main highway, I recalled what Sheriff Simms had told Mary Quest-man after yesterday's funeral: "Elections aren't as clean as they used to be."

No, they weren't.

Unless I was seriously mistaken, someone had just tried to kill me.

PART THREE

Hearing Is Believing

When the doorbell chimed, Mister Puss darted into the front hall and waited near the door, twisting his neck to peer up through a side window.

Mary Questman called, "I'll get it, Berta." She'd been looking forward to the sheriff's arrival all morning and had changed clothes twice for the occasion. Now, shortly past noon, her chunky-heeled Ferragamos clacked on the parquet floor and then softened for the last few steps along a Turkish silk runner. The lock clicked open as she turned the heavy brass knob and swung the door wide. "Welcome, Thomas. So nice of you to make time for me today."

Sheriff Simms stepped inside, saying, "Always a pleasure, Miss Mary."

Mister Puss nuzzled his shin.

Smiling, Simms leaned and offered a quick pat. "Good to see you, too, puss-cat."

Mister Puss followed as Mary led Simms into the little parlor adjacent to the hall. Mary perched at the end of a tidy loveseat; the cat hopped up and sat next to her.

The Sheriff sat facing them. "I find this really embarrassing, Miss Mary."

"Thomas? Whatever are you talking about?"

He shrugged. "Campaign contributions. You've been more than generous already. I wouldn't dream of asking for more."

"But I insist," said Mary. "And besides, circumstances have changed—with that horrid deputy of yours." She fumed at the very thought of Deputy Kastle, whom she considered nothing less than a traitor. "We *can't* let him get away with this."

"Can't argue with that," agreed Simms.

Mary had propped an envelope against a lamp on the table next to the loveseat, wanting to make a nice presentation. She plucked it up and extended it to Simms. "So I want you to have this. I hope it's not too late to make a difference."

Simms stood to accept it, then sat to open it. Mister Puss leaned in his direction, stretching his neck, watching.

Mary said, "If it's not enough, I want you to let me know."

The sheriff's eyes bugged as he pulled out the check. "*Thank you*, Miss Mary. If this won't do it, nothing will."

Mister Puss pawed Mary's arm and reached for her ear, purring loudly. Mary told the sheriff, "If I were younger, I'd be out there knocking on doors for you." Mister Puss pressed his nose to her ear.

Cash is king.

"You're far too kind," said Simms.

"Now, why didn't *I* think of that?" said Mary.

"Beg pardon?" said Simms.

"Would you prefer cash, Thomas? Unless I'm confused, there's no limit on cash contributions—and I could give you far more." Yes, she thought, Mister Puss had made a brilliant suggestion. Why *hadn't* she thought of that? And tucked away in her bedroom, as always, was a plump roll of bills that would make her check seem measly.

Simms laughed. "Miss Mary, you amaze me. Actually, the same limits apply to cash, assuming it gets reported. And I've been elected to enforce laws, not skirt them. So this check will do very nicely." Pocketing it, he added, "I'll send a receipt tomorrow."

Berta appeared from the hall and rapped her knuckles lightly on the doorway. "Excuse me, Mary. Will the sheriff be staying for lunch?"

Mary asked, "Won't you, Thomas?"

"It's thoughtful of you to offer, but I really need to—"

Mary raised a finger. "Now, I thought you might be busy, so I asked Berta to prepare something that would allow you to eat and dash, if you need to. So she made a lovely carrot soup—nice and hearty for a cold afternoon."

Berta said, "Cornbread, too."

Mary grinned. She knew what *that* meant.

Simms asked Berta, "Did you just bake it? I thought I knew that smell."

"I make it with honey and a little cinnamon—that's probably what you smell."

Mary told her, "I think we've convinced the sheriff to stay, Berta."

A few minutes later, they were in the dining room, a grand space with a long, gleaming mahogany table and twelve chairs, set with lunch for two. Mary sat at the head; Sheriff Simms sat near her along the side, where he could look out upon the front lawn through tall windows framed by silken drapes of misty rose.

Berta stepped forward and removed silver domes from two bowls containing a rich, creamy-orange soup.

"Looks wonderful, Berta," said Simms. "Sure beats a sandwich at my desk."

"I'll be right back with the cornbread." She winked at Mary, then left.

While Mary and the sheriff tried the soup, agreeing that Berta had worked some magic in the kitchen, Mister Puss peeped up from the edge of the table across from Simms, following their conversation with his golden eyes.

Mary set down her spoon and heaved a little sigh. Sitting back in her chair, she said, "I can't help feeling a bit guilty, Thomas."

Simms gave her a quizzical look. "*You,* Miss Mary? Guilty of what?"

She tossed her hands. "This whole FlabberGas mess—if I hadn't encouraged Dr. Frumpkin with his business plans, none of this would've happened."

"I'm not so sure of that," said Simms. "First, if Frumpkin was intent on building a chain of gas clinics, he would've ended up pitching it to investors with or without your help. Second, and most important, Jason Ward's death wasn't accidental; it was homicide. So it's safe to assume the killer had a strong motive and was waiting to strike whenever the opportunity presented itself."

"That's reassuring," said Mary, adding, "in a perverse sort of way."

Berta returned with a basket of cornbread, still steaming, and two bread plates, each holding a sizable slab of butter. Setting everything on the table, she nudged the sheriff's shoulder, telling him, "Try it while it's hot." Then she disappeared.

Mister Puss lifted his nose above the edge of the table, sniffing. His eyes widened.

Mary and Sheriff Simms helped themselves to the cornbread. Tasting it, Simms responded with a rapturous moan. Mary broke off a crusty corner and held it off to her side, making kissy sounds at Mister Puss. When she dropped the morsel to the floor, the cat leapt from his chair and pounced on it. Then Mary buttered a piece for herself and nibbled it, swallowing with a petite, ladylike groan of approval.

Dabbing her lips with her napkin, she said, "The funeral yesterday—it was nice—I mean, nice for a *funeral.*"

Simms nodded. "It was a beautiful service."

"But Father Sterling is slowing down now—getting on in years—it really shows." Mary fed another tiny scrap of cornbread to Mister Puss, who was pawing her knees.

"Any talk of retirement?" asked Simms.

"Plenty," said Mary with a laugh, "but not from Father Sterling."

"Good," said Simms, "I'd miss him. Sure, he's a good-hearted old guy—you'd expect as much—but above and beyond that, he's a truly gifted orator."

Mary nodded. "He certainly helped bring a measure of closure to the Frumpkin family. I hope he was a comfort to them." Mister Puss was begging again, so Mary pushed her chair back and patted her knees, inviting the cat to jump up to her lap.

"I hope so, too," said Simms. "Murder takes such a terrible toll within the victim's family. I've seen it too often."

"Poor Dr. Frumpkin. Somehow, I thought he'd be stronger in the face of this tragedy, but I'm afraid the healing will be slow." Mary didn't want to give Mister Puss more of Berta's cornbread, so she swiped a finger through the butter and offered it to the cat, who licked the swirl from her pinkie with a grateful purr. She said to Simms, "And then there's Sarah. That poor woman, a widow so young, facing so much uncertainty." Mary fed Mister Puss another swipe of butter. His purring intensified. "But on a brighter note," said Mary, "little Olivia seemed to be dealing with everything surprisingly well. She's been going through a difficult phase lately, but yesterday? She was quite the little lady."

Mister Puss had pawed his way up Mary's chest and stretched his snout to her cheek. Then he slid his nose to her ear. His purr droned.

There's something wrong with that sasspot.

Mary laughed. Petting the cat, she said, "Yes, Mister Puss, you've already made your feelings perfectly clear on *that* topic."

Simms eyed Mary with a look of evident concern.

Mary smirked. She understood that the sheriff, like most of her friends, had heard the gossip that she conversed with her cat. She also understood that they were skeptical—naturally—and even a bit worried. She herself had reacted the same way, at first, but now, a half year after Mister Puss had arrived, she had grown comfortable with a simple, objective conclusion: hearing is believing. She said, "Humor me, Thomas."

He broke into laughter. "Of course, Miss Mary."

The doorbell chimed.

Mister Puss shot out of the dining room and into the front hall. The sound of Berta's footfalls emerged from the kitchen and moved toward the door.

The chimes rang again.

"Coming," called Berta.

The massive brass knocker pounded on the door.

Berta opened it. "Mr. Norris—is something wrong?"

"I need to speak to Sheriff Simms. I believe he's here?"

Alarmed, Mary called out, "Brody, love, we're in the dining room." She and Simms rose from their chairs as Brody rushed into the room, looking disheveled and flustered. His necktie was loose, with his collar unbuttoned. He carried his sport coat in one hand and a small leather portfolio in the other.

He said, "I'm sorry to intrude, but—"

"Nonsense, dear. What's wrong?"

"Thomas," said Brody, "someone just tried to kill me."

Berta brought soup. Mary and Sheriff Simms huddled with Brody at the table. Mister Puss sat near Brody's chair, watching from the floor.

"I should take some notes," said Simms, slipping a pad from his pocket and opening it on the table. He clicked a pen and began writing.

"And I should review mine," said Brody. He put down his soup spoon and unzipped his portfolio.

Berta delivered a fresh basket of cornbread, setting it in their midst.

Brody said, "The carrot soup is incredible, Berta. Marson was telling me about it—he loved the 'aggressive spark of nutmeg.' It's a great pairing."

Obliquely, Berta said, "It's a little more complicated than that." She turned to leave for the kitchen, adding, "But thanks— glad you like it."

Mary told Brody, "You'll *love* the cornbread."

"Maybe later."

Simms clicked his pen again. "Let's see if I've got this straight: You visited Dr. Phelps at his vet office and concluded he'd had no role in the FlabberGas murder—assuming his story about the conference in Green Bay checks out. Then he showed you the work area at the rear of the office, and you saw that he keeps a supply of nitrous oxide, as well as oxygen and other gases. When you returned to your car and began driving back to town, you discovered a tank of nitrous in the backseat area—with the valve open, hissing."

"Right," said Brody, jotting a few notes of his own. "The car was cold, so the windows were up, and the heater was on, recir- culating the air. The radio was on, playing way louder than I'd left it. So it took me a while to notice the hiss. And by that time, I was starting to feel woozy. I was barely able to pull over and stop the car."

Mary fretted, "What a horrible turn of events. Why, you could've ... you could've been ..." But she was unable to speak the word she was thinking.

"And then," said Simms, "you got out of the car and cleared

your head. And now you feel normal, right? You don't need medical attention?"

"I'm fine," said Brody. "Just shaken."

Simms asked, "And that's it? You drove directly here?"

Brody paused, crossing his arms. "One more detail." He looked Simms in the eye, explaining, "After I cleared my head, got back in the car, and began driving again—out there in the middle of nowhere—someone pulled out of hiding, practically cutting me off, and then blasted away in front of me. Guess who."

Simms and Mary asked in unison, "Who?"

"Ready for this?" asked Brody. "It was none other than Deputy Alex Kastle. In uniform. In a police cruiser."

Mary gasped. This was beyond her worst suspicions—the deputy was not only a traitor, but the would-be assassin of her dear friend Brody.

Simms set down his pen, closed his eyes, and pinched the bridge of his nose. Then he stifled a laugh.

"*Thomas,*" said Mary, appalled. "Surely you can't find this funny."

"I'm sorry, Miss Mary." Simms sat back in his chair. "And my apologies to you, too, Brody. Obviously, someone attempted some serious mischief out there today. And I plan to get to the bottom of it. But I'm pretty sure Deputy Kastle wasn't behind it." He turned a page in his notebook and began drawing a grid.

"Why?" asked Brody. "Why do you think it wasn't Kastle? I saw him."

"I believe you, Brody. It makes perfect sense that you saw him. You see, that county road is sort of isolated and quiet—not much traffic—which tempts some drivers to roar through there. That's dangerous enough in itself, but with all the curves and blind spots, it can be deadly. So we've set up an enforcement zone."

Brody said, "A speed trap."

"In common parlance, correct. Kastle found a nicely concealed observation spot, which he mans for about an hour most mornings. You saw him when, Brody? Maybe twenty minutes ago?" Simms checked his watch. "Kastle's shift was just ending, and he must've been rushing off to lunch. I'll have a word with him about the posted speed limits—doesn't look good when citizens see officers ignoring the laws they're supposed to enforce."

With a disgruntled sigh, Brody shook his head, then ate some more soup.

"Granted," said Simms, "this doesn't prove that Kastle *didn't* plant the gas canister, but it does explain why he happened to be there. Tell you what—I'll take the canister as evidence and start looking into this. Can I borrow your keys?"

"Uh," said Brody, hunching sheepishly over his bowl, "you won't need them. The car isn't locked."

"Brody," said Simms. "After what happened today?"

"Lesson learned. God, back in L.A., I wouldn't *dream* of leaving the car unlocked, but here in Dumont, it seems like a different world."

"Not so different," Simms reminded him. "Be careful, now."

After Simms left, Mary insisted that Brody should stay for another bowl of soup, telling him, "You've had such an *awful* scare—you need your strength." She sat with him as he ate it, and Mister Puss hopped up into her lap.

Between spoonfuls, Brody began drawing a grid on his pad, which sat next to his bowl on the table.

Mary peered down at it. "Sheriff Simms drew something like that as well. Is it a game?"

"Only in a manner of speaking." Brody drew an *X* in one of

the squares, explaining, "It's a suspect grid. It helps make a visual comparison of everyone's motive, means, and opportunity to commit the crime."

"Oh, my," said Mary, "how clever. So you just fill in the squares—and then you have your answer?"

"That's the idea, but in practice, it's not so clear-cut. At the outset, it's great for eliminating certain suspects. But along the way, other details, other circumstances, other *questions*—they seem to muddy up the finalists."

"What sort of questions?"

Brody paused before answering, "Questions like: What did they know? And when did they know it?" He paused again. "I wonder …" Then he flipped the page and started another grid.

Mary noticed that as Brody added X after X to his chart, he seemed to grow more agitated. She cooed at Mister Puss, who purred, and she gabbed about this and that with Brody, who looked preoccupied as he scratched and stabbed at the pad. She asked, "Why don't you try some of Berta's cornbread? I think you'd enjoy it."

"Thank you, Mary, but not now." He turned the page and drew another grid.

She tittered. "Sheriff Simms was so funny. He really doesn't know what to make of Mister Puss. He must think I've lost my marbles."

"I'm sure that's not the case …" Brody's eyes were focused on the grid as he slashed another X and then tried another spoonful of soup.

"Mister Puss doesn't seem to care for little Olivia at all. He calls her a 'sasspot.'"

Brody froze.

Mary continued, "But I think it's just because she played rough with him." Rubbing the cat's ears, she asked him, "Is that the problem?"

Mister Puss purred loudly.

Brody set down his spoon and turned to Mary, asking, "You heard Mister Puss call Olivia a 'sasspot'?"

"Twice, in fact. He told me, 'There's something wrong with that sasspot.'" She laughed merrily. "Such a droll expression, isn't it? *Sasspot*—I haven't heard that in years."

"I have," said Brody. He looked at Mister Puss, who had stopped purring and stared back at him.

"Well, then," said Mary. "You know what they say: hearing is believing."

Brody stood. He glanced over his notepad, then closed it, zipping the portfolio. "Forgive me, Mary, but I need to run."

"Oh, *no*—already?" she asked, standing as Mister Puss pounced to the floor.

"Please thank Berta for me. I need to take care of something." Brody grabbed his jacket and his notes, gave Mary a quick peck, and stepped briskly out to the hall.

Mary scooped up the cat and followed Brody to the door. As he opened it, she said, "Be careful, Brody. And watch out for that *nasty* Deputy Kastle."

"Not him," said Brody as he crossed the threshold. "He's not my problem."

Mary watched him trot down the tile-bordered walkway to the street. Then she nudged the door closed while petting Mister Puss beneath his chin.

The cat broke into a rolling purr.

13

What a freaking weird day, and it was far from over.

That Wednesday had begun routinely enough with a few hours of work at the office, where I mentioned to Marson that I couldn't join him for lunch. "I have an appointment with Dr. Phelps, the veterinarian, and I'm not sure how long it'll take."

"I hope it's nothing serious, Brody," said Marson, deeply concerned. "Hairballs?"

Funny, yes. But it was no laughing matter when I left Phelps's office and someone tried to replicate the FlabberGas murder by planting an open tank of laughing gas in my closed car. And it was no laughing matter when I narrowly escaped injury—or worse—and spotted Deputy Alex Kastle speeding away from the scene.

So I rushed over to Mary Questman's house, where I knew I'd find Sheriff Thomas Simms. It was no laughing matter when I reported to Simms what had happened, but then he couldn't help laughing when I detailed my suspicions that Deputy Kastle had been the culprit behind the attempt on my life, which turned out to be yet another blind alley—a concoction of an architect's overly creative sleuthing skills, pressed into service to help solve the original mystery of who had murdered Dr. Jason Ward.

And although it *should* have been a laughing matter when Mary informed me that Mister Puss had called little Olivia a "sasspot," I nearly choked on my carrot soup (and its aggressive spark of so-called nutmeg) when I realized that the cat had used the same unusual word in an earlier, verbatim conversation with me (pooh-poohed as the product of my so-called imagination). What—just what *exactly*—was I to make of this development?

That quandary, however, was soon back-burnered by yet another laughing matter when Mary asked me if the sheriff and I were playing games—with our suspect grids. Which prompted me to ask these questions concerning our remaining field of possible killers: What did they know? And when did they know it?

Drawing a new grid, focused solely on this pair of linked questions, I recalled a small detail, previously assumed insignificant and therefore dismissed. I recalled—with a jolt—what someone knew, and when. And it was no laughing matter.

Now, around one o'clock, on this freaking weird day that was far from over, I got out of the car at the First Avenue offices of Miles & Norris and rushed inside to find Marson at his desk, tattering away at his keyboard.

He looked up from the computer, smiling. "Hi there, kiddo." Then he frowned. "What's wrong?"

When I had brought him up to date, he said, "Maybe it's time to step back from this, Brody. Last week, when you signed on as Simms's 'sidekick,' it was sort of a lark, a favor to Mary. But now, someone must think you're getting too close to the truth. I'm a big believer in community involvement. And I think it's great that you're doing your bit. But suddenly, you're in *danger*. As far as I'm concerned, that's way beyond the call of civic duty. Let Simms wrap this up."

"But he's nowhere *near* solving the murder, and he's running out of time."

"That's his job. It's *his* problem."

I asked, "Is it? If Alex Kastle takes Simms's job, then it's *our* problem. Then sleepy little Dumont will be headed toward a zombie apocalypse."

"A valid point," Marson admitted, "though you might be overstating the consequences."

We were sitting in his office with the door closed. He was still at his computer; I had perched near him on the edge of his desk; our legs touched. I told him, "I figured something out today, at Mary's. Something clicked, and I don't like it. And unfortunately, I'm in a far better position to get to the bottom of it than Simms is."

Marson placed his hand on my knee. "Explain, please."

I took a deep breath and held it for a moment. Then I stood, paced around to the front of Marson's desk, and asked him, "Remember Saturday night—at the loft?"

"Sure. We had Dahr over for dinner. Nice evening."

I nodded. "Right. And the purpose of that dinner was two-fold. Aside from our wanting to get to know him, socially, as a friend, *my* underlying purpose was to sound him out about the murder. Simms had already expressed his suspicions of Dahr, whereas Dr. Frumpkin had told both Simms and me that Dahr 'would never harm a fly.' I wanted to believe Frumpkin and prove Simms wrong."

"And unless I'm mistaken, Dahr passed the test with flying colors." Marson paused before adding, "He even gave you a doozy of a good-bye kiss."

"Yes, there was that." I didn't mention that I had since received more than one e-mail suggesting Dahr's interest in taking that kiss to another level. I had not responded, hoping to defuse the sexual tension—both his and mine. Simply put, I had been avoiding him. "But now," I told Marson, "I'm having second thoughts."

Marson sat back in his chair and folded his arms. With a soft smile, he said, "I'm listening, kiddo."

"Remember when Dahr was telling us about the nature of his relationship with Frumpkin?"

"Indeed I do. It was rather more detailed than I expected."

"Right"—I laughed—"and one of those details, a seemingly minor one, slipped past me in the recitation of their sex habits. He was talking about the night before the murder. They had dinner at Frumpkin's place, and then, afterward, they were 'getting cozy, getting in the mood,' but they were interrupted by a phone call from Sarah, with news that Mary Questman had backed out as guinea pig for the next day's demo. This put Frumpkin in a dither, and it took them an hour to get their groove on again."

"Well," said Marson, "I admire Dahr's persistence, and presumably his stamina. Good for Francis Frumpkin—all's well that ends well."

"But don't you see?"

"What?"

I leaned across the desk toward Marson. "They *knew*. Dahr *himself* knew that Jason Ward would be the new guinea pig— the night before he was killed."

Marson shrugged. "So?"

"Today at Mary's, things fell together for me when I reviewed the field of suspects and asked myself, 'What did they know, and when did they know it?' Sheriff Simms has already determined that the killer must've rigged the gas lines the night before the demo. And that fact alone rules out some of the people we've considered: Glee Savage, Phelps the veterinarian, and maybe Deputy Kastle. Simms also concluded that the killer must've had a working knowledge of medical gases, which rules out Berta the housekeeper and Zakarian the rug man."

Marson asked, "So who's left?"

"By my calculation, just three: Dr. Frumpkin, Sarah Frumpkin Ward—and Dahr."

Marson's features wrinkled in thought. "Okay: All three of them had knowledge of gases. They all had access to the clinic the night before. And they all had knowledge that the new guinea pig was Jason. However: Sarah had no motive at all. And while Frumpkin might conceivably have wanted to settle a score between his son-in-law and his lover, he had far too much to lose. The murder has jeopardized his current practice, and it trashed his big plans for FlabberGas. Which leaves only … Dahr."

I summarized: "Dahr checks all the boxes, and everyone heard him tell the victim, 'I *know* what I'm doing, Doctor.'"

Marson let it all sink in. Then he told me, "Call Simms."

I shook my head.

"Why not?"

I was not inclined to explain to my husband why I felt the need to confront Dahr myself. I was confused by the feelings he had shown for me, and I felt guilty for the attraction I had felt for him in return. What's more, I was shaken by the deadly mischief that had been plotted against me only a few hours ago. And I was angry that a man who had played with my emotions—and tickled my lust—had now apparently tried to kill me. I told Marson, "I don't want to send Simms down another blind alley. If I'm wrong about this, why spread the shame?"

"You're playing with fire, kiddo."

Since Marson could not convince me that I should not confront Dahr, he suggested, "Don't do it alone. I should be with you."

Actually, this made sense. Marson's presence would surely put a damper on any amorous impulses Dahr might bring to our meeting. What's more, if my suspicions were correct, and if

Dahr felt suddenly accused and trapped ... well, I didn't much want to think about that. I told Marson, "Good idea."

He asked, "Maybe invite him over for a drink after work?"

Another good idea. So I crossed the hall to my own office and sat down to write an e-mail. Subject line: Up for a drink?

Hi there, Dahr.

It's been a hectic week, hasn't it? And it's only Wednesday! With the funeral over, I hope things are getting back to normal in Dr. Frumpkin's office. Today has been anything but "normal" for me, though. Maybe you'd like to hear about it.

How about a quick drink or two this evening at the loft? Anytime after five is fine. Let me know.

Brody

Dahr did not respond immediately—I assumed he was working at the clinic, busy with patients—but twenty minutes later, *ping*, his reply popped onto my screen.

Dear Brody,

What a pleasant surprise! So great to hear from you. Yes, absolutely, let's do drinks after work. I want to run home for a quick shower first, so I'll try to be there by six. Will it be "just us"?

xoxox,

Dahr

I sent a brief response: Yes, just us—you, me, and Marson. See you at six.

A moment later, *ping*: Great, got it. xoxox.

I sent Marson a short message, letting him know the plan, which he confirmed. Then I sat back at my desk, wondering why

Dahr thought it necessary to shower for a midweek cocktail hour. Was he compulsively clean? Or expecting more?

The afternoon dragged. There was no shortage of projects needing my attention, but I was worn down by the day's events, and my mind was adrift with questions and worries.

Sheriff Simms phoned to let me know that, as expected, the only fingerprints found on the canister of nitrous oxide were my own. He asked if I felt the need for police protection, and I said, "Of course not, Thomas," but I wasn't so sure.

Later, Marson popped over to my office, looking a bit ashen. I asked him, "Something wrong?"

"I have a conflict," he said sheepishly.

I asked, "Man versus nature? Man versus machine?"

He smirked. "No, wise guy. I'm needed on a conference call for the Oregon project at four o'clock—their time. Six here. And I'll need to be at my desk."

"Oops."

"Do you want to reschedule with Dahr?"

I checked my watch. "Sorta late for that. I'll be fine."

"Are you sure?"

I gave him a confident smile. "Of course I'm sure." But I wasn't.

He said, "I'll come home as soon as I can."

I wondered what Dahr would wear that evening. I wondered how he would react when he learned that Marson couldn't join us. I wondered if he would become physically aggressive—wanting sex, or wanting to finish the failed plot that had begun with the nitrous oxide in my car, or perversely, wanting both sex *and* murder.

Puttering in the kitchen, assembling a basic bar setup on the center island, I wondered what Dahr would want to drink.

Checking the time, I wondered when he would arrive.

Grrring.

Six sharp. Yanked from my grim thoughts by the sputtering old bell at the loft's street door, I wondered why Marson and I had never bothered to replace it with a more modern update—less authentic, perhaps, but decidedly less grating.

When I opened the door, the sun had set, and I had not yet turned any lights on. My visitor stood silhouetted against the twilight. I said, "Good evening, Dahr."

"Good to see you, Brody. Thanks for asking me over." He stepped inside, offering an easy hug. I smelled the leather of his jacket as he leaned close.

I shut the door and flipped a nearby row of switches, which dispelled the gathering darkness. The last time Dahr had visited, he'd worn all black, but not tonight. His leather coat was not a tailored black blazer, as before, but a puffy brown bomber jacket with a shearling collar, worn to fend off the cold of a waning October in Wisconsin. He unzipped it and pulled a plaid wool muffler free from his neck.

I offered to take them, and as I set them aside, he strolled toward the center of the main room. The rest of his clothes—button-down shirt, V-neck sweater, wide-wale corduroys—were not so mysterious or seductive as his previous outfit, but equally attractive, in a more cozy sort of way.

In the dead quiet of the vast space, he looked about. "Marson's not here?"

"He needed to stay at the office for a conference call." Fudging, I added, "He should be home any minute."

"Great," said Dahr.

I moved toward the kitchen. "What can I get you?"

Dahr followed me to the makeshift bar. "Last time, you fixed me your 'winter drink.' Winter's in the air tonight, so maybe the same—Scotch and soda, please."

His comment about winter tempted me to suggest that I could light the candles in the fireplace, but I quickly nixed that notion because of its overtly romantic overtones. Instead, I mixed our drinks, adding a twist of lemon peel to each, and then led Dahr to the conversation area at the front of the loft, in front of the dark fireplace, inviting him to sit.

When he was settled on one of the loveseats, I moved to the one across from him and sat. I asked, "Are things getting back to normal at the office?"

"Well, we're *open* again, but it's far from normal. We were closed for a week, and Jason's gone, so things are pretty frantic now, making up for those missed appointments. Plus, everyone who comes in, they all talk about the murder and offer condolences—naturally—but it's an unhappy atmosphere, to say the least." He took a generous sip of Scotch.

I asked him, "And what about Dr. Frumpkin? Have his spirits improved any?"

"Not much, I'm afraid. His world is upside-down now. Not just the business issues—but the anguish over Jason's death. Francis truly loved the guy, grooming him to take over the practice. Jason wasn't just 'the son-in-law.' He was also Olivia's father. Francis has always been highly sentimental about that link to his granddaughter."

"And yet," I noted, "you and Jason found yourselves at odds."

Dahr set his glass on the low table between us. "Jason had some strange ideas, some insecurities, I guess. I can't say I understood his feelings; I'm not wired that way."

"But you must have felt some animosity toward him—the way he treated you."

"Actually, no, I didn't. Jason's issues weren't *my* issues. I worked—and I still work—for Francis." Dahr picked up his glass and drank again.

Swirling my own glass, I said, "Sorry it's been so hard on Francis. May I ask, where is he tonight?"

"He's having dinner with Sarah and Olivia—needed a little 'family time,' and I didn't want to intrude. So I'm glad you asked me here. Feels good to decompress."

Odd choice of words. Jason Ward had died in an oxygen compression chamber.

Dahr continued, "Olivia is bouncing back nicely, but poor Sarah—if anything, she seems to be sinking even deeper into her grief."

I reminded Dahr, "Jason died only ten days ago. There's no timetable for grief, and we each set our own rules."

"Of course. One bright little glimmer, though. Sarah's been flummoxed about Olivia's after-school schedule; it seemed to work out just fine when Jason was still with us. So after the funeral yesterday, the sheriff's wife offered to pick up Olivia after school today for a play date with their son, Tommy."

I nodded, recalling, "I was there when Gloria suggested it."

"It worked out great," said Dahr. "It took some pressure off Sarah this afternoon and let her focus more on the office—probably a good distraction right now."

I swallowed the last of my cocktail, then told Dahr, "I know the after-school issue has been weighing on Sarah. She was here on Monday afternoon and brought Olivia with her. We had a bit of drama with Mister Puss."

Dahr gave me a quizzical look.

I explained, "I was doing some cat-sitting for Mary Questman's Abyssinian. Olivia played with the cat and got sorta rough with him. In fact, the situation came to a tense climax, but it was peaceably resolved." With a soft laugh, I reminded Dahr, "Mary claims to communicate with Mister Puss."

Dahr smiled. "And vice versa."

"Right," I said. "And it seems Mister Puss has grown somewhat wary of Olivia. He told Mary, and I quote, 'There's something wrong with that sasspot.'"

Both Dahr and I laughed. I was not inclined to mention that I had heard—or wondered if I *might* have heard—the same words from the cat.

Dahr's laughter trailed off. "Believe it or not, Olivia is a sweet little girl. I've watched her grow up, and this recent phase of hers—well, I hope it's *just* a phase. And while Mister Puss is entitled to his opinions, I think it's a bit harsh to dismiss Olivia as a 'sasspot.' I'd prefer to call her 'troubled.' I don't see her as a problem child, but as the victim of some larger problem, some psychological turmoil, whatever that may be. Point is, she's a child. And like all children, she needs—and deserves—unconditional love."

Jeepers. I felt like a heel again. Dahr had come to Olivia's defense during his prior visit to the loft, and now he had reminded me that it was not only cavalier, but cruel, to judge conditions that are not understood. I also felt ashamed that I had lured him to my home to confront him with suspicions of murder—which had all but evaporated.

I said, "Know what, Dahr? You'd make a great parent."

He grinned. "Don't I wish."

Yes, I knew that was what he wished. I also knew that the parenting issue was the crux of his reticence to commit to Francis Frumpkin, who clearly loved him.

Noticing his empty glass, I asked, "Can I get you another?"

He hesitated. "Sure. But if you'll excuse a request from an impolite guest, may I ask if you have any snacks? Chips, anything like that? I'm starved."

"Ughhh"—I tossed my arms and stood—"how thoughtless of

me. Come on." Leading him back to the kitchen, I realized that I, too, was hungry. While Berta's carrot soup was, for lack of a better word, transcendental, it was not a meal.

I rummaged. "Let's see: macadamia nuts, lavash, some decent-looking apples, a round of brie, and—sorry to admit—a party-size bag of Cheetos. Any preference?"

"Cheetos!"

"Good call." As I opened the bag, I handed him a wad of paper napkins. "You'll need these." Then I poured us another round of drinks.

After eating several fistfuls, he explained while wiping his hands, "We were booked solid today, and I assisted with a Mohs surgery for a basal cell at eleven. It required removal of more tissue than expected, lasting well into the noon hour."

I asked, "So you never got out for lunch?"

"God, no. It was nonstop for me today."

His story could easily be checked, if needed, against office schedules, insurance records, and such. So he had no reason to make this up. And I had every reason to abandon the notion that he had planted a canister of laughing gas in my car between eleven-thirty and twelve-fifteen.

"But hey," he said, "enough of my woes. You mentioned in your e-mail that you'd had a rough day and that I might like to hear about it. What happened?"

"Just ... stuff." It no longer seemed important to confront him with this. In fact, it seemed important to keep a lid on it. "However," I said, raising my glass and touching it to his, "there's something we haven't talked about, but should."

He returned the skoal and swallowed a slug. With a slow nod, he said, "I'm sorry, Brody. I humbly apologize."

"For what?"

"For coming on to you like I did. You're a hot man, about my age, openly gay—a rare bird around here. But you're also married, and both you and Marson have offered me your friendship. I was way out of bounds to ask for more. It took me a few days to realize that. But yesterday, the funeral changed everything. Even though I haven't *committed* to Francis, he needs me, and I was glad to be there for him. So I'm sorry if that 'special kiss' last Saturday caused you any problems."

"I admit, it threw me." Heaving a little sigh, I added, "But it was fabulous."

"Good, huh?"

"One of the best. I still enjoy the memory."

"I do, too, Brody. So let's just keep it that way. And most important, let's be friends." He winked. Or was it a tic?

"Awww," I said, "of *course* we're friends."

As we stood there sharing a smile, it was the most natural thing in the world for us to wrap each other in a big, friendly, innocent hug.

And then Marson said with a laugh, "Hope I'm not interrupting anything," as he stepped through the back door.

I froze, certain that the hug could not have looked innocent at all.

Dahr joined in Marson's laughter and stepped over to give him the same big, friendly hug, telling him, "Your beautiful husband and I were just clearing the air on a few matters."

"Glad to hear it," said Marson. Turning to me, he asked, "Another blind alley?"

Although Marson misunderstood the details of how Dahr and I had cleared the air, he had nonetheless reached the right conclusion. I replied, "Yep, another blind alley."

"Guys," said Dahr, I don't want to take up any more of your evening. And I want to check on Francis—see how he's doing. So it's time for me to run."

We saw him to the front door, helped him into his jacket, and wrapped the scarf around his neck.

He gave Marson a nice little parting kiss. I was expecting the same as he turned to me and grasped my shoulders.

What I got, however, was another doozy—as masterfully delivered as the one he'd planted on me under the streetlamp. My knees went weak.

"I know," he said, laughing, "I promised. But that was just one for the road."

And he left.

Munching on Cheetos while Marson fixed himself a martini, I pondered aloud, "I'm running out of alleys—blind or otherwise."

Marson said, "Your instincts were right about Sheriff Simms, though. Good thing you *didn't* convince him to give Dahr the rubber-hose treatment."

Ignoring that, I asked, "Know what Mister Puss said?"

"No," said Marson, suppressing a grin. "What?"

I rephrased: "Know what Mister Puss said—to Mary—about little Olivia? He said, 'There's something wrong with that sasspot.'"

"Most observant of him." Marson lanced a cocktail onion with a toothpick and dropped it into the gin. "He certainly has an ear for catchy dialogue."

I wiped my fingers with a napkin, smearing it orange. Then I took out my phone. "Think it's too late to call Mary?"

"The night is young, kiddo. She's old. Not bedridden."

I tapped her number. When she answered, I said, "Good evening, Mary. It's Brody. No, nothing's wrong. I was just wondering if I could ask a small favor."

14

The next afternoon, Thursday, I drove over to Mary Questman's house and parked at the curb shortly before three.

For the past two weeks, since the FlabberGas pitch session delivered by Dr. Frumpkin at Mary's, little Olivia had been popping up in conversations with everyone—from her parents and her grandfather, to Dahr and Mary and even Mister Puss. What's more, Olivia herself had been popping up in person—at the pitch session, at my loft, and most recently at her father's funeral—generally behaving like a hellion, or as her mother had termed it, "acting out," but finally undergoing some attitude adjustment and summoning the self-control to make a respectable appearance at the funeral.

It was now only four days until the start of early voting in the sheriff's election, and the prospects weren't looking good for my friend Thomas Simms, who was singularly qualified to serve another term, but who was facing an unexpectedly strong challenge from one of his own deputies. Alex Kastle, a racist wingnut, had successfully reframed the election as a test of Simms's ability to solve the FlabberGas murder—and quickly.

Having been flattered as a first-class problem-solver, I had foolishly assumed that my design skills as an architect would somehow translate into amateur sleuthing skills as an unofficial sidekick to Sheriff Simms, who welcomed my input. To date, however, I had managed only to lead him down one blind alley after another. And the clock was ticking. Clearly, I needed to rethink things. I needed a fresh approach.

Which had led me to consider a more focused appraisal of Olivia. Mister Puss had called her a sasspot. Dahr Ahmadi had called her a sweet little girl, but troubled, a victim of the psychological turmoil that can arise out of nowhere to haunt anyone's childhood—in other words, she'd been going through a phase of routine growing pains. But I wanted to take another look at her.

I'd hit upon an idea last night and phoned Mary Questman. Recalling that Sarah Frumpkin Ward, Olivia's mother, was having trouble adjusting to her new circumstances—needing to balance her dual roles as office manager and single mom, needing to make arrangements for Olivia's after-school hours—I asked Mary if she would mind offering to supervise an afternoon play date for Olivia with Mister Puss. Mary readily agreed, and then, so did Sarah. It was all arranged: Olivia would be dropped off at Mary's today around three-fifteen.

Now, shortly before three, I got out of my car, remembered my hard-learned lesson to lock it, then strolled up the walkway from the street to Mary's front door. I thought I saw her peeking from the sidelight. When I rang, she answered at once.

Offering a peck as I entered, she said, "Brody dear, *welcome*. I've been on pins and needles all day."

"Oh?" I asked with childlike innocence. "How come?"

She shot me a wry expression, then whispered, "I haven't yet told His Majesty that you-know-who is coming over." Mister Puss moved from Mary's ankles to mine.

I looked down at the cat and suggested to Mary, "Maybe it's time for a talk."

Mary nodded. "In here."

She led me and the cat into the parlor off the front hall and settled on the loveseat, which seemed to be her customary spot in the room, as the cat simultaneously hopped up to sit next to her. I sat across from them in a quilted-chintz armchair.

Mary slowly stroked the cat's spine, which soon had him purring. She told him, "Someone's coming to see you today." He stepped from the cushion and into her lap, leaning against her chest to look up at her. "I'm sure you remember little Olivia." His purring halted for a moment, then resumed. Mary said, "She'll be here soon, and we'd like you to spend some time with her. Alone." The cat climbed to her shoulder and reached his snout to her ear. Mary nodded. "Yes, I know you've had some bad experiences with her, but Brody and I will be nearby if you need us." The cat nuzzled Mary's ear again.

I said, "Mister Puss?" In spite of mounting evidence to the contrary, I remained thoroughly skeptical that the cat was capable of conversation, but he did recognize his name, turning to peer into my eyes. I recalled yesterday's meeting with Dr. Phelps, when he mentioned that, as children, we've all talked with animals, dolls, or imaginary friends—a normal exercise in creativity.

Having captured the cat's attention, I returned his stare and wondered what to say to him. Mary hadn't baby-talked him, so neither did I. "Mister Puss," I said, "I saw Olivia recently, and she was sorry for playing so rough with you. I think she wants to apologize and be friends. She told me she's been confused lately. Maybe you could help us straighten this out."

The cat twisted his head to look up at Mary.

She said, "Maybe you could wait in the dining room. Find a place where you feel safe and comfortable—probably under the table. When Olivia arrives, we'll send her in. If she misbehaves at all, let out a yowl. We'll be listening."

With a purr, Mister Puss stretched to give Mary a nose-bump, then hopped to the floor. While pussyfooting out of the room, he paused near my chair and flashed me an expression that looked a lot like a grin. Do cats *grin?*

When the doorbell rang, Mary told me, "I sent Berta out on some errands—thought we should have the house to ourselves. Let's see who's here." Then she led me out to the front hall.

Opening the door, we found Olivia, as expected, but not with her mother. Instead, Dahr Ahmadi had brought her over.

He said, "Hello, Mrs. Questman. And hi there, Brody! I didn't know you'd be here, but I thought I recognized your car."

I couldn't recall when he might have seen me in my car. Giving him a breezy hug, no smooches, I explained, "Actually, this visit was my idea. After you told me how Olivia's play date with Tommy Simms worked out so nicely for everyone, I thought Mary might like to look after Olivia this afternoon."

"And I was *happy* to offer," said Mary, beaming.

Dahr said, "Sarah was so pleased to hear from you, Mrs. Questman. She'll thank you herself when she swings by after work to pick up our little princess here."

Olivia tugged the sleeve of Dahr's jacket. "I don't think I like that name anymore. Okay, Dahr?" She was apparently ditching not only the name, but the costumes as well. She wore a normal little frock, not as dressy as the charcoal pinafore she'd worn to the funeral—just a nice, cheery school dress well suited for a girl of seven.

Dahr told her, "Okay, punkin, I'll call you whatever you like."

With a sweet smile, she reminded him, "My name's Olivia."

"Got it, Olivia." He tousled her hair. "You'll be good today, right?"

She gave an earnest nod.

Dahr said to Mary, "Thanks so much for helping out. I need to get back now—just call the office if anything comes up." And he left the girl on the doorstep.

Mary took Olivia's hand and brought her inside. I closed the door. It was heartening to witness the change in the girl—her overall deportment as well as the clothes. She was as well mannered and deferential as she had been at the funeral, which I had assumed was the result of a stern lecture regarding "best behavior" that day. But now, two days later, it seemed the lesson had stuck.

I crouched to ask her, "What would you like to do this afternoon?"

Mary suggested, "We could have some milk and cookies. When I was little, that's what I liked after school. Berta baked them just today."

Olivia looked around. "Is Mister Puss here?"

Mary said, "He might be sleeping in the dining room. I think I saw him under the table. Tell you what: Mr. Norris and I were in the middle of talking about something important, so maybe you'd like to go visit Mister Puss while we finish up our business"—she wagged her jowls—"which is *very* dull stuff indeed."

Rising from my crouch, I said, "And then, later, we can all enjoy the cookies." I wondered what was in them. Surely, I thought, Mary and Berta had sense enough not to dope a child. I asked Olivia, "Sound like a plan?"

She nodded.

Mary and I moved off to the parlor, improvising chitchat as we paused in the doorway to watch Olivia take a few exploratory steps down the hallway. Finding the dining room, she went inside.

Mary lifted a finger, signaling me to wait while she slipped out of her suede pumps and placed them on the carpet inside the parlor. Then she led me on our stealth mission across the hallway's parquet flooring. Despite our best efforts, the floor emitted occasional quiet pops beneath our traversing feet, which moved with slow, short steps. A full minute passed before we arrived outside the dining room's double doors, one of which was wide open. Mary slipped into position against the wall.

I hid behind the closed door and peeped in through the opening of the other door. As Mary had suggested, Mister Puss was settled in a safe spot beneath the large table, near its middle, protected by a spindly forest of mahogany chair legs. He sat calmly in the recumbent sphinx position, with front paws extended. His eyes caught mine for a moment and blinked. Then he returned his careful gaze to Olivia.

She was busy dragging a few of the chairs away from the table, which would afford her a path of entry. When her way was cleared, she got down on all fours and began a slow crawl beneath the table, toward the cat. "It's just me, Mister Puss," she said in a loud whisper. "Don't be afraid."

His gaze didn't waver. He remained still as stone.

"I'm sorry I was mean. I won't play rough. Promise."

His eyes widened as she neared.

"Won't you be my friend?" When Olivia came within inches of Mister Puss, she settled on the floor facing him, mirroring his sphinx pose. She didn't have the cat's haunches, though, so her butt stuck up. With her hands extended on the carpet, she reached a pinkie to touch the tip of one of the cat's paws. He did not pull back, so she reached a little farther and stroked the velvety, ruddy fur. She told him, "You have such pretty little hands."

Mister Puss—a sucker, it seemed, for flattery—broke into a purr.

Olivia giggled, stretching her head closer to the cat.

As Mister Puss reached to give her a nose-kiss, his mouth drooped open and the purr gurgled loudly.

Laughing, Olivia reached under his chin and stroked his neck.

His purring intensified as he slid his snout up her cheek. When his nose reached her ear, they both froze briefly. All was quiet for a few seconds. Then Olivia began laughing again, telling the cat, "*No,* I don't think so."

Mary and I exchanged a curious glance.

Under the table, Olivia sat up, crossing her legs. Mister Puss stood, then stepped into her lap. She petted him; he purred. She gabbed about school and a game they had played and a new song they had learned, singing a few lines about the sun and Mercury and Venus and so on. Then she got quiet. After a long pause, she told the cat, "I've been so confused."

Mister Puss tilted his head up to her, as if asking, Why?

She said, "I feel bad for Mommy. She's so sad that Daddy died."

The cat leaned into Olivia's chest, as if offering a hug.

Olivia snapped out of her fleeting slump and told the cat about another song she'd learned at school. Then she sang some sprightly lines about counting by fives.

Mary caught my eye and shrugged.

With a jerk of my head, I implied we should retreat.

When we had tiptoed back to the parlor, Mary replaced her shoes. I called into the hall, "Where'd everybody go? Did you find Mister Puss, Olivia?"

"We're in *here,*" called the girl, followed by the sounds of some bumping and jostling as she got out from under the table.

When Mary and I strolled into the hall, Olivia darted out of the dining room to meet us, saying, "Mister Puss and I are friends now."

I said, "That's wonderful, Olivia."

Mary took the girl's hand. "Ready for some cookies?"

Olivia answered with an enthusiastic nod. As they headed toward the kitchen door, she said, "Mister Puss was *snoring.*"

Mary told her, "That's called 'purring,' Olivia. Cats purr."

"And guess what—Mister Puss *talked* to me."

"Oh, *did* he now?" said Mary with a hearty laugh. "And just what did he say?"

"He called me a *sasspot*. Isn't that funny?"

"Very funny," said Mary, sharing the child's laughter. "I have *no* idea where he picks up these things."

"Mrs. Questman?" said Olivia as they walked into the kitchen. "What's a sasspot?" The swinging door whooshed behind them and closed.

Mister Puss sauntered out of the dining room and crossed the hall to me, sitting at my feet.

I looked down, studying him.

He looked up, studying me. Then he reached his paws to my knees.

When I took him in my arms, he revved up his purr, climbed to my shoulder, and stretched his snout to my ear.

Did you get that?

Yes, I thought. I did indeed get that. I pondered Olivia's words: "I feel bad for Mommy. She's so sad that Daddy died."

Sheriff Simms needed to know what I'd been up to that afternoon, but a phone call or e-mail wouldn't cut it. What I wanted to discuss was both complicated and iffy. This would require some face time.

When I returned from Mary's to the office and called Simms to ask if we could meet that evening, he asked, "Is it urgent?"

"I'm not sure."

"Here's the thing, Brody: little Tommy has a pack meeting tonight."

I asked, "He has a ... what?"

Simms laughed. "Cub Scouts. He's new to it this year. There's a monthly pack meeting at the school hall, and I like to go with him. You know—the bonding thing."

"Of course, Thomas. But, um…"

"Look," he said, "I need to get him there by seven. Maybe we could stop at your place first, six-fifteen or six-thirty. Will that screw up your dinner?"

"Not at all—we'll make it work. Thanks, Thomas."

When I told Marson the plan, he said, "Don't worry about dinner. We can go out afterward, whenever you're ready." Then he asked, "Do you want me at home for this? If not, I could just stick around the office and catch up on a few things."

"Actually," I said, "I *would* like you at home for this. Simms will have little Tommy with him, and I'll be explaining how I eavesdropped on Olivia, who goes to school with Tommy, and—get the picture?"

"Got it. You might need me to distract the boy."

Grrring.

At the loft that night, around twenty past six, I answered the street door and greeted Sheriff Simms and his son.

Simms looked dapper as ever in a dark business suit, white shirt, and jaunty necktie. The suit appeared so fresh and unwrinkled, he must have changed out of his day duds before heading out for the evening. But Simms was never truly off duty; a polished leather shoulder holster glinted beneath the flap of his jacket.

Tommy looked adorable in his crisp blue uniform, with its yellow neckerchief, gold sliding clasp, and button-topped cap—which his father reminded him to remove as he stepped indoors. Tommy could have been a model for a recruiting poster, and the sheriff's pride in his little guy beamed from ear to ear.

And yet, I felt uneasy seeing Tommy like this. Inez, my radical-lesbian single mom, had not only raised me as a heathen, but had also instilled in me a dose of the pacifism she'd embraced during the Vietnam era. I recalled one day when we were picnicking in a local park, where a nearby table was occupied by a group of scouts, grilling hot dogs. As she eyed them with a disapproving gaze, she leaned to tell me from the corner of her mouth, "Putting kids in uniform. They teach'em young, and before you know it, they'll be a new crop of cannon fodder."

Knowing Thomas Simms, I was certain he had no such motive for putting his son in uniform. But still, the paramilitary overtones were unmistakable. And Tommy was only seven. In a sense, it struck me as the flip side of tarting up little girls—like Olivia in a princess dress.

Marson stepped over from the kitchen to greet our guests. After shaking Simms's hand, he turned to Tommy and, standing ramrod stiff, offered a comical salute, telling him, "Good evening, young man."

Tommy laughed. "Good evening, Mr. Miles." He offered his little hand and shook a few fingers of my husband's hand, which suddenly looked as big as a holiday ham.

Marson said, "I know you guys need to talk. Can I get you anything? Something to drink, Thomas?"

"Nah," said Simms, "but thanks."

Marson told me, "If you need anything, just holler." And he returned to the kitchen, where he fussed with something.

Simms, Tommy, and I settled around the low table in front of the fireplace with its rows of fake candles, which Marson had switched on. Simms said, "I'm all ears, Brody. What's this about?"

"Yesterday," I said, "Tommy had a play date with Olivia after school." The boy's head snapped in my direction. I continued, "And I understand it worked out pretty well, considering that the girl's behavior has been less than sterling lately."

"Right," said Simms, "Gloria told me all about it. Seems everything went fine." He turned to his son. "Right, Tommy?"

The boy nodded.

"So," I said, "Mary Questman asked Olivia's mother if she'd like to send the girl over to play with Mister Puss after school today. I was there, too."

"Nice. How'd it go?"

Tommy's attention ping-ponged from his father to me, following our every word. I called over my shoulder, "Uh, Marson?"

He stepped over to us. "Yes?"

I said, "Tommy's never seen the loft before. I'll bet he'd enjoy having a look from upstairs. Maybe give him the grand tour?"

"Happily. Come on, Tommy." And Marson led the boy over to the spiral stairs, explaining that the space had once been a haberdashery.

"A what?" asked Tommy as they started clunking up the metal stairs.

Smiling, Simms leaned in my direction. "Okay, coast is clear. What happened?"

With a grin, I told him, "The whole setup was pretty slick."

Simms laughed. "You *set up* that sweet little child?"

"Yes. I wanted to give her some alone-time with Mister Puss. Children sometimes speak more openly with pets than with grown-ups."

"So you set her up with the cat—and then *spied* on her?"

"You bet. So did Mary. We heard every word. It was mostly just kid talk—goofy gabbing and singing—but finally, Olivia said something I'd call *relevant*."

"Oh?" said Simms, getting interested. He pulled out his notebook and readied his pen. "What did she say?"

"She had sort of a 'down' moment, telling Mister Puss that she's been confused lately. Then she told him, 'I feel bad for

Mommy. She's so sad that Daddy died."

Simms made note of it, then studied it. He shrugged. "So? Makes sense."

"Don't you see—?" I started to ask, but then Simms's phone made an urgent-sounding racket.

He whipped it out and answered. "Simms. What's up?"

I turned in my seat and glanced up to the mezzanine, where Marson stood with Tommy at the railing, giving an animated lecture on some aspect of the rehab.

"Okay, what's the address?" said Simms, jotting on his pad. "I'll be there in a couple minutes." He hung up and told me, "Thwarted robbery—under control, but I should get over there." Then he thwacked his head. "Tommy. The pack meeting."

Too quickly, I suggested, "I'll take him, Thomas. Happy to help." What was I *thinking*?

Simms stood and called up to the mezzanine, "Tommy? Daddy's gotta run—it's important. But Mr. Norris will take you to the meeting. I'll meet up with you as soon as I can, okay?"

"Okay, Dad."

All right. I hadn't eaten, but had been looking forward to a night out with my refined and sensitive husband, expecting a leisurely meal somewhere nice, somewhere quiet. And now, instead, I was in the car with a boy in uniform buckled up securely in the backseat, driving him to a long meeting in a grubby school hall that would be swarming with possibly hundreds of other little men in uniforms, with their sashes and their merit badges and whatnot. I also envisioned their potbellied fathers tagging along in their quest for a second childhood, looking ridiculous in their stretched old uniforms, popping their buttons, strutting their stuff, redolent with the musk of heterosexuality.

Or was I being too harsh?

If Tommy Simms was in any way typical of current-day scouting, he was a fine tribute to the organization. While plying the dark streets of Dumont, I looked over my shoulder to ask him, "So, Tommy—what have you been doing in Cub Scouts?"

"Learning to fold the flag."

I imagined my mother's voice in my ear: Uh-huh? What did I tell you, Brody?

"But now we've started a new project," said Tommy. "I'm building a birdhouse out of Popsicle sticks."

"Really? How do you do that?"

"It takes a lot of glue and shellac."

"I'll bet it does."

He asked, "Mr. Norris? What's shellac?"

I thought hard before admitting, "I have no idea." We both laughed. Then I asked, "So you've been eating a lot of Popsicles lately?"

He shook his head. "They got a big bag of the sticks somewhere. They're all clean."

A few minutes later, I slowed the car as we pulled into the school parking lot and found one of the few remaining spaces—between a pristine pickup with a jacked-up suspension, and a hunting van with a camouflage paint job, plastered with trout decals. I really wasn't sure how to handle this. Would I have to pledge allegiance?

I parked, killed the engine, and unsnapped my seatbelt. "Well, Tommy, let's do it." I was about to open the door when I glanced in the mirror and noticed that the boy hadn't moved. He was still strapped in, sitting perfectly still. I turned in my seat, asking, "Something wrong, Tommy?"

His head was lowered. "Can I ask you something, Mr. Norris?"

I reached back to pat his knee. "Of course."

"Back at your house, you told my dad that you saw Olivia this afternoon."

"That's right," I said. "Mrs. Questman and I thought she'd enjoy a visit after school—the way she went to your house yesterday."

The boy looked up at me. "I was just wondering if maybe she told *you* the same thing she told *me*."

"I'm not sure, Tommy. What did she tell you?"

He hesitated. "I think it might be kinda dirty."

With sudden apprehension, I asked quietly, "What did she say?"

"I don't know what she meant, but she said—" He broke off, hesitating again, and then told me, "Olivia was talking about her dad, and she said, 'His penis was icky.' She said, 'It hurt me.'"

I felt as if all the oxygen had been sucked from the car. I felt the blood pulsing in my temples as my mind raced to piece together the events of the weekend when Jason Ward was murdered.

When I could summon the breath to speak, I asked Tommy, "Have you mentioned this to your father?"

"Gosh no, Mr. Norris. I'd *never* tell him that. He wouldn't like it."

15

When that exhausting day at last came to an end—after the pack meeting, after regrouping with Sheriff Simms, after deciding on our next steps, and after a late meal with Marson at a loud, bright Applebee's because everywhere else had closed— when at last I bedded down with my husband and kissed him good night, I feared that my mind would never stop spinning, that I would never fall asleep.

But I was wrong. I drifted off quickly. And my sleep was unperturbed by dreams of the murder or its method or its motive. In fact, it seemed as if I didn't dream at all that night—a peculiar sensation that I had experienced only once before, as a young boy, when I was four or five, when I had gone to bed, fallen asleep, turned over, and opened my eyes to discover the broad daylight of morning, as if no time whatever had passed during the night, as if I had rocketed from one day to the next.

Now, Friday morning, I awoke upstairs in the loft—dazzled by the brightness from the skylights, wondering where Marson had gone, puzzled by the sound and the smell of coffee brewing downstairs, and bewildered by the very same sense of accelerated time travel that had astonished me as a child. More surprising still, this existential fast-forward had left me suffering no queasy effects of jet lag, as one might assume, but quite the opposite. I felt thoroughly rested, refreshed, and ready to take on the important events of the day ahead.

I shrugged into a robe and wound my way down the spiral stairs.

Marson looked up at me from the kitchen island. "Hark," he said. "Has my Sleeping Beauty at long last arisen?" He was dressed and primped for the office, lingering with his coffee and the morning paper.

I padded over to him for a kiss, then poured a mug of coffee. "What a weird night," I said. "I was so whipped, I didn't even dream."

"You were dead to the world when I got up, so I didn't want to rouse you. How do you feel?"

I clinked my mug to his. "Raring to go." Glancing down at the front page of the *Register*, I noticed the headline of the daily election update: EARLY VOTING BEGINS MONDAY MORN-ING. Sheriff Simms now had a mere seventy-two hours to convince the people of Dumont that he was better suited than Deputy Kastle to serve as the county's top lawman. And the most efficient means of achieving that was to name Dr. Jason Ward's killer.

It was shortly after eight o'clock. I assumed Simms had already arrived at headquarters, so I phoned his office.

Taking the call, he said, "Hey, Brody. Can you be here at ten?"

"Sure."

"Late last night, I had a long talk with Heather Vance," he said, referring to the medical examiner. "And just a few minutes ago, I phoned both Frumpkin and his daughter, telling them that Heather needs help with a few questions regarding some newly discovered physical evidence. I said we'd like to meet at ten."

"How'd they react?"

"Frumpkin was sorta flustered, but cooperative. Sarah just seemed annoyed, since the short notice meant they'd have to cancel several patients. But she agreed to come. She said, 'If it'll help get to the bottom of this, I'll be there.'"

A few minutes before ten, I arrived outside the sheriff's office, and a deputy showed me in, leading me back to the conference room with the big windows, the dusty bookshelves, and the cracked, inscrutable old painting that depicted a man with a horse and a monkey.

Already present was Heather Vance, who stood at the table, digging through files in a bulging briefcase, as well as Simms, who paced the room, checking something on his phone. I greeted Heather with a hug and Simms with a handshake, telling them, "Thanks for letting me sit in today."

They glanced at each other. Deadpan, Simms told me, "It wouldn't be quite the same without you."

While we were still standing, comparing notes, the deputy opened the door again to admit Dr. Francis Frumpkin and Sarah Frumpkin Ward. The doctor had apparently begun the process of emerging from his grief, as his snappy outfit was no longer muted by the somber hues of the funeral, but had blossomed anew with the silken jewel tones more typical of his splashy wardrobe. His daughter's attire, which never varied much, was still as drab in grief as it had been in happier times, but the lines that etched her face made it plain that her healing had not yet begun.

The doctor shook Simms's hand. "It was a wonderful surprise to get your call this morning, Sheriff. It seems you've made some progress?"

"Maybe. I hope so. I'd like to get this wrapped up for you."

Frumpkin countered, "And I'd like to get it wrapped up for *you*. The election's only three days away, you know."

Simms grinned. "Yeah. I heard."

Heather introduced herself to Sarah. "I'm so sorry for your

loss, Mrs. Ward. All of us in the medical examiner's office are deeply committed to resolving your late husband's case."

Sarah managed a weak smile. "Thank you, Heather. My father and I appreciate your efforts. I understand you have some new evidence."

"Well," said Heather, "it seems so. That's what we need to talk about—that's why we're all here."

"Excellent," said Dr. Frumpkin. He turned to Simms. "Where would you like us to sit, Sheriff?"

"Wherever you want," said Simms. "Please, make yourselves comfortable."

Frumpkin didn't hesitate to choose the chair at the head of the table, seating himself beneath the cryptic, yellowed painting. He extended his arms and comfortably gripped both corners of the table that extended before him, as if signaling his permission for the rest of us to carry on.

Sarah took a chair adjacent to him, along the side of the table.

Simms seated Heather Vance at the other end of the table, facing Frumpkin. Then Simms and I sat across from each other, with Simms adjacent to Heather. He laid an attaché case on the table and opened it, removing his notebook and a few folders.

"Now, then," said Frumpkin, taking charge and checking his watch, as if wanting to move things along, "what's this all about? The sheriff said something about 'newly discovered physical evidence,' I believe. That leads me to assume you have some late test results from the postmortem."

With the slightest turn of his head, Simms deferred to Heather Vance.

She said, "Actually, Dr. Frumpkin, we have no new test results. What we do have, however, is a whole new theory as to how—and why—your son-in-law died." She paused.

Frumpkin tossed his arms. "Then let's hear it."

Heather turned to me. "Care to explain this, Brody?"

I said to Frumpkin, "Let's back up a bit. Since the day of Jason's death, we had a fairly sound theory regarding how he died in the hyperbaric chamber. Sarah herself suggested it—he was administered something other than oxygen. And we quickly determined that, yes, the gas lines had been rigged and Jason died of asphyxiation by nitrous oxide. That's the 'how,' the means of murder and the cause of death—clean and simple."

Frumpkin nodded. "Nothing new about that."

"But," I continued, "the 'how,' the means of murder, always has a corollary—namely, opportunity. And early on, we determined it was necessary for Jason's killer to have had the opportunity to rig the gas lines on the night before the murder. That's the only way it could have happened."

"All right," said Frumpkin. "Old news, if you ask me."

"Which leaves us with only one other major variable," I said. "The 'why,' the motive. We determined that this tragedy could not have been an accident, so someone *must* have had a very strong reason for wanting Jason dead."

Sarah, Jason's widow, looked at me with tears welling in her eyes. "How can you possibly *say* that? Why would *anyone* want to kill my husband?"

I told her, "I admit, that question has been the sticking point all along. We've identified a whole field of *plausible* suspects with *plausible* motives, some of them checking one or both of the other boxes, but none of them truly nailing all three—motive, means, and opportunity." I paused. "Until yesterday."

Frumpkin and his daughter shared a quizzical glance. They both brightened a bit.

"You mean you've *solved* it?" asked Sarah.

With a trace of skepticism, Frumpkin said, "Tell us more."

I hesitated. Now it would get difficult. "I spent some time

with little Olivia yesterday afternoon."

Sarah flashed me a smile. "I know. It was kind of you and Mary to look after her."

"And then," I said, "last evening, I spent some time with Tommy Simms."

Sarah turned her smile to the Sheriff. "It was sweet of Gloria to offer the play date with Tommy. Please thank her for me."

Simms returned Sarah's smile and gave her a nod.

Dr. Frumpkin asked me, "But what does Olivia have to do with any of this?"

"Plenty, I'm afraid." With a woeful shake of my head, I added, "Way too much."

Getting testy, Frumpkin said, "What the hell are you talking about?"

Sarah asked, "Why would you try to drag my daughter into this? She lost her father—she's a *victim* of what happened."

"Yes, Sarah," I said. "And she was also a victim *before* it happened."

Frumpkin blustered, "You're talking in riddles, Brody."

There was no more dancing around it. So I braced myself and said it: "We're fairly certain that Jason had been abusing Olivia—sexually."

Frumpkin and Sarah froze for a moment before rising and screaming at me in unison. He: "You're out of your fucking mind!" She: "That's a *vicious* lie!"

I told them calmly, "You need to hear this." There must have been something in my voice, in its surety, that penetrated their rage and sapped their outburst. Dazed, they both sat and listened as I began to lay out my theory:

"From the moment when I first encountered Olivia, two weeks ago today, at the FlabberGas pitch session at Mary's house, I was mystified by the girl's odd manner and terrible behavior, which struck me as something more serious than a childhood 'phase,' as Sarah described it. And each successive encounter only struck me as more bizarre. Then, yesterday at Mary's, after school, Olivia had a private conversation with Mister Puss, which Mary and I overheard. She told the cat, 'I feel bad for Mommy. She's so sad that Daddy died.' Now, when you think about it, isn't that remarkable?"

"Remarkable?" said Frumpkin. "What would you expect her to say?"

I looked Frumpkin in the eye. "I'd *expect* her to say: 'I'm so sad that Daddy died. I miss him.' But instead she said, in effect: 'I'm so sad that Mommy misses Daddy.' It doesn't take much digging to find Olivia's subtext. She was really saying: 'I'm not sad that Daddy died. I don't miss him.'"

"Preposterous," said Frumpkin.

"I don't think so. In fact, I found her words so extraordinary, it made me wonder how Olivia could possibly react that way to the death of her own father—her parent and protector. But then, last night, I was alone in my car with Tommy Simms, and he confided something to me that not only confirmed a horrible suspicion, but nearly made me ill with the scope of its depravity. He told me that during his play date with Olivia, she was talking about her father, and she said, 'His penis was icky.' She said, 'It hurt me.'"

Sarah planted an elbow on the table and dropped her forehead into her hand.

Frumpkin insisted, "Kids don't say 'penis.' When I was seven, I called it my—"

"Dad," said Sarah without looking at him, "times have changed. We raised Olivia to speak of anatomy without the priggish euphemisms."

"Even so," said Frumpkin, "kids make things up. They live in a make-believe world."

"Some do," I acknowledged, "but if I know Sheriff Simms and his son—which I certainly do—I know that Tommy would never lie about such an important matter. As for Olivia, I don't know her well enough to vouch for her honesty, but why on earth would a seven-year-old accuse her apparently loving father of rape unless it were true? Where would someone so young even get the *idea* unless it were true?"

Frumpkin had no answer. Sarah seemed unable to raise her head from her hand.

"Further," I said, "there was a strange and troubling incident I'd rather not even broach, but I'm afraid it's highly germane. This past Monday, Sarah, you came to my loft to let me know that the FlabberGas project was officially cancelled. It was in the afternoon, after school, so you brought Olivia with you. I was cat-sitting Mister Puss for Mary Questman that day, and Olivia went up to the mezzanine to play with him. You saw what happened—she threatened to drop him over the railing. Later, while you were leaving, she said Mister Puss tried to bite her. But she didn't tell us why. I have reason to believe that she attempted to insert her finger into the cat."

No one was expecting *that*—everyone at the table gave me a wide-eyed stare.

I explained, "It's a well-documented pattern that young children who are victims of rape often play-act the abuse they're suffering as a silent cry for help. In fact, all of Olivia's history of bad behavior over the last several months, all of her 'acting out'—she wasn't just going through a childhood phase. *All* of that was a cry for help, but the only one who understood it was her father."

Tears now streamed down Sarah's face in tacit recognition of the truth of my words.

"Think back again," I said to Dr. Frumpkin, "to the pitch session at Mary's. When Olivia arrived, you asked her to give

Grampa a kiss. She skipped over to you and delivered the kiss. But then Jason also asked for a kiss, saying, 'Hey, princess, what about Daddy?' And Olivia backed off, refusing."

Frumpkin bowed his head. "Good God," he mumbled.

Sarah looked up. "Those damned princess dresses, they were *his* idea—Jason's."

"I'll just bet they were," I said. "And since the funeral, those princess dresses have disappeared, and so has Olivia's erratic behavior. Yesterday afternoon, she was a perfect little lady. An amazing transition—but it's easily explained as the result of her knowledge that the monster in her life is now dead and buried."

Frumpkin sucked a bubble of snot from his upper lip.

I said to Sarah, "This past week, you've had a hard time adjusting to Olivia's after-school hours. Dahr Ahmadi mentioned to me that her schedule hadn't been an issue before Jason died. How come?"

Sarah raised her puffy, reddened eyes to the ceiling, saying nothing.

Frumpkin answered for her. "Jason arranged his schedule to come into the office early and leave by three. Sarah stayed till five. Meaning"—Frumpkin choked—"meaning, each afternoon, at home, Jason had two hours alone with Olivia."

"And there you have it," I said.

Frumpkin trembled with his conflicting emotions of grief and rage, telling the room, blaring to the heavens, "Why, it's *horrifying*. It's *disgusting*."

"It's more than that," I told him. "It's a strong motive for murder—by the one person whose every instinct commanded her to protect her daughter."

As the weight of my words sank in, all heads turned to Sarah. But the only gaze she returned was mine. She said, "You're out of your mind. You may be right about Jason—which is totally shocking, if it's true. And if it *is* true, you may be right that I would've been tempted to protect Olivia at any price. But the point is, Brody, until today, I had *no* idea this was going on. I'm stunned."

"No," I said, "I think the moment you were stunned took place two weeks ago, on Saturday, in Green Bay, when you took Olivia to see Dr. Hammond, the renowned child psychologist you'd been trying to book for so long. The day before, at the pitch session, you described how you and Jason had been taking Olivia to appointments with several doctors, none of whom seemed able to get to the root of her problem, so you'd been especially eager to get her in with Dr. Hammond, which wasn't easy. And suddenly, he had a last-minute opening on Saturday—when Jason couldn't go along because he was booked up with his own patients. So you insisted on taking Olivia to see Dr. Hammond by yourself. And when you were there, without Jason for a change, that's when Olivia finally opened up. Right?"

"We, uh"—she waffled—"we didn't end up going that day after all."

"I think you did, which is easily checked. And while you were there, Olivia said something, maybe not enough to tip off Dr. Hammond, but *you* understood her, or maybe you coaxed more out of her during the ride back. Either way, by the time you got home, you were determined that Jason would never harm your daughter again. Then, late that afternoon, I phoned to let you know that Mary Questman had backed out as the volunteer guinea pig for the next day's FlabberGas demo. On the spot, while I was still on the phone, you recruited Jason as Mary's stand-in. That evening, you went over to the surgical center to take care of some supposedly forgotten last-minute preparations, switching the gas feed to the hyperbaric chamber—and leaving the outside door to the gas closet unlocked, to spread suspicion. And then finally, on Sunday, you watched coldly as your husband drifted off, not in the mild euphoria of an oxygen buzz, but in a massive, suffocating overdose of nitrous oxide." I paused for effect before concluding, "You had the means, you had the opportunity, and most important, Sarah, you had an overwhelming motive to protect your daughter by killing her father."

Sarah smirked. "You're *so* sure of yourself. You think you've figured out every little detail. But you're pulling this out of thin air."

"No, I'm not. I admit, I didn't have an inkling you were involved until just recently. But as early as the day after the murder, you said something that didn't make sense to me, and I wasn't sure why. We were here in this room with Sheriff Simms, and you mentioned that you'd kept Olivia home from school that day. You said she seemed surprised by that, and you explained that you were concerned about how her classmates might react to the news—you were afraid all the fuss might disturb Olivia."

Sarah shot me a stupefied expression. "So?"

I looked her in the eye. "When a little girl's father dies on Sunday, you keep her home from school on Monday because she's *sick*—sick with *grief*—not because the fuss might disturb her. You, however, understood the bigger picture. You knew that your daughter wasn't grieving at all."

She spit her words: "You're full of *shit*."

Frumpkin, looking drained and destroyed, patted Sarah's arm. "Honey," he said, "things are bad enough. Don't make it worse."

"But it *did* get worse," I told him. "Did you know that, two days ago, someone tried to kill me?"

Staring at me, aghast, he asked quietly, "You, Brody? Why would anyone—"

I explained to him what had happened outside the veterinarian's office, in my car, with the laughing gas. "And the *reason*," I continued, "was because Jason Ward's killer was afraid I was getting too close to the truth. On Monday, when Sarah visited me at the loft, I assured her that the investigation of Jason's murder was 'focusing on a new lead,' one that 'checks all the boxes,' and I noticed that she seemed more agitated than relieved by this news. Then on Tuesday, after the funeral, Sheriff Simms told her, 'This is starting to move fast now. Brody's been a huge help. We're getting to the bottom of everything.' And once again, her reaction seemed odd. At the time, I had no reason to suspect her, but now I understand that I should have. In fact, I should have *feared* her, because on Wednesday she tried to set up a *second* murder with nitrous oxide. I assume she simply followed me when I left my office that morning, not knowing where I was going, but waiting for the opportunity to strike—and then finding it when I went inside the vet's office."

Dr. Frumpkin removed from his jacket a flowing pocket square of crimson silk and blotted his eyes with it, then wiped his nose. "Sarah honey," he said, "this can't be true. *Please* tell me none of this happened."

Instead, she said, "I had to do *something*, didn't I? Of *course* they were getting too close to the truth. But going after the sheriff would be too risky. I thought Brody would be easier to deal with."

"Well, *thanks.*" Indignant, I asked, "You intended to pick me off because I was the low-hanging fruit?"

"In a manner of speaking, yes, I suppose you were."

Sheriff Simms had not said a word since we'd all sat down. But now he spoke. "Sarah," he said, taking a small recorder out of his case and setting it on the table, "I wonder if you'd mind repeating that for me—on the record." Then he recited her rights and switched on the gadget.

At the far end of the table, Dr. Frumpkin wept.

Over his shoulder, however, the monkey danced.

16

News traveled fast. That Friday afternoon, the *Dumont Daily Register* broke the story on its website, and within minutes, word began to spread through town—and beyond—via social media. On Saturday morning, the *Register* published a full report in its print edition.

Early voting just two days away

Sheriff Simms, amid "shocking revelations," arrests alleged FlabberGas killer

Compiled from *Register* staff reports

•

OCT. 23, DUMONT, WI—The race to solve the two-week mystery of Dr. Jason Ward's bizarre murder came to a stunning finish on Friday when Dumont County sheriff Thomas Simms arrested Dr. Ward's widow, Sarah Frumpkin Ward, and charged her with the crime.

Sheriff Simms reported that Mrs. Ward was taken into custody peaceably at his office yesterday morning after she was confronted with an accumulation of circumstantial evidence, which he described as "solidly convincing." When asked about the motive for the murder, Simms declined to give details, stating, "The particulars of this case are extremely sensitive, with a child's welfare involved. The shocking revelations that led to the arrest will be aired in due time before a judge and jury."

The murder case has taken on added significance in Dumont, as its timing has become a factor in the community's upcoming election for county sheriff. The incumbent in that office, Thomas Simms, has faced a surprisingly strong challenge from one of his own deputies, Alex Kastle, whose campaign strategy has focused on framing the election as a test of Simms's competence in solving the so-called FlabberGas murder.

That tactic, however, appears to have backfired for Kastle. As word spread yesterday that the mystery had been solved, the *Register* sent its reporting team back to the local Walmart to sample the mood of shoppers in the aisles. The voters we polled were unanimous in their praise of Sheriff Simms.

Emily Schmidtt, mother of two preschoolers who rode in her cart, echoed the responses of many others, telling us, "I've always liked Thomas Simms. I never doubted for a minute that he'd pass this test, which wasn't very fair to begin with. His deputy should be ashamed. Bottom line: four more years."

"Four more years" was a sentiment expressed over and over ...

Sunday morning, I awoke upstairs at the loft, with Marson still dozing deeply at my side. All was quiet, except for the lullaby rumble of the furnace. And the room felt unusually warm. I couldn't recall having woken up to the sound of the furnace in an overheated room since the prior winter—it meant that the night had turned very cold.

In the nearly two years since I'd moved to Dumont, I'd learned to recognize signs of the transitions between four distinct seasons, which had been more of a blur throughout my earlier life in Southern California. But now, overnight, there'd been a hard freeze.

Winter wasn't here yet. This was just a foretaste, a warning. There would still be warmer days, even a few hot ones—Indian summer, as they called it here. But the first hard freeze was a turning point.

Like it or not, it marked a new beginning. And it wasn't only the weather that had changed that weekend. The mystery of Jason Ward's murder had been solved. The trajectory of Sarah Frumpkin Ward's life had been derailed and sent down an uncertain but ominous course. Sheriff Simms's election challenger had been all but vanquished. And my brief foray into amateur sleuthing had come to an end. I could now return to my true calling. No longer would this mild-mannered architect tussle with the vagaries of murder or justice or death threats. No longer would I flirt with such nonsensical notions as gas clinics or infidelity—or talking cats.

On that cold morning, I woke up to reality. I woke up to my *own* reality. Brody Norris, architect. Brody Norris, husband of Marson Miles.

I rolled over to kiss him good morning.

He stirred, asking groggily, "Time to get up, kiddo?"

"It's early," I said. "Sleep all you like. I'll start the coffee."

I threw on a robe and traipsed down the stairs. The view of the street through the big front windows was frosty and still, with not a trace of green remaining on the trees; all the leaves were yellow or brown or gone. Swinging through the kitchen, I switched on the coffeemaker, then heard its first few gurgles as I crossed the main room to the front door.

When I opened it, the rush of dry, arctic air made the hair bristle on my legs and arms. I stooped to retrieve the morning paper, grabbed it, and ducked inside, thumping the door closed behind me.

Back in the kitchen, I set the bulky Sunday edition of the *Dumont Daily Register* on the granite countertop. The paper flopped open, revealing a rare front-page editorial. Headline: FOUR MORE YEARS.

Mary Questman had invited a small group of friends to her home that morning for a casual brunch, beginning at eleven. When Marson and I arrived in his Range Rover and parked at the curb, Glee Savage pulled up behind us in her vintage fuchsia hatchback, greeting us with a toot of the horn.

"*Brody* love," she gushed, hugging me as we stood in the street. "I understand *you* came up with the breakthrough that cracked the case." The steam of her breath mingled with ours, forming a tiny cloud of conversation in the chilled morning air, like a dialogue bubble in a newspaper cartoon.

I said, "Sheriff Simms seemed grateful. But it was his case, and he welcomed my input. I'm not looking for any credit. Just glad to help him out."

Marson added, "Glad to help him out—and get him reelected."

"Bingo," said Glee. "A double win for Dumont."

Marson told her, "I saw your big story this morning about the orchestra's fund-raiser—ought to be fun."

"My, yes," she said, "the anniversary ball should be *quite* the gala. And did you notice my interview yesterday with the Dumont Players' new executive director?"

"We did," I said. "Great to see that you're back on the arts beat—and on solid ground with the paper. After that Flabber-Gas blowup, we were concerned."

"So was I, sweets. But the only way I'm leaving the *Register* is feet-first." She stepped between us and locked arms with both of us. "Come on. It's cold out here." Then she marched us up the walkway to Mary's front door.

Berta answered when we rang and shooed us indoors, instructing us, "Don't let the cold air in."

Marson gave me a look. Yes, Berta could be impertinent. But she was loyal and caring, an important presence in Mary Questman's later life.

While Glee fished inside her big purse and extracted a bag of cookies, handing them to Berta, Mary trundled down the hall to greet us, tailed by Mister Puss.

"Marson dear"—one kiss—"and Brody dear"—another kiss— "how wonderful to see you this morning. We should do brunch more often."

Mister Puss nuzzled my shins as I said to Mary, "So kind of you to invite us."

Marson gave her a petite wrapped package, a hostess trinket.

She thanked us with a warm smile. "Well, it's a bit of a celebration, isn't it?"

Glee said, "*I* certainly think so," as Berta reappeared with a tray of filled champagne glasses. Glee plucked one and held it aloft.

"Then again," said Mary, weighing her words, "I know it's a terrible time for the Frumpkin family. It's a relief to have the crime solved, but I'm sorry things turned out the way they did."

"Blind justice," said Glee, hand on hip.

Mary said, "Given what's happened, I wasn't sure if I should include Francis today, but then I thought, Do unto others. So I invited him."

Glee looked stricken. Her last couple of encounters with Dr. Frumpkin had not gone well—they'd been explosive.

"But he declined," said Mary. Glee downed a gulp of bubbly as Mary continued, "He did ask, though, if he could send his friend instead—his nurse? I believe the young man's name is Dahr."

"Really?" I asked. "Dahr's coming? Nice." I tried the champagne.

"Delightful," added Marson.

"And of course the Simms family. They'll be along right after church." Mary then led us to the living room, where we could await the arrival of the others.

Mister Puss followed at my heels as I took a seat on one of the sofas. Marson sat a few inches away from me, on the adjacent cushion. Mister Puss hopped up between us, negotiating the crack.

"Is he bothering you?" asked Mary.

"Not at all." I twiddled the cat's ears. He purred.

When the doorbell rang, Mister Puss stayed put, rather than darting out to the hall. A few moments later, Berta showed Dahr Ahmadi into the living room. Everyone rose; the cat plopped down to the floor.

Dahr looked great—as always—though a bit somber, in light of recent events. He greeted Mary with a tidy bouquet of autumn flowers, which she passed off to Berta while thanking Dahr and welcoming him.

Marson and I greeted him with hugs—no kisses today—and expressed our sorrow for the horrible outcome of the Flabber-Gas calamity.

When we were all seated, he told us, "Francis asked me to send his regrets. He'd like to be with you today, but he's deeply shaken. The murder was awful enough, but now, with Sarah's role in it—I'm surprised he can even find the strength to breathe."

Everyone mumbled words of understanding.

"But you know what?" asked Dahr. His features brightened some as he said, "There's that old truism: every cloud has a silver lining. When Jason was killed two weeks ago, Francis lost his colleague and his son-in-law, and it seemed that things couldn't get much worse. But now, Francis has lost his daughter as well. It's hard to say what Sarah's chances are before the law. There may be some leniency in the matter of Jason's murder—the incest, the mother's instinct to protect her child—but Sarah won't just walk away from this with a rap on the wrist. Plus, she tried to kill Brody, which has *no* arguable defense. Even in the best-case scenario, even if Sarah gets off easy, it could take *years* to grind through the legal machinery. Beyond that, her future is permanently disrupted. So Francis feels, regardless of how everything plays out, that he's already lost his daughter."

Marson said, "I hesitate to ask, but what's the silver lining?" I was wondering the same thing. This did *not* sound like the preamble to a happy ending.

"Oddly," said Dahr, "the silver lining is little Olivia."

We must have looked aghast. Olivia was a seven-year-old victim of repeated incest whose father had been murdered by her avenging mother, now behind bars. Olivia's troubles were far from over.

Dahr acknowledged, "Olivia has already suffered way more than *any* child could be expected to endure. She needs sympathy and respect, she needs tons of therapy, she needs love and reassurance." Dahr paused. "And she needs parents."

Marson and I glanced at each other. Aha. Was there indeed a happy ending to be snatched from the depths of this tragedy?

Dahr smiled. "Francis and I have been involved for quite a while now, and he's always wanted to take it to the next level—a committed future together. But he's never seen children in our future, which I've wanted. Now, though, his granddaughter needs him badly, and he needs *me* to help complete a little family for the girl. We've talked about it nonstop since Friday, when Sarah was arrested, when everything changed for both Olivia and Francis. We've agreed: Francis and I will become Olivia's 'two daddies.' He's with her right now."

Marson and I—Mary and Glee—we all stood and rushed

to Dahr with open arms, who laughed as he rose to receive our group hug, our best wishes, our congratulations. I had never quite been able to imagine Dahr settling down with Frumpkin, but now it seemed that, although they were an unlikely match, their coupling would work beautifully for all concerned.

Mary asked, "Will you live here in Dumont?"

Mister Puss wandered into our circle, looking up from face to face.

"Yes, Mrs. Questman, at least at first. But after Sarah's fate is known, we may rethink things. Francis has been looking forward to a 'chapter two' in California, and maybe that'll make sense for the three of us."

Marson asked, "Francis is ready to retire?"

"Yeah," said Dahr with a single nod. "He's been flirting with it anyway, but now, you bet, he's ready to close shop. The Milwaukee office, he'll sell out to his partners. The Dumont practice, that'll disappear quickly."

Glee said, "I don't suppose *any* of this is intended for public consumption?"

We all shot her a look. I said, "Don't press your luck, honey."

The doorbell rang. As Berta barreled out of the kitchen to answer it, the rest of us, including the cat, filed into the hall to greet the Simmses.

"Welcome, Thomas," lilted Mary as the Sheriff stepped inside with his wife and their son. "And congratulations." We all joined in a round of hoots and applause.

"Thank you, Miss Mary, but don't jinx it—the election's not over till it's over."

Mary tittered. "I was talking about the *murder* case."

"Oh, that," said Simms. "Just between you and me? That was pretty much Brody's doing."

I saw Glee digging for her notebook and stopped her with a

glare of warning.

"Nonsense," I told Simms. "And the election? I have a hunch congratulations won't jinx it."

Gloria Simms leaned into the conversation, beaming. "I think you're right, Brody. Thomas won't tell you, but he got a hero's welcome at church today." Then she turned to their young son. "Don't you have something for Mrs. Questman, sweetie?"

He looked so adorable in his Sunday best—ten years from now, that kid would be breaking hearts all over Dumont. He lifted a small box, Tiffany blue with a white satin bow. Offering it to Mary, he said, "This is for you, Mrs. Questman."

Mary scooched down to take it from his hands. "Why, *thank* you, Tommy. I can't wait to open this later."

Bright-eyed, he told her, "You can open it now, if you want."

Rising, Mary glanced at Tommy's smiling parents, who gave subtle nods. Then she pulled the bow open and lifted the lid from the box. "How absolutely *darling*," she gushed, setting the box aside and showing us a little broach that looked like a sleek, golden cat swatting at a ball, which was a pearl.

Tommy said, "It looks like Mister Puss!"

"It certainly does," agreed Mary.

Everyone moved closer to peer at it, marveling at the resemblance. I hoisted Mister Puss from the floor, asking him, "What do you think?"

Purring, he nosed the pin for a moment, then crawled to my shoulder. While the others gabbed merrily, he reached my ear.

I've seen better.

Mary asked the sheriff, "Could you help me pin it on, Thomas?"

"Gladly, Miss Mary. There now. Hope you'll enjoy wearing it."

"I *love* wearing it, but I wish you hadn't done this. It's far too generous."

Simms crossed his arms. "Miss Mary. I could *never* repay all you've done for me. No exaggeration—you helped save my job."

So did Mister Puss, I thought.

Berta leaned to tell Mary, "Everything's ready."

And we all chattered as Mary led us into her gracious dining room, where the long table had been draped in white linen and set for nine. Arranged down the center were flowers, including the ones Dahr had brought, and pitchers of this and that, as well as a champagne bucket, plus an array of serving dishes brimming with all manner of brunch items, elegantly garnished and perfectly presented.

Mary took the single chair at the head of the table, saying, "Nothing formal today, nothing fancy, just friends. Please sit wherever you'd like."

When we had arranged ourselves around the table, there were eight of us—Mary, Glee, Dahr, the three Simmses, Marson, and me—so one chair remained vacant. Berta stepped over from the sideboard to ask Mary, "Are we expecting someone else?"

"No"—Mary's glance circled the table—"I don't think so."

Berta indicated the empty chair. "Who's sitting there—His Majesty?"

We chuckled as Mister Puss sauntered from the base of Mary's chair to sniff at the empty seat.

"Actually, Berta," said Mary, "I was hoping to convince you to join us today."

"Gosh, Mary, no—I couldn't."

"Why not? Everything's ready. Nothing left to do but eat it."

Glee piped in, "Come on, Bert. Join the party."

The rest of us cajoled her as well, even Marson, who told her, "It's all your doing anyway."

Berta hesitated. "Suit yourself," she said, pulling out the last chair and sitting.

As everyone settled into the convivial mood of our gathering, we sampled the various dishes set before us, all the products of Berta's kitchen wizardry: chicken quenelles, baked eggs with ham, a layered concoction of French toast with bacon and syrupy fruit, and a cheesy feel-good casserole studded with sausage—liberally spiced with something like oregano. More than once, Mary told us, "Save room for dessert. You'll *love* Berta's brownies."

Our table chat covered the gamut, from the mundane to the heavy. In a lighter vein, we talked about the house Marson and I were building—immodestly dubbed "the perfect house"—which was still in the early stages of construction.

Glee said, "Anytime you want to wrap it up, you'll get a full-blown Sunday feature. I have some open slots to fill, so pedal-to-the-metal, boys."

I replied, "Cool your heels, doll. It's at *least* a year away."

Dahr said, "The drawings were amazing. Can't wait to step inside the real thing."

"You'll be among the first," Marson assured him.

How would I react, I wondered, when that day arrived? When Dahr came visiting, he would surely be in the company of Dr. Frumpkin, probably married, along with their little girl, Olivia. They would land on our new doorstep as a family, to which Dahr would be committed as one of "two daddies." I found it a difficult leap to imagine him in such a context, having known him as the exotic stranger in black who had kissed me (and *how*) in the drizzle beneath a streetlamp. I would simply have to adjust my image of him—unless, of course, his freshly hatched family had scooted off to California by then. Either way, I was content that the fantasy had flared, but faded.

Mary plucked a piece of sausage from the casserole on her plate and made kissy sounds at Mister Puss, who jumped up to her lap and chomped at the greasy morsel between her fingertips. She asked Sheriff Simms, "Was there a decent crowd at St. Alban's this morning?"

"Yeah," he said, "decent. I talked to Father Sterling afterward and mentioned we'd be with you today. He asked me to give you his best—and to tell you he misses seeing you on Sundays. In fact, we all do."

"Well," she said wistfully, petting Mister Puss, "sometimes we need to move on." It was now common knowledge that she had lost her faith, claiming the cat had convinced her that God is a myth. "Besides," she said, wiping her fingers on a damask napkin, "they need some new blood over there at St. Alban's—and I'm old."

Everyone, of course, begged to differ, joking about how she outran all of us, how she'd outlive the whole bunch of us.

She laughed at our silly assurances.

But time and again, our banter took on a more sober tone as we returned to the aftermath of the FlabberGas murder.

Marson said, "At least it didn't screw up the election."

"So it seems," said Glee, "but it really peeves me that someone so deranged as Alex Kastle could even pose a threat. He actually made some headway—until he didn't."

Following Mary's example, I dug a piece of sausage out of the casserole and lifted it for Mister Puss to see. He abandoned his mistress and moved under the table before reappearing in my lap, where he erupted into a loud purr as I fed him the meat.

Simms said to Glee, "It's a sad sign of the times. Kastle's campaign was based solely on his ability to criticize and degrade. He never once offered a single productive idea."

"Wonder where he picked *that* up," Marson said with a harrumph.

Some of us laughed; the others, apparently, could find no humor in the devolution of American politics.

Mary said to Simms, "But you're an honorable man, Thomas. Without ever lowering yourself to Deputy Kastle's level, you stood up to his challenge—and along the way, you solved the murder."

We chimed in with a round of hear-hears.

Simms modestly shushed us with both palms. "I know you never doubted me, but to be honest, I sometimes doubted myself—and I had no idea how this would turn out. Brody? You were a tremendous help. Without you, it might not have ended this way. Thank you."

Marson told me, "Nice job, kiddo. Like I've always said, you're a first-class problem-solver."

I reached over to hold my husband's hand. With the other, I petted Mister Puss. "I appreciate all the high praise, but I had a bit of help myself. Some of my encounters with Mister Puss were downright … revelatory." The cat looked up at me. "And finally, there was little Tommy." I smiled at the boy, telling him, "Thanks for opening up to me in the car Thursday night."

Gloria Simms stroked her son's head. "We've had a long talk about that."

Sheriff Simms wrapped his arm around Tommy's shoulder. "We explained to him that he should never be afraid to come to us with anything that's troubling him. There's nothing he could say that we wouldn't want to hear. And I'm sorry if I've seemed too busy or too stern." He held his son's chin and peered into the boy's small round face. "Okay, Tommy?"

"Sure, Dad."

Mary said, "How sweet. Dessert, everyone?" She was still pushing those brownies—literally pushing the platter in Tommy's direction.

His eyes widened.

Before he could reach, Glee snatched the platter and replaced it with the plate of her signature cookies with chocolate chips and whole giant cashews. "I think the brownies are sort of *bitter*. You might not like them, Tommy. How about these instead?"

With an eager nod, Tommy helped himself to one of Glee's fabulous cookies. I took one, too. Marson chose a brownie, and

I didn't say a word.

By the time we helped ourselves to seconds, the pitcher of milk on the table had run dry. I asked Berta, "Is there more in the kitchen?"

She nodded, wiping her mouth. "I'll get it."

"No, stay put," I said. "You've done way too much already."

"Suit yourself."

So I moved Mister Puss from my lap to the floor. Grabbing the pitcher, I got up from the table and walked to the kitchen. Mister Puss followed. With a whoosh, the swinging door closed behind us.

The cat jumped up to the countertop near the refrigerator. When I set the pitcher down, he stuck his head in it. "Stop that," I said. "You'll get plenty." Checking inside a cupboard, I found a saucer, which I set on the counter. The purring began as I removed the milk from the fridge; the rumbling grew to a pint-sized roar as I poured milk into the saucer, then filled the pitcher.

I leaned with my hip against the counter, watching Mister Puss polish off the puddle of milk. When he pawed my chest and reached his face to mine, his purr smelled like baby's breath. I lowered my ear to his chin.

Nice job, kiddo. Mystery solved.

Getting into the spirit of things, I said, "Know what, little guy? I couldn't have done it without you."

The damp velvet of his nose tickled my ear. His purr spoke to me.

Let's do it again.

•

Michael Craft is the author of fifteen novels, including the acclaimed "Mark Manning" mystery series, three installments of which were honored as finalists for Lambda Literary Awards: *Name Games* (2000), *Boy Toy* (2001), and *Hot Spot* (2002). In addition, he is the author of two produced plays, and his prize-winning short fiction has appeared in British as well as American literary journals.

Craft grew up in Illinois and spent his middle years in Wisconsin, which inspired the fictitious setting of this book. He holds an MFA in creative writing from Antioch University, Los Angeles, and now resides in Rancho Mirage, California.

In 2017, Michael Craft's professional papers were acquired by the Special Collections Department of the Rivera Library at the University of California, Riverside. A comprehensive archive of his manuscripts, working notes, correspondence, and other relevant documents, along with every edition of his completed works, is now cataloged and available for both scholarly research and public enjoyment.

Visit the author's website at www.michaelcraft.com.

The text of this book was set in Adobe Caslon Pro, a 1990 digital revival designed by Carol Twombly, based on the original specimen pages produced by William Caslon between 1734 and 1770 in London. Caslon is a serif typeface classified as "old style."

William Caslon's enduring typefaces spread throughout the British Empire, including British North America, where the family of fonts was favored above all others by printer Benjamin Franklin. Early printings of the Declaration of Independence and the Constitution were set in Caslon. After a brief period of decline in the early nineteenth century, Caslon returned to popularity, particularly for setting printed body text and books.

Numerous redesigns of Caslon have reliably transitioned the face from hot type to phototypesetting to digital. Among its many conspicuous uses today, Adobe Caslon is the text face of *The New Yorker*.

CPSIA information can be obtained
at www.ICGtesting.com
Printed in the USA
LVHW031529111118
596723LV00002B/550

9 780692 135990